POSSESSION

Also available from Headline Liaison

Private Lessons by Cheryl Mildenhall
Intimate Strangers by Cheryl Mildenhall
Dance of Desire by Cheryl Mildenhall
The Journal by James Allen
Love Letters by James Allen
Aphrodisia by Rebecca Ambrose
Out of Control by Rebecca Ambrose
A Private Affair by Carol Anderson
Voluptuous Voyage by Lacey Carlyle
Magnolia Moon by Lacey Carlyle
The Paradise Garden by Aurelia Clifford
The Golden Cage by Aurelia Clifford
Vermilion Gates by Lucinda Chester
Sleepless Nights by Tom Crewe and Amber Wells
Hearts on Fire by Tom Crewe and Amber Wells
A Scent of Danger by Sarah Hope-Walker
Seven Days by J J Duke
Dangerous Desires by J J Duke

Possession

Kay Cavendish

Copyright © 1996 Kay Cavendish

The right of Kay Cavendish to be identified as the Author of the Work has been asserted by her in accordance with the Copyright, Designs and Patents Act 1988.

First published in 1996
by HEADLINE BOOK PUBLISHING

A HEADLINE LIAISON paperback

10 9 8 7 6 5 4 3 2 1

All rights reserved. No part of this publication may be reproduced, stored in a retrieval system, or transmitted, in any form or by any means without the prior written permission of the publisher, nor be otherwise circulated in any form of binding or cover other than that in which it is published and without a similar condition being imposed on the subsequent purchaser.

All characters in this publication are fictitious and any resemblance to real persons, living or dead, is purely coincidental.

ISBN 0 7472 5244 0

Phototypeset by Intype, London
Printed and bound in Great Britain by
Cox & Wyman Ltd, Reading, Berks

HEADLINE BOOK PUBLISHING
A division of Hodder Headline PLC
338 Euston Road
London NW1 3BH

Possession

Prologue

June 1794

Climbing the steep hill from the village, they left the rest of the wedding party behind them. Every now and then a shout, a laugh would be carried to them on the breeze, but neither looked round as they made their way towards their new home.

Sensing the impatience in her new husband, Demelza stopped to kick off her wedding slippers, running to catch up with him in her bare feet. The grass felt dry and scratchy beneath them, but she barely noticed; all her attention was fixed on Jago.

Ah, but he was handsome! Tall and strong and dark, a gentleman, with a way of looking at her that sent her legs to water. He smiled at her now, his full, sensuous lips curving beneath his neatly trimmed whiskers, his brown eyes intense. Demelza felt something kick in the centre of her body, a kind of clutching of her insides that made her feel soft and wanton as she caught up with him.

'Is it far?' she asked him, her voice sounding breathy

and small in the wide open spaces of the moorland.

'Aye, a little way. Can you manage it?'

She nodded, her pride not allowing her to tell him how her legs ached and her lungs burned in her chest. He must know she would run to the four corners of the earth for him if he should ask her.

They walked for an hour or more and Demelza lost track of time. The sun burned down mercilessly on the top of her head, and she began to feel faint and dizzy. Gradually, as she left the familiarity of the village and her friends and family behind her, she clung to him, drawing courage from his strength as he strode along beside her, shortening his step so that she could keep up.

At last they reached the the top of the cliff and there it was. Rearing up like a monster from the rocks, a building like none she had ever seen before.

'Pengarron's Folly,' Jago announced and, hearing the pride in his voice, Demelza forced herself to smile. This, after all, was the house he had built for her.

Turning towards her, Jago drew his new bride to him and kissed her. Demelza clung to the reassuring breadth of his shoulders, revelling in the sensation of his firm, well-shaped lips imprinting themselves on hers. He had kissed her before, of course, but never with such unleashed passion, and she leaned heavily against him, half afraid, half exultant. They were husband and wife now, they need not stop at chaste kisses.

Sinking with him onto the grass, she looked at him in surprise. Surely he would not take her now, on the top of the cliff? But yes, his hands were roaming her body, feeling its shape beneath the lace and fine silk of the wedding gown he had had made for her. Demelza felt her body respond, her breasts swelling and hardening, a strange liquid warmth spreading outward from the pit of her belly.

Jago was kissing her, his lips pressing urgently against her face, her neck, the swell of her bosom beneath her gown. Impatient with the hindering fabric, he suddenly wrenched it asunder with both hands so that it fell from her body, leaving her naked and exposed to the glare of the sun.

Demelza lay very still and watched Jago's eyes devour her nakedness. All thought of her ruined dress fled as he lowered his head and began to kiss her white skin. Wherever his lips touched she felt that they burned her. Her breathing became shallow and rapid as he blazed a trail from her neck to her breasts and lower, crossing her stomach to the fiery red curls at the apex of her thighs.

Of their own volition her legs fell softly apart to expose the tender, virgin folds of her sex. She gasped as Jago buried his face in the dew-soaked flesh, and she felt the probe of his tongue, swirling around the secret entrance to her body. Trembling, she tangled her fingers in his hair, wrapping her legs around his shoulders as his tongue found the centre of her pleasure and lapped at it as if it were the most delicious sweetmeat.

Demelza tried to summon some vestige of modest restraint, but found that she could not. For what he was doing to her was delightful, wonderful, opening her eyes to the true purpose of her intricate womanly places. She murmured her distress as he slid himself further up her body, sucking in her breath as he plunged his tongue into her mouth. She could taste the juice of her own body on his lips and tongue, could smell the musky, secret scents of her sex.

Jago's hands were on her breasts now, moulding, squeezing, pinching the hardening nipples until she cried out.

'Tis good,' he murmured against her ear, 'do not be afraid of pain.'

She felt the nudge of his penis against the gateway of her sex and tensed in spite of herself. She had wanted this for so many weeks, dreamed of his possession of her for so many long, lonely nights, yet now she was afraid. He loomed above her, his body covering hers, blocking out the glare of the sun. Though it was in shadow, she saw that his face was intent as he stared into her eyes. Then he pushed into her, breaking through the barrier of her maidenhead with one swift, sure thrust.

Demelza opened her mouth to cry out, only to find it plugged by his tongue, her cry pushed down into her body, never to be released. For several minutes, as he moved in and out of her, she thought the pain would never end, the stinging, burning sensation in her passage filling her mind to the exclusion of all else. Then slowly, gradually a new sensation crept beneath the discomfort, no more than a glimmer at first, a creeping, tingling tendril of pleasure that gave her new strength.

Jago sensed the moment when the transformation began to take place and took his mouth from hers, watching her face as realisation dawned. Slowly, Demelza drew back her knees and fastened her legs over his hips. She wanted to feel him deeper inside her, to intensify the rippling pleasure which travelled along the walls of her passage and suffused her entire body with heat.

'Yes! she whispered. 'Oh, yes!'

Jago quickened his pace, pumping his hips up and down with increasing rhythm as the seed gathered at the base of his shaft. He cried out as it surged along it, spilling into Demelza's now welcoming body.

Demelza saw the ecstasy written clearly on his handsome face and she was suffused by a rush of power so great that she laughed out loud. He kissed her face as he withdrew from her and she stretched, like a cat in the sun.

'Oh Jago!' she said, smiling.

He ran his hand down the front of her body, marking her as his. Incredibly, she felt the warmth beginning to spread through her again.

'I knew it would be like this between us,' he told her, his voice low and intense. 'I built this house for you so that we can be together, always. We will bring others here, when it suits us for our pleasure, but we will never allow the world outside to intrude.'

Listening to him, seeing the intensity in his fathomless dark eyes, Demelza felt the first stirrings of alarm. It sounded as if he would make a prisoner of her here, she who thrived on company and freedom. She wanted to tell him this, but his hands were playing with her body, drawing a response from it that she could not ignore. Jago loved her, that was all, it was apparent in his every gesture, his every word.

'I would do anything for you, my husband,' she

whispered as the emotion surged up in her.

He smiled, a satisfied, almost secretive smile, and his fingers slipped into the now sticky channels of flesh between her legs.

'I know,' he said, beginning to move his fingers in and out of her, bringing them up to stroke the burgeoning nub of flesh at the apex of her labia. 'And you will, my love, you will...'

Again, Demelza felt that uncomfortable fluttering of alarm, almost of fear, but she pushed it away, refusing to examine it. For she wanted him again and nothing else mattered, nothing at all...

One

July 1995

James Lawrence rolled towards the middle of the big double bed, blindly seeking the warmth of Emma's body. Sleepily, she curled herself around him, settling from force of habit into the cup of his shoulder.

She smelled of sleep and talcum powder and other, less distinct scents which were womanly and mysterious. Her long, satiny nightdress had ridden up her thighs, bunching in the crease between legs and bottom and one breast had escaped the confines of the bra-like bodice. James's body, deprived of such visual delight for too long, responded instantly to the stimulus, becoming fully awake in the darkness.

'Emma?' he whispered her name, not too loudly, not really wanting to wake her. Awake she would never have moved so easily into his arms, crossing the invisible barrier which had lain between them in the bed for so many long weeks.

Holding her in the velvety darkness made him ache for all that they had lost. It hadn't always been like this.

Before the accident, which had caused Emma to lose the child she was carrying, they had been happy. Sex had never been a problem, certainly it was never used by either of them as a weapon with which to wound the other.

For two months now he had watched, helpless, as Emma withdrew from him, withholding some vital part of herself in a mute expression of recrimination and blame.

Her long, coppery-coloured hair lay like a soft blanket across his chest, reminding James of the times it had caressed him before. Vivid images of it shielding her face as she lowered her head to take him in her mouth tormented him and he stroked the silky tresses aside.

Her face was a pure, white oval in the darkness, her features indistinct. Lifting the covers cautiously, his eyes slid down her body, lingering on the ghostly white swell of the breast which had spilled from her nightdress. It was more than flesh and blood could stand!

She didn't stir when he pressed his lips against her forehead and, encouraged, he allowed his hand to drift over the exposed flesh. It felt warm and soft, pliant as he grew bolder and cupped her breast in his hand. To his delight, she reacted to his touch, her nipple hardening, rising to meet the skin on the centre of his palm. Emma stirred and murmured something incoherent. James held his breath, afraid she would wake and freeze him out with the look of wounded contempt which seemed to have become her natural expression whenever he came near.

Acknowledging that she would have every right to be

angry that he was caressing her while she slept, James told himself he wasn't doing any harm. After all, they had been married now for five years, he knew every centimetre, every nook and cranny of the lovely, feminine body now pressed against him.

Listening to her deep, even breathing, he knew that Emma was sound asleep. He stroked his palm down her back with the vague idea that she might on some subconscious level recognise the tenderness in the gesture. Tentatively, he caressed the exposed curve of one buttock, slipping his fingers under the nightdress and pushing it up, over her hips.

His mouth went dry as he thought of the vulnerable, exposed flesh he had revealed. As if she too was suffering from the hiatus in their sex life, Emma moved slightly in response to his stroking fingers, rolling onto her back and allowing her thighs to fall softly apart.

James could feel the heat of her sex as his hand passed gently over the plentiful hair at the apex of her thighs and he trembled. God, it had been so long since she had allowed him to make love to her, so long since he had touched and tasted the familiar body. Night after frustration-filled night he had lain beside her, aroused beyond endurance by the scent of her, the warmth emanating from her body, so close, yet so far, unable to penetrate the defences Emma seemed to have erected around herself.

Now he could not resist touching her, thrilling at the swift response of her nipples as he stroked them, aware that her belly had grown taut and her heartbeat had quickened. Perhaps she longed for this as much as he, but, having rejected him after the accident, did not know how to make the first move?

Convincing himself that this could be the beginning of the reconciliation he craved, James allowed his fingertips to edge closer to the erotic centre of her. Slowly, he drew delicate, ticklish circles on her skin as he traversed her stomach. The hair on her mons felt springy beneath his fingers and Emma gave a little sigh as his fingertips touched the beginning of the cleft between her labia.

Gently, he allowed his fingers to sink into the warm, petal-soft flesh between her legs. His cock twitched with excitement as he realised that she was wet, the swollen folds of her sex opening eagerly under his touch. The feel of her, the sensation of sinking into the hot, wet, pulpy flesh made his cock weep with anticipation. Suddenly it didn't matter that she was sound asleep, that she would have undoubtedly pushed him away had she been awake: her body was telling him that she still wanted him.

James kissed her gently on the lips before dipping his head to capture one tumescent nipple in his mouth. Closing his eyes for a moment, he rolled it on his tongue and was rewarded by the instinctive widening of her legs, giving him easier access to her body.

He could feel the hard bead of her clitoris rising to meet his fingers and he rubbed it rhythmically, bringing up the moisture from the lip of her vagina and swirling it around the sensitive bud. His lips lingered on the gentle swell of her belly, revelling in the way it quivered as the tension in her lower body mounted.

Deciding that he would enter her the moment she came, James levered himself up so that he was kneeling between her outspread thighs. His penis reared up eagerly from his loins, the angry red tip glistening with the thin film of pre-emission which leaked from its end.

Emma's head tossed restlessly from side to side, as if she was dreaming. James grinned, thinking how wonderful it would be to wake from what one thought was a wet dream to find that it was reality!

Though her eyes remained firmly closed, her mouth did not, falling open as the first warm spears of sensation began to travel through her body. Knowing she was about to come, James nudged the entrance to her body with the tip of his cock and eased the head inside. Pressing hard on the pulsating bead, he moved the hard core beneath the silken skin, knowing that this would be too much for her.

He felt the contraction of her vaginal walls, drawing him in, sucking the full length of his shaft into the heated channel of her sex. The soft walls rippled around him as her orgasm shook her and he broke out in a sweat.

'Oh Emma... darling...!' he moaned as he began to move inside her, too caught up in his own headlong rush into ecstasy to notice that she had opened her eyes and was staring at him in horror.

'James! What the hell do you think you're doing – ah!' she cried out as, deprived as it was, his body vaulted into a climax so intense that he heard the blood roaring in his ears. It seemed to go on and on, a never-ending outpouring that made him tingle right down to his toes.

It was several minutes before his breathing slowed and his heart rate steadied. Several minutes before he realised that the sweet recipient of his lust was lying rigid beneath him, emanating vibrations of anger so strong that he suddenly felt icy cold.

Daring at last to meet her eyes, James flinched from the blistering contempt he found there.

'Emma, I—'

'Pull down my nightdress when you've finished, won't you?' she said venomously.

Yanked unceremoniously out of his post-coital contentment, James was overcome by a sudden, searing resentment. He pulled out of her roughly and rolled onto his side of the bed.

'I thought you were enjoying it,' he said through gritted teeth.

Emma's voice was cold and hard.

'How could I be *enjoying* it – I was asleep, for Christ's sake! God, how *could* you? It's despicable!'

'Your body didn't think so!' he retorted, stung by her contempt. 'You might have been asleep, but you responded to me!'

Emma made a small, disgusted noise in the back of her throat.

'You're pathetic!' she threw at him as she leapt out of the bed and made for the en suite bathroom. 'That's about as close to necrophilia as you're ever likely to get!'

'Emma! That's disgusting!'

'*You're* disgusting!' she yelled, slamming the door behind her.

James lay in the gloom and blinked back angry tears. How dare she? He knew she was hurt and angry with him, but she had no right to destroy something as beautiful as what he had thought they had shared earlier. Did she think he'd deliberately crashed the bloody car? Didn't she understand that he had mourned the loss of their baby too?

On the other side of the door, Emma turned on the shower and tore off her nightdress. Stepping under the scalding spray, she refused to give in to the threatening tears. She'd thought she was dreaming. In her dream world she had allowed herself to feel, to respond, to set aside the numbness of her waking life and make love with James.

The shock of opening her eyes and realising how James had taken advantage of her had made her feel physically sick. She'd wanted to hit out at him, to wound him as she felt she had been wounded. Remembering the shocked anguish on his handsome face, she knew she had succeeded, but the thought gave her no pleasure. She was ashamed of what she had said, and sorry that he had felt the need to resort to what he had.

Worse, far worse, she acknowledged bitterly as she turned off the shower, she was ashamed that her own body had betrayed her in such a humiliating way.

Emma could barely bring herself to look at James as they sat across from each other at the breakfast table.

'I don't see why we have to go on this ridiculous holiday,' she blurted as he brought down the cases he had packed.

'We're going, Em, because I want us to get out of London for a few weeks.'

'We could have flown home.'

James glanced at her and shook his head.

'Once you're back in Connecticut your mother would take over and we'd never work this out.'

Emma had seen red at that.

'I'm not a problem you have to solve, James!' she protested vehemently. 'Carrying me off to deepest Cornwall isn't going to change what happened.'

'I'm not a fool, Emma, I know that,' he responded quietly, deliberately holding back his anger. 'But the house at Pengarron is booked for the whole of the summer and I think it would do you good to have a holiday.'

Knowing from past experience that it was useless to argue against that quiet determination, Emma watched James lock up their rented mews house and climbed mutinously into the car. As always, it had taken several miles before she had been able to control the erratic thumping of her heart that always accompanied the beginning of any car journey since the accident. Now she was resigned to spending at least a fortnight at the house her husband had rented for the summer, though after last night, she was damned if she was going to make it easy for him!

As they left London behind them and headed southwest, the weather gradually worsened from dullness to drizzle. By the time they passed the small town of St Ives and had found the concealed entrance to the road which would take them to Pengarron, the rain was falling in sheets.

Emma peered out of the window at the bleak, grey landscape, her spirits sinking even lower. She had thought that she'd grown used to the 'English summer' in the three years they had lived here, but that did not mean she could view grey skies and drizzle without feeling depressed. A sudden, sharp pang of homesickness overwhelmed her, adding to her low mood.

'It shouldn't be too far now,' James said, squinting through the rain-washed windscreen whilst trying awkwardly to unfold a map across the steering wheel. 'There's a turning off this road – damn! We just missed it!'

Stuffing the map between his teeth, he performed a three-point turn in the middle of the road and drove at a snail's pace to the point where he judged the turning to have been. It was a single-track road, Emma noticed without curiosity. Passing points had been devised at intervals, small encroachments onto the verge, so that if they met another car coming in the opposite direction, they would be able to squeeze past – just. It would be a hair-raising journey at the best of times, but now, in the gathering dusk, the rain pelting down like malicious arrows from the angry sky, it was nothing short of nightmarish.

Emma jumped at the sudden rumble of thunder and glared accusingly at James.

'That's all we need!' she snapped pettishly.

'It's not my fault! For Christ's sake, Em, you can't blame me for the weather!'

Emma clenched her teeth and looked straight ahead. The road seemed to have narrowed further still as they approached a particularly steep bend. Up ahead, she could just make out a signpost where the road split into two. James stopped the car so that they could read the blackened letters which appeared to have been scorched into the old wood.

'Pengarron,' James said slowly. 'That must be the way

to the village. The other side of the sign is blank – that must be our road.'

That sounded to Emma like a bad omen for the days ahead. Confirmation that they were going nowhere. Carefully, James manoeuvred the car around the left-hand bend and eased the car along the track. It was so narrow now that the tall grasses on either side of the track brushed against the windows like glossy wet fingers, making Emma flinch. It was like being in a giant car wash. Even James seemed put off by the rain now, sitting on the very edge of the seat and pressing his face towards the windscreen. His relief when the road opened out again was palpable.

'There you are,' he announced, triumphant, 'that must be it – Pengarron's Folly.'

Emma stared as they drove along the wide access road towards the house. It loomed up at them in the gloom, its solid, grey walls looking as though they had grown from the rocks on which it stood. The main doors were massive, dominating the front façade and dwarfing the mullioned windows. The walls ended abruptly in a crenellated line, rendered asymmetrical by the tower which rose up on the right-hand side, almost as tall as the house again. This turret gave the curious impression of weighting the house on one side, making it look as if it was listing, leaning irresistibly towards the sea.

Emma could hear the crash of the stormy waves as she got out of the car. The sound made her shudder, reminding her how close they were to the edge of the cliff. Pengarron's Folly seemed to be clinging precariously to the soil, as if it was threatened by the proximity of the waves.

'Is it safe?' she asked James nervously as he joined her, but the wind whipped her words away and he didn't hear her. Grabbing her by the hand, he ran with her across the stony ground and fumbled in his pockets for the key.

The key was old and intricately cut. Emma was relieved to find that the lock was kept well oiled; she had half expected the key to stick. As the giant doors swung back, Emma felt a waft of cold, musty air and she wrinkled her nose in distaste. James pulled her through when she would have held back, and closed the door against the storm. He found the light switch and the entrance vestibule was flooded with yellow light, making them both blink.

As if by tacit agreement, both of them stood and allowed their eyes to grow accustomed to the light before they ventured further inside. The flagstones beneath their feet were worn with age, uneven in parts. As she looked around her, Emma saw that the vestibule was a large, square room with several doors leading off. A staircase in the grand manner stood dead centre, its wide tread laid along its centre with a worn carpet which might once have been a rich ruby red, but which had been trodden to a dull burgundy by the march of endless feet across the centuries.

'God, no wonder it's cold in here – look at those bare stone walls! And these flagstones!' James shook his head in wonder. 'I guess you can't get much more English than this, can you, honey?'

'Cornish,' Emma corrected him absently as she walked over to the stairs. She found she was intrigued by the place in spite of herself. Unaccountably, the urge to walk up the stairs was strong.

'That's the same thing, isn't it?' James said, picking up the overnight bag he had brought from the car.

Emma turned and looked at him, one foot poised on the bottom stair.

'I don't think so,' she said firmly. 'Cornish and English – they're not the same thing at all.'

Turning away from him, she climbed the stairs. Halfway up, the staircase split into two halves. Without hesitating, Emma took the right-hand fork and made her way to the galleried landing. The walls up here were lined with dark wood panelling which Emma sensed was as old as the house. There was a large, square window, framed by dusty red velvet curtains, very heavy, pulled back by a scarlet rope. Looking out at the unrelenting rain, Emma knew instinctively that when the weather cleared there would be the most glorious view through the window.

James held back, watching her. He hardly dared draw breath in case he reminded her of his presence and the spell would be broken. For it seemed to him to be almost magical, the way Emma had changed the moment she walked into the house. Not for weeks had she shown the slightest interest in anything, so it was a joy to watch her exploring the house. There was even a hint of animation on her face.

It was almost as if she knew where she was going, as if she had been there before, for her step was sure as she made for one of the doors leading from the landing.

Following her through it, James stopped and caught his breath. This had to be the master bedroom. In the centre of the room, dominating the rest of the heavy, dark furniture which lined the walls, was the biggest four-poster bed James had ever seen. The twisted, dark wood dowel-posts were all but hidden by the extravagant gold-and-red-coloured damask drapes which Emma was fingering as if in wonder.

Emma gazed at the heavy, brocade bedspread, at the piled cushions with their gold tassels and rope-braided trim and felt a curious churning in her stomach. It had started as she stepped inside the Folly, and had grown steadily stronger as she had climbed the stairs. A sense of *déjà vu*, perhaps, a feeling of homecoming. She frowned. How odd to feel such a thing in such an ugly, forbidding place!

Her eyes glanced around the room briefly, but kept coming back to the bed. She was aware of a slow, insistent pulse beating gently between her thighs as she stared at it. Instinctively she knew that the bed had seen much pleasure across the centuries. It welcomed her like an old friend as she sank down onto it.

'What do you think?'

James voice sounded a discordant note and she looked at him in surprise, almost as if she had forgotten he was there, he thought irritably. Then she smiled and he forgot his irritation at once.

'It's quite lovely,' she said.

James smiled, relieved. He had been right to insist that they should come here. Perhaps it was going to be all right after all.

Two

James was relieved to find that Mary Helston, the woman from the village who looked after the Folly, had stocked the ancient-looking refrigerator. While Emma unpacked, he made coffee and read the note Mrs Helston had left on the vast deal table which stood in the middle of the kitchen. It was difficult to decipher her faint, spidery handwriting with its idiosyncratic spelling, but he understood enough to realise that there was a casserole waiting for them in the Aga which would only need warming through, and a panful of potatoes ready peeled and waiting to be boiled.

As he set the meal to reheating, James offered up a silent thank you to the thoughtful Mrs Helston. Taking the coffee up to Emma, he paused as he approached the bedroom. The door was standing ajar and he could see her reflected in the full-length, free-standing mirror which was positioned in the corner of the room. She seemed distracted, wandering from place to place, running her fingertips lightly across the surfaces of the furniture, pausing every now and then to pick up an object, examine it, then put it down again, precisely, on the spot where it had been before.

Emma stopped moving, standing in the centre of the room and wrapping her arms around herself. Her lips were moving, as if she was talking silently to herself. James's eyes widened as he took in her tall, slender form, too thin lately, but lovely nonetheless. Her long, red-gold hair lay loose about her shoulders, frizzing slightly around her face in the way she hated but he loved.

As he watched, a sudden flash of sheet lightning lit up the sky through the uncurtained window, flooding the room with neon-bright light. For an instant James thought he saw a second figure in the room, standing just behind Emma, and he took a step forward, alarmed. The thunder took him by surprise, coming as it did almost at the same time as the lightning, making the windows rattle. He realised that the storm must be right upon them and he hurried forward, afraid that Emma might be frightened. Since the accident she had hated sudden, loud noises.

She looked at him calmly as he walked through the door, her eyebrows rising slightly as his eyes darted around the room, checking that she was indeed alone. Of course she was alone! he berated himself. It had been a mere trick of the light which had made him see the figure in the shadows.

'It's cold in here,' he said, handing her a cup of coffee.

Emma regarded him with surprise.

'Do you think so? I was just thinking how cosy it is for such an old house! Oh – don't!' James paused, his hands poised on the curtains and turned to her quizzically. 'I was watching the storm,' she said.

James looked out at the cold, forbidding landscape and shuddered. With a decisive snap, he brought the curtains together and said briskly,

'Dinner is almost ready – why don't you come down to the kitchen?'

Shooting him a reproachful glance, Emma turned and walked out of the room without a word. Damn! What had made him act in so high-handed a manner? If she was enjoying the storm, there was no need for him to spoil it for her. James passed a weary hand across his eyes. He couldn't seem to get anything right! It was just that the room had felt so cold, so unwelcoming.

A slight draught drifted across the back of his neck and he shivered. Funny – the windows were shut tight, there was nowhere for a breath of air to squirm through. He could feel the tiny hairs at the base of his skull rising up and he shivered again, Deciding that he didn't like this room, he quickly followed Emma downstairs.

Emma was laying the table ready for dinner, moving from drawer to table to Aga to check on the potatoes. James pulled out a chair, wincing as it scraped discordantly on the ancient flagstones.

'There's a strange atmosphere in this house,' he said as Emma began to serve the food, 'have you noticed it?'

'What do you mean?' she asked, ladle in hand.

'Can't you feel it? It's ... kind of *cold* ... unwelcoming ...' he trailed off uncomfortably.

Emma looked at him in surprise.

'I was thinking exactly the opposite! It's a lovely old house with so much history – can't you feel the passion that has seeped into the walls?'

James began to eat, more than a little perplexed. Normally he and Emma were perfectly in tune about such things. It disconcerted him to find that her first impressions of Pengarron's Folly had been so different to his own. It was such a momentous change, though, to hear Emma being positive about anything that he decided to let the subject slide.

'This is great stew,' he said, tucking into the thick, dark gravy. 'Mrs Helston certainly knows how to make an impression!'

Later, as they prepared for bed, James's sense of unease returned. He had the strangest feeling that he should not be in the bedroom that Emma had picked, as if he was actually intruding.

'Are you sure you want to sleep in here, Em?' he asked, pulling on the cotton boxers he used for sleeping.

'Of course – why?'

She was sitting at the dressing table, brushing her hair. James noticed that she had parted the curtain again slightly. The rain had eased a little and a milky shaft of moonlight fell across the bed.

'Well, we haven't so much as glanced at any of the other rooms—'

'I don't need to – this is the one I want,' she interrupted him firmly. 'What is the matter with you? You've done nothing but whinge and complain since we arrived. This was your idea, remember?'

James grimaced.

'All right. I guess I'm tired, what with the driving and the storm...'

Emma looked at him thoughtfully, her head held slightly on one side.

'You do look a bit drawn. Things'll seem better in the morning. When the sun comes out you'll see the Folly in a new light.'

'I expect so,' James answered doubtfully, watching as she turned away and began to rub cream into her face. 'What's that you're wearing?' He frowned as he realised she was wearing a white cotton nightdress he had never seen before.

Emma glanced down at herself, her fingers flying to the ribbon ties at her throat.

'Isn't it lovely? It was lying on the pillows when I pulled back the cover. I figured the mysterious Mrs Helston had put it there for me.'

James shook his head.

'But why would she do a thing like that? She doesn't know you and that looks awful expensive—'

'Stop fussing, James,' Emma cut him off sharply and he frowned at her, impatience with her quickening his pulse.

She rose and he saw that the nightdress fell in voluminous folds to her ankles. It looked like something out of a period costume drama, certainly not something he would ever imagine would appeal to his thoroughly modern, sophisticated wife.

'It might belong to someone,' he suggested reasonably, but Emma waved his half-hearted protests away with a flick of her wrist.

'Then I'll have to pay them for it, won't I? Though I

hardly think it likely that someone would leave their nightgown between the covers of a bed which has been freshly made up for us, would you?'

Slipping into the bed, she lay back on the pillows. Her hair spread out across the crisp white pillowslip, making her look very young – vulnerable in a way that made James's irritable mood ease and caused his heart to beat a little faster in his chest. Pushing the mystery of the nightdress to the back of his mind, he climbed into bed beside her. Turning to gather her in his arms, he drew back, the frustration zinging through his veins as he felt her stiffen.

'Not now, James,' she whispered into the moon-silvered darkness.

'Then when?' he said sharply. 'For Christ's sake, Emma! I only wanted to hold you, that's all. No need to panic.'

He sensed she had turned her head towards him. He saw the glitter of her eyes in the gloom.

'Give me time. Please?'

James felt a lump rise in his throat and swallowed it down with anger.

'Sure,' he drawled, his voice dripping sarcasm. 'Like I've got all the fucking time in the world.' Hardening his heart to her almost palpable hurt, he dragged the covers viciously up to his neck, trying to ignore the heavy ache at his groin as he rolled away from her.

It was not many minutes before Emma's deep, even breathing told James that she was asleep. He lay, wakeful, waiting for sleep to claim him too. Somehow, though, he could not seem to get comfortable. He tossed and turned, pummelled the pillows, tried throwing the covers back because he was too hot, then pulled them up to his chin again when he started to shiver.

He felt guilty for the way he'd spoken to Emma, but Christ, a man could only take so much! Nevertheless, he was left with the uncomfortable feeling that his anger demeaned him, made his less. He wondered if they would ever recover from the wounds they persisted in inflicting on each other.

The bed felt lumpy underneath the immaculately starched lower sheet. Every time James changed position, something seemed to dig uncomfortably into his hip, or his lower back, or his shoulder. Eventually, in exasperation, he sat up. Emma was sleeping like a log, a gentle smile curving her lips. James wondered what she was dreaming about. She was obviously supremely comfortable, he thought resentfully. It was clear that their row hadn't affected her anything like as much as it had him. His anger against her renewed itself and he sat up, running an agitated hand through his dishevelled hair.

He was so tired after the journey that his eyes felt gritty and even his jaw ached. In desperation, craving sleep, he slipped out of the bed. Wrapping himself into his old towelling robe, he walked in bare feet across the room to the door. There must be other bedrooms, other beds he could sleep in, just for tonight.

Padding along the corridor, he tried each door that he passed. The first two had clearly been shut up for some time, for the furniture was draped in white sheeting, the curtains closed against the intrusive thrust of the light. At the far end of the galleried landing, the room which was the farthest away from where Emma lay sleeping came as a surprise.

A bedside lamp glowed softly beside a mahogany tester bed. A very masculine-looking dresser was laid with shaving equipment and toiletries and the crisp white bedding was folded back invitingly. James was too tired to wonder at it for long, the bed looked too welcoming.

He frowned as he saw something poking out from under the covers. Pulling the sheet back further, he saw that it was a pair of red plaid pyjamas, neatly folded as if just removed from a cellophane store wrapper. James tried them on and was at once seduced by the crisp but soft feel of the fabric against his bare skin. He had never in his life worn pyjamas, but these were so comfortable, so *comforting* that he decided to leave them on.

The bed welcomed him like a lover, the mattress sinking blissfully under his weight, moulding itself to the contours of his body. Reaching for the light, he found the switch and plunged the room into a blanketing, velvety darkness. James sighed deeply. The pillowslip smelled faintly of mothballs and camphor and reminded him of his grandmother. The quilt which lay around his shoulders was feather-light, and yet gloriously warm. Within seconds he was sound asleep.

Emma stirred and rolled onto her back in the big four-poster bed. Gentle fingers were stroking her hair. So James wanted to make up, did he? A part of her knew that she should tell him to stop, that if she didn't he would regard her silence as an invitation to go on to take greater liberties and she didn't see why she should let him off the hook that easily. But it felt *so* good.

The caress was light and rhythmic, soothing. She moaned softly, arching her neck so that he would stroke her there, yearning for the tenderness she felt in his touch. Somewhere in that mystical place between sleep and wakefulness, Emma felt warm breath, perfumed with cinnamon and the faintest whiff of tobacco, waft across her cheek. She sighed deeply as gentle fingers ran through her hair and she felt their feather-light touch on the patch of naked skin between her nape and the neck of her nightgown.

Somewhere in the back of her mind, she registered surprise that he did not immediately try to lift her nightdress. James did not usually have the patience for such long foreplay. If he had followed his familiar pattern and undressed her at once, she knew she would have allowed herself to waken fully and put a stop to his caresses. Instead, to her delight, he began to stroke her through the thick cotton, his fingertips skimming her form, as if relearning her shape.

As they brushed over her breasts, Emma knew that her nipples rose and crested, yet he did not return to them, instead, he stroked the gentle swell of her stomach, tenderly, as if comforting her. Though his touch aroused her, it was not with a burning passion which clamoured for release, but with a spreading, languorous warmth which invaded every part of her. Slowly, without being fully aware of what was happening to her, Emma sank into a deeper sleep.

In her dreams the gentle caresses continued, though

with greater purpose. The slow, comforting circles widened, creating a referred vibration in the heated, secret folds which nestled between her legs. Emma was beset by trembling as her body responded, swelling, moistening, opening like a flower in the sun. It had been a long, long time since she'd felt able to let herself go in this way and her body felt stiff with disuse. Her lungs hurt in her chest, her throat grew dry and constricted.

The more the gentle yet insistent fingers played with her, the more she craved their touch, yearning, she was shocked to realise, for more than their tender, respectful caress. She longed for them to handle her more harshly, to wring out of her the pleasure that she was so reluctant to release.

But the caresses continued as they were, coaxing a response from her, making her give as much as she was taking. Her breath caught in her chest, whirling in little eddies of excitement as the fingers dipped and swept along the insides of her thighs, their backs brushing as if by accident across the bulge of her mons.

Shifting restlessly in her sleep, Emma longed to pull the nightdress away from her body so that she could feel the fingers against her naked skin. Yet no matter how hard she tried to move, she felt immobilised, shackled, unable to express her desire. Her arms and legs felt as if they were weighted down, incapable of independent movement, though she jerked and writhed with the sheer pleasure of what he was doing to her. Like a marionette with tangled strings.

Beneath the discreet folds of her nightdress, her thighs rolled apart, exposing the moist, warm centre of her. As they did so, the fingers trickled slowly up from her legs to her stomach, dragging at the tender channels of her sex before leaving her. Emma cried out as the caresses stopped, leaving her frustrated, longing for more.

She felt firm, cool lips press against the corner of her mouth. The unmistakable tickle of a silky moustache teased her sensitised flesh and she frowned, sighing as the tip of a tongue pushed suddenly, shockingly into her mouth. It plundered the heated recesses of her mouth, drawing the sweetness from it and grinding her lips back against her teeth. She felt the rasp of a beard against her chin, then his tongue withdrew as suddenly as it had entered her, and she sensed that he had gone,

Feverishly, she tossed and turned, squeezing her legs together tightly to try to relieve the tension which had been building, inexorably, towards a crisis.

Sleep coiled around her, dragging her down, leeching from her the energy she needed to bring herself to the peak. With a small sigh of distress, Emma gave in, and slept.

When she woke the next morning, Emma was alone. For several minutes she lay, watching the dust motes dance in the shaft of early-morning sunlight which fell across the elaborate bedclothes through the gap in the curtains. The covers were dishevelled, testament to her restless night, and she felt hot and uncomfortable, her night-clothes damp with cooled sweat.

She frowned as she remembered what had happened in the night, forgetting her own complicity in the act in her anger at James. It really was too bad of him – just because her body seemed to want to rebel against her self-imposed celibacy, it was low of him to take advantage. Sex, after all, was more than a mixing of bodily fluids. The mind, the emotions had to be involved too. Emma winced as she realised just how cut off she had become from her emotions. As if by denying her own desires she could atone for her guilt, absolve herself from blame over the loss of her child.

The door opened, startling her. She frowned as she saw James's foot appear, followed by the rest of him carrying a breakfast tray. Opening her mouth to berate him for taking advantage of her again, she swallowed the words back as she saw that he was fully dressed. It was rare for her not to wake before him. When he spoke, she was glad she'd held her tongue.

'I've brought you some breakfast,' he said brightly. 'I'm sorry about deserting you last night.'

'Deserting me?' she asked carefully, dragging herself up against the pillows and smoothing a place for the tray on the counterpane.

'I couldn't get comfortable and I was worried that my tossing and turning would disturb you. There was another bedroom made up along the landing. You looked so peaceful – did you sleep well?'

Emma frowned. The dream had been so real, she could have sworn ... still, this was probably the closest James was going to come to an apology for the row they'd had when they first went to bed. Grateful for the truce, Emma shrugged slightly.

'I had a strange dream,' she admitted, trying to smile.

James looked at her oddly.

'So did I.'

Emma glanced up in surprise.

'Really? What . . . what was yours . . . about?'

It seemed to her that James made a meal of pouring milk and tea into the two cups he had set on the tray. As if he didn't want to meet her eye as he answered.

'It was nothing. Disjointed, you know?'

Handing Emma her cup, he gave her a meaningless grin, thinking of the mysterious, flame-haired beauty who had slipped in and out of his dreams all night long. At first he had assumed it was Emma – same build, same colouring and with the same air of overwhelming sadness that he was beginning to find so difficult to cope with. But the woman in his dream had been different somehow. Quieter, more frail. Less likely to recover. Yet despite her air of fragility, there was a powerful, earthy sexiness about the woman which had left him feeling frustrated and confused.

The thought of her made James feel uncomfortable and he pushed it away angrily.

'And yours?'

'The same.'

She smiled at him and he knew that she too was lying. Surely now Emma would admit that there was a curious atmosphere about Pengarron's Folly. He opened his mouth to ask her, but just then they both heard the unmistakable sound of footsteps crossing the flagstones in the hall. They looked at each other, Emma's eyes widening questioningly.

'That'll be Mrs Helston,' James said, 'I'll go and introduce myself to her. Eat up.'

Emma watched him as he left, aware that he was in a strange mood. What was it he hadn't told her about his dream? Could it be that it had been as disturbingly erotic as hers? She grimaced, aware that she was being absurd. People didn't share dreams, did they?

Drinking her tea, she picked at the toast James had made and thought of her dream lover. His caresses had been so real, she had been convinced that it *was* James. Even now, she could feel the echo of that orgiastic building of sensation. Squeezing her thighs together experimentally, she felt the heavy, dull pulsing begin in her sex, as if it had been waiting patiently all night for the release that it had been denied.

Emma put the tray carefully on the floor beside the bed and lay back against the pillows. Keeping one eye on the partially closed bedroom door in case James returned and began to ask awkward questions, she rucked her nightdress up around her waist and sank her fingers into the warm, slightly sticky flesh between her thighs.

It all came back to her as she began to stroke herself: the warm, cinnamon-scented breath against her skin; the gentleness of the fingers as they coaxed a response from her slumberous body. She grew hot and her breathing became more shallow as her sex lips swelled and grew slick with fresh moisture.

Closing her eyes, she tried to conjure up a picture of her dream lover, but he was as elusive as dandelion seeds on the breeze, nothing more than a configuration of touch and scent. The feeling was building now, the sensations which had been radiating out through her body concentrating themselves on that tiny mass of nerve endings at the apex of her labia. Reaching down with her other hand, she held them apart as she concentrated her efforts on he clitoris, slippery and hard as a small bead, straining now towards her fingertips.

She cried out as she came, stuffing her fist into her mouth to muffle the sound as her body convulsed with pleasure. At last, as the final vibrations began to ebb away, Emma dragged down her nightdress and curled herself into a ball. She yearned for strong, masculine arms to come about her to rock and soothe her before taking her on to new heights. Emma squeezed her eyes tightly closed as if trying to block out the realisation that it was not James's arms she craved, but those of her dream lover. His absence was like an open wound, painful, inescapable. She had never felt more alone in her life.

James walked into the kitchen, fully expecting to see a homely, grey-haired Cornish matron bending over the stove. So the sight of a firm, beautifully rounded bottom encased in skintight denim shorts rather took him by surprise. Allowing his eyes to run appreciatively down the slender, tanned length of the legs emerging from the shorts, he lingered at the kitchen door, unwilling to alert the owner of the legs, and the delectable rear end, to his arrival until he had fully appreciated the view.

'Mrs Helston, I presume?' he said ironically as the woman straightened.

She turned, and James caught an impression of short, bottle-black hair, a small, if pugnacious chin and wide grey eyes before her mouth stretched wide in a grin and the brightness of her smile obliterated everything else.

'*Ms* Helston actually – the granddaughter. Morgana.'

She stuck out her hand and James took it automatically, raising his eyebrows at the unexpectedly firm handshake.

'James Lawrence.'

'I know.'

James felt as if he had been kicked in the stomach. The cool grey eyes were staring at him appraisingly, a small gold ring which had been set in one of her finely arched eyebrows glinting at him as she raised them.

'Can I have my hand back? Only I find it comes in useful for unpacking groceries.'

James dropped her hand as if it had suddenly become red hot, flushing with embarrassment.

'Here, let me give you a hand,' he offered.

She'd brought milk and fresh bread, meat and vegetables. They worked together to put the groceries away, James trying very hard not to watch the gentle, unfettered swing of Morgana's breasts in the black jersey halter-necked top she wore as she bent down and reached up. To his intense discomfort, his cock had hardened in his jeans and stubbornly refused to deflate.

'Thanks – I'd best be getting on. Gran said I should wave a duster round all the rooms you'll be using.'

'Does your grandmother normally look after the house?' James asked, more because he wanted to keep her with him in the kitchen than because he was interested.

'Yeah. Her arthritis is playing her up today though –

all this wet weather – so I offered to help out.'

'You . . . you live with your grandmother?'

'You're joking! This place is dead in the winter. I'm at Bristol Uni – came back for the holidays. This'll be my last carefree summer, I take my finals next year.' Morgana grinned again, fixing James with a steady, mischievous grin. 'This year I plan to have fun – like, non-stop.'

'Cleaning up here hardly qualifies as fun, does it?' James said, aware that his voice had become unnaturally hoarse as he thought of all the ways Morgana would find to 'have fun'.

She laughed, a rich, sensuous sound that curled around his senses and made his cock leap in his jeans.

'That's why I want to get on now,' she told him, picking up a duster and a tin of furniture polish. 'Be seeing you.'

James watched her bottom roll in the tight-fitting shorts as she walked across the kitchen and he swallowed hard. *Christ, I wish I could escape from this place with her!* he thought guiltily as he refilled the kettle and switched it on before reluctantly returning to Emma upstairs.

'Who was it?' Emma asked as she pulled on a pair of white jeans and a close-fitting pink sun top.

'Mary Helston's granddaughter. I've put the kettle on for some coffee.'

'Let's make it a quick one, James – I want to explore.'

James watched her as she brushed her hair, unable to stop himself from comparing her to the girl whom he could now hear whistling merrily downstairs. Morgana was like a breath of fresh air, full of life and fun. Emma used to be like that, it was what had first attracted him to her.

Would she ever be like that again? More to the point, did they have a future together if she did not recover her old self?

Catching his expression, Emma moved over to the window, more to escape it than out of any interest in looking outside. A movement caught her eye further down the garden and she pulled the curtain back to get a better view. It was a man, dressed in dark coloured breeches which ended mid-calf and, despite the heat of the day, a waistcoat over a wide-sleeved shirt. He was wearing a curious-looking hat and little puffballs of smoke rose above his head from the pipe he was smoking.

'I wonder who that is?' she remarked curiously, turning back to James.

James, who had been picturing himself peeling the cotton jersey top away from Morgana's soft, unfettered breasts, started guiltily. He frowned.

'What?'

'I said, I wonder who that is in our garden?' Emma repeated, giving him a strange look.

Striding over to the window, James looked out. He saw a large, sun-soaked garden, stretching back as far as the eye could see, overgrown and very green. It was also empty.

'I don't see anyone,' he said, looking quizzically at Emma.

Emma looked out at the path where she had seen the man walking, and frowned. There was no one there.

'That's odd – I can't see where he could have gone that

we wouldn't be able to see. I wonder who it was?'

James shrugged and turned away.

'Probably the gardener or something. What's that on your chin?' he said suddenly.

'What?' Emma's hand flew to her chin as she saw that James was frowning at her.

'Some kind of rash . . . it looks sore.'

Emma bent towards the dressing table mirror to look, the man in the garden all but forgotten. There *was* a rash on her chin and she ran her fingers over it, the faint flicker of a memory making her frown. It looked suspiciously like a shaving rash . . . or as if a beard had recently rasped against her tender skin.

She jumped as James spoke.

'I'm going to have that coffee – are you coming?'

With a last puzzled glance at her own reflection, Emma followed James downstairs.

There was no sign of Morgana in the kitchen, but a fresh pot of coffee was waiting for them on the table. Aware of an irrational sense of disappointment that she wasn't there, James was subdued. He and Emma looked at each other in bemusement as the sound of a telephone ringing somewhere in the house reached them. It struck a discordant, modern note which jarred the atmosphere. James found it oddly reassuring.

The telephone was answered somewhere, and after a few minutes footsteps could be heard crossing the flagstones in the hall. This time when Morgana appeared he was prepared for the effect she had on him.

'It's for you, Mr Lawrence,' she said, throwing a 'hello' grin at Emma. 'Someone from London. They said it was urgent,' she added when he didn't move.

'Right. Sorry, Em – you'd think they could leave us alone for five minutes, wouldn't you?'

But Emma was staring moodily into her coffee cup and appeared not to have heard him. Shrugging slightly, James went with Morgana to the telephone.

Emma waited until the door had closed behind them before stirring herself. She was glad of the phone call; it gave her the opportunity to look round the gardens on her own. Leaving her cup half full on the table, she pushed her feet into her shoes and wandered out through the back door.

The mid-morning sunlight was blinding, the clarity of the light making her eyeballs ache. Shielding her eyes with her hand, Emma paused on the patio and looked around her. She found herself in a formal garden, slightly overgrown, as if someone was fighting a losing battle with the elements to keep it in order. The path leading away from the house which meandered across the lawn seemed to beckon her and she began to walk along it.

The air was redolent of sea spray and summer flowers and Emma found herself breathing it deeply into her lungs. The sudden screech of a seagull wheeling overhead made her jump and she smiled, her spirits lifting. She could hear the sea, hidden from view by a high hedge of grasses to her right, and the constant *whoosh* and hiss soothed her.

It was then that she heard it. She stopped in her tracks, sure she must have misheard. Cocking her head to one side, she strained her ears, praying that her mind was playing tricks on her. But no, there it was again, coming from further down the garden.

'Oh no!' she whispered, trembling. 'Please, no!'

There was no ignoring it, no turning away, for the noise grew steadily louder, more insistent – a woman's cry, thin and distressed, like an echo of her own despair. Something kicked in Emma's chest, an urgency that she had never felt before, a need to find the weeping woman, to bring her comfort.

With a strangled sob, she began to run.

Three

Emma's shoes caught on the uneven pathway, making her stumble along. The woman's sobs were growing nearer, her anguish reaching out and urging Emma along. Hardly noticing where she was going, she veered to her left instinctively, ducking beneath an overgrown archway of climbing roses. She found herself in a garden within a garden; a small, hexagonal patch of lawn with an ancient wooden summerhouse presiding to one side.

Emma stopped in her tracks, aware that she could no longer hear the woman crying. She was breathing heavily, her heart pumping wildly in her chest and she made a conscious effort to steady herself. *In through the nose, out through the mouth*, she chanted in her head, channelling all her concentration into regulating her breathing in the hope that she could tame her thoughts the same way.

'Demel-*zaa*.'

She twisted her head as she heard the name, like an expulsion of breath whispered on the breeze.

'James?' But even as she spoke, she knew that it wasn't her husband. Her ears must be playing tricks on her for there was no one else there. What was happening to her? Had grief finally slipped into dementia?

'Demelza!'

There it was again, more urgent this time, a sing-song calling carried in the air.

'Who's there?'

Emma walked further into the garden, her eyes scanning the dark shadows in the shrubbery, passing over the summerhouse. A part of her said she should feel afraid, and yet she wasn't, not at all.

'Oh-*h* Demelza!'

The voice, low and caressing, unmistakably male, sighed as a lover might sigh and Emma felt her skin prickle. She closed her eyes. The sun, though not hot, bathed her in its warm light, washing over her like silk against her skin. She could smell the sea and the heady, pungent odour of freshly mown grass. Emma frowned, wrinkling her nose as she realised that underlying such ordinary, everyday scents, there was the heavy, musky smell of fresh male sweat close by. She had been told that hearing voices was a classic sign of mental imbalance, but surely one could not imagine smells as well?

It wasn't an unpleasant odour, rather she found herself physically responding to it, a hard knot of desire settling in the pit of her stomach, her mouth and throat growing suddenly, unaccountably dry. She didn't want to move, holding herself taut in the middle of the lawn, the adrenalin pumping steadily through her body.

She drew in her breath and held it as she sensed the man come closer. There was no hint of threat, no feeling of intimidation, only of acceptance as he touched her hair. Emma recognised that touch from the night before, and a part of her mind, the sensible, still-rational part, told her that she should open her eyes and confront him.

Sensation very quickly triumphed over sense and she let out her breath on a sigh.

'So beautiful...' he whispered. 'I had thought you would never come.'

His voice was rich as golden syrup, his accent unmistakably local. Long, sensitive fingers played over the tendons of her neck, making her shiver.

'Who... who are you?'

He chuckled and Emma felt his warm breath brush across her cheek. It smelled of cinnamon and tobacco.

'Do you not know me, my love? Could it be that you have forgotten me already?' His voice was light, teasing, yet Emma felt the pain behind his words.

She shivered, the goosebumps rising on her flesh as his fingers ran lightly down her arms.

'Please... I-I would like to know your name,' she whispered, hardly knowing what she was saying.

He lifted her hair away from her neck and she felt the prickle of his beard against her skin as his lips pressed against the exposed nape. They were warm, no figment of her imagination, she was sure. They curved into a small smile as he answered her.

'It is I – Jago,' he whispered.

'Jago?' she breathed, her voice barely audible.

Her whole body felt over-sensitised, responding to the lightest touch on her skin. Knowing she was acting out of character, she found she could not muster the strength to care as he continued to caress her. Perhaps it was his very anonymity that she craved, for she felt his touch was setting her alight.

'Do you remember me now?' he asked her, his large hands coming up to touch her breasts.

Recalling those same hands on her the night before, Emma nodded.

'Oh yes...' she whispered.

The man groaned softly and nibbled at her ear lobe.

'And this...' he whispered, pinching her nipples between his thumbs and forefingers, 'and this...' He bit gently on the soft flesh behind her ear and Emma made a small protest, making him chuckle softly.

'Ah, Demelza... I have searched for you for so long...'

'My name is Emma,' she protested half-heartedly. Her tongue felt as though it had swollen in her mouth and her words were slurred, drunken.

'Do not tease me, my own love,' Jago murmured as his hands kneaded her breasts. 'Think you that I would not recognise you? We are one, you and I. I am Jago, and you are Demelza, my one true love. Do not be so cruel as to deny me now.'

Suddenly it did not matter who he was, or who he might think her to be, Emma went beyond reasoning as his clever hands began to roam her body, seeking out its most responsive areas and coaxing her into an ever-widening vortex of sensation. Allowing her head to fall back onto his shoulder, Emma welcomed his kiss on her upturned face.

James put the telephone down on his London-based editor with a frown of irritation. This extended period of leave had been fully explained and he had thought that Jeff Brawn had given it his blessing. So what did the slave-driving swine think he was doing butting into their peace on the first day of the holiday?

'Something wrong, Mr Lawrence?'

He looked up in surprise to find Morgana, duster in one hand, aerosol polish in the other, regarding him frankly from the other side of the room. He hadn't realised she was still there and the fact that she was, and had clearly heard his side of the conversation, irritated him.

'Nothing serious,' he replied, hoping she would take the hint and go back to her work.

'Nothing you can't handle, then,' she said, her eyes shining with merriment at his stuffiness.

James found himself smiling at her in spite of himself. It was difficult to stand on his dignity when she was looking at him like that. She had a small face, perfectly set off by the severe crop of her hair. Her skin was tanned to a shade of light caramel, glowing with good health and time spent in the fresh air. James found her colouring a welcome contrast to the pallor Emma's skin had acquired under the weight of her depression.

'I'm a journalist,' he explained, wanting to make up for his former tetchiness. 'Apparently the paper has tracked down Andrew Joiner to a hotel in St Ives. I suppose I'm the obvious choice to cover the story since I'm more or less on the spot.'

'Even if you are on holiday.'

'Quite.' James pulled a face and Morgana laughed.

'Ah well – St Ives is a nice place to visit. Mrs

Lawrence'll probably like it, her being artistic and all.'

James looked at her in surprise. How could she have known that Emma worked as an illustrator?

'I've seen her name on some of my nephew's picture books,' Morgana said, as if she had read his mind. She looked thoughtful for a moment. 'Andrew Joiner – isn't that the producer who did a bunk on that play in London?'

'That's right. The press have been searching for him for weeks.'

'Quite a scoop for you then,' Morgana commented with a grin.

James regarded her with new respect.

'I didn't think you'd have heard of that particular scandal,' he said, realising at once that he sounded even more condescending than before. 'I mean—'

'We do have newspapers down here in the sticks, you know,' Morgana interrupted him without rancour. 'Even in Pengarron!'

Laughing, she passed by him on her way to the door. As she did so, she unexpectedly ran the tip of her forefinger over his lips. It was a perfectly harmless, playful gesture, but James felt rocked to the core. It was as if there was electricity in her fingertips, so violently did his lips tingle where she had touched them.

'I'll be in again on Wednesday,' she told him as she left. 'Or Gran will be, if she's up to it. If you run out of anything, Mrs Jordan in the village sells most things.'

Then she was gone, leaving James staring wordlessly after her. He knew his disappointment that it would be two whole days before he saw her again was irrational, yet he could not deny it. There was something about Morgana which he found powerfully disturbing – perhaps, on reflection, it would be better if her grandmother did recover by Wednesday!

Smiling ruefully at himself, James went back to the kitchen. It was empty. Guessing that Emma had started off without him, he muttered a curse under his breath. Damn Jeff Brawn and his bloody story! He would not allow anything to distract him from his purpose in coming here – the need to save his marriage.

Not even Morgana Helston? a small, mischievous voice taunted him in his head. *Especially not Morgana Helston*, James answered himself angrily, pushing the delectable memory of her tanned skin and soft breasts away. There was no electricity in that young woman's fingertips, only a willingness to make mischief. Well, whatever Morgana might think, he wasn't in the market for mischief – not just now.

Setting his jaw in a determined line, James set off in search of Emma.

He found her in the small, secret garden which had been created to one side of the main landscaped area. James smiled as he saw that she was enjoying the sun, arching her body and raising her arms as if to embrace it. Her long hair flowed down her back like a sunlit waterfall and there was a stillness about her, as if he had surprised her at prayer, that filled him with awe.

She was standing with her back to him, so she did not see his approach. James was still suffering from the effects of Morgana's nearness and the sight of his wife looking so infinitely desirable was too much. Without stopping to think, he strode across the lawn and slipped his arms around her waist. When she did not immediately pull away, he nuzzled the sun-warmed skin of her neck and caressed her breasts beneath their thin cotton covering.

Her body responded to him immediately, her nipples rising up eagerly under his palms, her buttocks pressing against the hardness at his groin. James groaned, hardly able to believe his luck as her arms reached up and back, behind her own head to caress the back of his.

She was smiling, a wide, contented smile, full of sensual promise. James felt his pulse quicken as he sensed the erotic tension in her and his cock hardened, fitting itself to the denim-covered crease of her buttocks.

He could feel the heat travelling through her, the arousal buzzing through her limbs, almost vibrating, transmitting its urgency through to his own body. Her skin tasted slightly salty, warm as toast as he kissed and licked a path from the sensitive area behind her ear down her neck to her collarbone.

Emma responded by arching her neck, twisting it round so that she could meet his lips. It had been so long since her lips had opened so sweetly under his, so long since she had offered herself with such generosity. Sure that they could not be seen from the house, James pulled the close-fitting top out of the waistband of her jeans so that he could feel the soft, fine skin of her stomach beneath his searching fingers. She was naked beneath her sun top and her breasts sprang free, spilling into his waiting hands as he rucked it up, under her arms.

James was breathing heavily now, and he fought to control himself. He didn't want to rush, to give in to the tide of passion which was already threatening to overwhelm him. But it seemed that Emma too was being carried away by the moment, for she turned in his arms and began to fumble at the buttons to his shirt with feverish fingers.

Wanting to feel his naked skin pressing against hers, James helped her, almost tearing off his shirt and flinging it, unregarded, to the grass. Their teeth clashed as their mouths came together. Hot tongues parried as Emma raised her arms to enable him to pull her top over her head.

Her skin felt hot against his, the softness of her breasts flattening against the muscular wall of his chest, the tumescent nipples pressing like two hard pips against him. James ran his palms up and down the familiar contours of her back, his fingers slipping easily over her damp skin and fumbling with the fastening to her jeans.

Emma helped him, undulating her hips as he pulled the jeans down. She was wearing plain white cotton panties which just adequately covered the dark auburn hair at the apex of her thighs. Ordinary, everyday underwear worn with comfort rather than titillation in mind, but James thought they were the most erotic panties he had ever seen. Slipping his fingers beneath the elastic, he eased them down over her hips, catching the scent of feminine arousal as he released her sex from the confines of the tight white cotton.

Pressing his face against the soft skin of her thighs, he breathed in the heady perfume. Emma sank to her knees onto the soft turf in front of him. Without a word, she pushed him back so that he was lying, looking up at the sun. She seemed desperate to divest him of his clothes and James did all he could to help her, still half believing that at any moment she could stop in her tracks and have second thoughts. She couldn't, not now! He was so hard he ached and the skin of his balls was stretched tight over his testes, uncomfortable in the constricting briefs.

James gave a ragged sigh as Emma released him. His penis reared up like a sentinel, pointing to the sky. He gasped as Emma took it between her cool, soft palms and ran them up and down its length. The skin pulled against the hard core, setting up a tingling at the base.

'Emma . . . oh God!'

She stood up, placing her feet either side of his hips so that he was staring straight up into her sex. It was open like a split peach, the inner lips suffused with colour, the delicate membranes glistening with juice.

James dabbed at his dry lips with his tongue as he gazed up at her. With her back to the sun, she was cast in shadow, so he could not see the expression on her face. The impossible blue of the sky was shot through with golden threads which shone like a nebula around Emma's red-gold hair. He felt dizzy, gazing up at her. He could smell the grass and the dry soil beneath him, the salt tang of the perspiration shining on Emma's skin and the sweetly sour musk of her arousal as she bent her legs and sank slowly to her knees.

'Emma . . . ?'

He did not resist as she clasped him by the wrists and drew his arms up, above his head, though the action puzzled him. It was so unlike her to take the initiative like this and her sudden show of dominance troubled him. So far she hadn't said a word and the intensity of her unspoken feelings worried him almost as much as her uncharacteristic sexual assertiveness.

There was no time to dwell on such things for his body was already in thrall to her. The parted lips of her sex rested lightly against the stem of his cock in a wet, open-mouthed kiss that made him tremble with anticipation.

Dipping her head to capture his lips with hers, Emma thrust her tongue aggressively through his teeth to probe the softness of his mouth. The tips of her nipples grazed the hair-roughened planes of his chest and he moaned incoherently against her teeth.

Raising her head, Emma's eyes locked with his and James gasped. Her eyes were glazed, as if, though she was looking straight at him, she was not seeing him at all. Her pupils had dilated so much that there was the barest of green circles around the rim and there was an intensity reflected in their depths which both excited and appalled him.

'What—' She cut him off by kissing him again, grinding his lips back against his teeth until he tasted the sourness of blood on his tongue. Breaking away, she thrust one breast against his lips, encouraging him to take it into his mouth. James obliged, gorging himself on the pliant flesh and suckling on the puckered teat, now hard as a nutshell.

Emma was making curious, mewling sounds against his ear, full of passion and need, yet, somehow, disconnected from what they were doing together. Aware that she was not altogether with him, James tried to break away, to roll her onto her back so that their positions were reversed. He wanted to make his mark on her subconscious, persuade himself that she was aware of him. Emma proved surprisingly strong and he gave up, gazing into the intense depths of her eyes with growing unease.

'Are you all right? Em? Ahh!'

Lifting her hips, she had positioned herself so that the very tip of his penis was poised at the entrance to her body. He could feel the heat of it, luring him in, the flexible inner lips fastening around the bulbous head as if about to devour him.

Emma was looking past him now, her gaze fixed at a point some way behind his head. James brought his hands down so that he could cup her face, trying to make her look at him, but she knocked his hands away with furious impatience. Slowly, controlling every move, she lowered herself down onto his straining rod, drawing him in, claiming the use of his body as if it was her right.

James had the uncomfortable feeling that, as a person, he might just as well not be there. All that was required of him was the use of his penis as Emma held him inside her, squeezing gently with her inner muscles. It seemed churlish to complain since the sensation was such a pleasurable one, but James could not help but wonder if this was what Emma had meant when she had accused him of using her the other night?

He gasped as she squeezed a little harder, setting up a ripple along the length of his shaft that added to the feeling of fullness in his scrotum. It wasn't the same, he told himself, closing his eyes as she began to rock her hips back and forth. He had never used her as if she was nothing more than a masturbatory tool.

James held his breath as Emma slowly raised her hips so that he withdrew almost completely from her. She held him there, poised for what seemed like interminable seconds, before plunging back down again, her spread buttocks bouncing against his thighs as she took the full length of him in.

Dammit, she might be using him, he might object later, but now... oh Jesus! Now he was rushing headlong into a vortex of sensation where rational thought had no place.

Grasping Emma's hips tightly, James held her still as the seed gathered at the base of his cock before rushing along its length. Emma arched her back, flinging her head back as she was filled by him. She cried out, her voice breaking on a sob which was carried by the wind to the far corners of the garden.

James froze, the ecstasy evaporating as soon as it was spent. For it wasn't his name that Emma cried to the gulls wheeling overhead. Though it started in the same way, it certainly did not end so.

James pushed her roughly away, anger making him brusque as he confronted her.

'Who the fuck is *Jago?*'

Four

Waking from the nap she had taken in the afternoon, Emma washed her face in a bowlful of cool water, trying to splash away the last vestiges of sleep. Her stomach still churned when she thought of James's reaction after they had made love in the garden earlier.

'I want some answers, Emma, right now! Who the hell is Jago?' He'd demanded for a second time, pulling on his clothes.

Emma watched him warily as she too dressed, trying desperately hard to hang onto the sense of detachment she had experienced while they were screwing. Inevitably, she failed and she sat down on the grass, hugging her knees close to her chest protectively as that detachment splintered around her.

The voice in her head which had encouraged her to take the lead with James had deserted her now. Without the murmured obscenities spurring her on, the low, seductive words of appreciation, she was on her own. It felt as though she had been cast adrift, left bewildered and defenceless to face the consequences of her actions. James kept up a continuous stream of questions and accusations until her head ached.

'I said "James", of course I did!' she protested as soon as she could get a word in edgeways.

But he had merely looked at her coldly, for all the world like the emotionally repressed Englishmen who were his colleagues, and said, 'We both know perfectly well that you did not. I want to know who you were thinking of, Emma, while you were ravishing me.'

His choice of words made her laugh.

'I hardly think that laughter is appropriate right now, Emma,' James rebuked her stiffly and the laughter had died on her lips.

'No,' she said at length, 'no, I don't suppose it is. Perhaps you could let me know what is "appropriate" in the circumstances?'

'Maybe just a little respect for my feelings,' he said furiously, 'if that's not too much to ask.'

Emma sighed heavily.

'All right. It's a name from a dream – I dreamt about a man called Jago last night.'

She flinched in the face of James's disbelief.

'Sure. And this guy's made such a deep impression on you that when you're fucking with your husband, you call out *his* name. And you think that's an explanation?'

'I don't have to explain anything to you!' Emma had retorted angrily, scrambling to her feet.

'What?' James looked shocked, then angry. 'I'd say I'm entitled after all I've put up with these past few months.'

They stared at each other in the golden sunlight, each afraid to say any more in case they made the situation worse. Eventually, Emma had shrugged.

'Well, that's tough, James, because that's all the explanation you're going to get.' *Because that's all the explanation I can find for myself*, she added silently. 'Look, I'm tired, James. I mean, *really* tired. Could we talk about this later, do you think?'

He hadn't replied, but neither did he try to stop her from walking away. With a small shrug, Emma turned back towards the house and made her way to what she had come to think of as *her* bedroom, as opposed to theirs.

She hadn't been lying – she *was* tired, bone-achingly so. Stripping off her grass-smeared outer clothes, she lay between the crisp white sheets dressed only in her underwear and slept like the proverbial log for four solid hours. No dreams this time. And no explanations.

Presumably James was waiting for her downstairs now. The thought gave her no pleasure, for he had had four hours to dwell on what had happened, while she, well, she had been dead to the world. It didn't matter anyway, for how could she explain when she didn't even know what had happened herself?

She remembered hearing the woman's cry – a cat, she supposed now, howling for its mate – and it had spooked her, made her run. The scene in the garden was etched clearly in her mind's eyes, but beyond that her recollections were hazy. All she could really recall were sensations rather than specifics: the clutch of fear, the pain of loss, but, above all, the vibrant surge of sexual energy. Thank God James had come into the garden when he did for she had been about to turn in the other man's arms and lie down on the soft, green grass for him . . .

Where had he gone when James arrived? And why

hadn't James seen him, heard him? Emma frowned as the uncomfortable thought crept into her mind that she had been making love to a ghost, some incubus who thought that she should know him, who believed that she was someone else.

What was it he had called her? *Demelza*, that was it. At that moment it mattered less to Emma who Demelza might be, than her own willingness, no, *eagerness* to allow the man to think that she was Demelza for fear that he would stop if he realised that she was not.

How she could have responded to him like that when she had been sexually dead for James for so long, Emma could not begin to imagine. It must have something to do with the amount of time it had been since she had last wanted sex, she mused as she dressed in clean jeans and a T-shirt. Her libido must have been resurfacing quietly from beneath the blanket of her grief, waiting for the chance to spring into life.

But that didn't explain why she had found it easier to respond to a figment of her imagination, a dream lover who came to her in the depths of the night. Nor how that night-time dream had materialised into a real, flesh-and-blood man in the sun-soaked garden of the Folly, making love to her in broad daylight. The night before she had mistaken him for her husband, then, in the garden, she had made love to James thinking that he was Jago...

James was reading in the sitting room. He looked up when she entered.

'Are you all right?' he asked, laying his book aside and leaping to his feet. Emma eyed him warily as he approached and he picked up both her hands in his. 'I thought you were never going to wake up! I'm sorry I lost my temper with you.'

Emma smiled.

'I'm sorry too.'

Then it came, the same voice, whispering in her head. 'Show him how sorry you are.'

Emma knew it was *him*, and she glanced up at James's face in alarm to see if he had heard it too. He was smiling at her, unconcerned, glad their disagreement was resolved. So it was only to her that Jago came, then. To his Demelza. Emma smiled, suddenly feeling glad. As this Demelza she could behave in ways Emma would never dream of behaving.

She reached up as if on automatic pilot to press her lips against the corner of James's mouth. His skin tasted warm, slightly salty, as Emma ran the tip of her tongue along the closed line of his lips.

'Aye, my lovely,' came the voice, swirling around in her head, 'do it for me, like you used to. Let me watch your clever mouth at work.'

Emma sensed the air pressure change, could smell the now familiar odours of cinnamon and tobacco as he whispered in her ear. James stood rigid in front of her, as if not quite trusting what she was doing.

'Em . . .'

'Ssh! Be still . . .'

Her fingers were deft on the buttons of his shirt, slipping them through the buttonholes and peeling back the side to reveal the strong, hard planes of his chest and stomach. He had a good body, toned from regular visits to the gym, and Emma revelled now in the well-defined hills and valleys of his torso while James held himself still.

'A fine figure, is he not, my lovely? Feel the tension in him, see how he holds himself back for you.'

He was right, Emma could sense the leashed passion in James and she felt fingers of excitement crawl down her spine. She heard his sharp intake of breath as she unfastened his belt and slipped the leather slowly through the loops. Her fingers brushed across the bulge in his jeans and he shuddered.

'Emma—'

'Quiet!'

James's eyes widened at the note of command in her voice, but he said nothing, merely watching her through darkening eyes as she unzipped his jeans and reached into his underpants with a cool hand. His cock throbbed against her palm as she released it from his pants and ran her hand quickly up and down its length.

'A fine prick, my lovely,' the voice in her head remarked as she fondled it. 'So white and slender – a veritable sweetmeat at my lady's table.'

There was a note of teasing in the tone of the voice, yet Emma knew that this was threaded through with barely suppressed excitement. She knew what he wanted her to do, and knew that she would comply. For some reason she could not yet fathom, it pleased her to give him pleasure.

Slowly, she sank to her knees before James and guided him into her mouth. The tension in the room was impenetrable, Emma could sense the rising excitement in both James and the watcher, unseen, in the shadows. A dull pulse began to throb between her thighs as she recognised the power of her position.

She began to suck, gently at first, then harder, drawing James's rigid shaft into the warm, wet cavern of her mouth. The bulbous head knocked against the back of her throat and she resisted the impulse to gag, wanting him to feel how totally she was swallowing him.

James was breathing fast, the skin of his belly growing taut and damp with sweat. Feeling his balls swelling beneath the layers of denim and cotton, Emma cupped them gently with one hand and squeezed with a steadily increasing rhythm.

'Ah, Demelza – so sweet do your red lips look stretched wide around that lewd shaft! Milk him dry – let me see the stain of his seed upon your soft lips!'

Urged on by the softly whispered obscenities, Emma sucked harder, drawing the sperm along the shaft of James's penis, until, with a shout, he came, spilling into her mouth in a series of short, hot jags. Emma swallowed what she could, suckling on the now angry red tip of his penis until she could take no more. Rocking back on her heels, she looked up at James.

The atmosphere in the room seemed to have changed; she was aware of a surge of strong emotion, negative this time, as if Jago had thought better of his encouragement of her and was now consumed by jealousy. Emma glanced around nervously, half expecting to see some physical manifestation of anger disturbing the air. Then, as suddenly as it had come, the feeling eased. Gradually she became aware that Jago's strength was now fading, he was slipping away from her, back into nothingness. Then he was gone.

'Christ, Emma!' James choked as he tucked himself

away and bent down to help her to her feet. Watching him scan her face, Emma read the confusion in his eyes and gave a small, inward sigh. Was he going to want her to explain this too?

When, at last, he broke the silence, it was as if nothing had happened between them. His voice was quite conversational in tone as he said, 'I've booked a table for dinner in St Ives – would you like that, Em? To go out to dinner?'

Emma felt hysterical laughter bubble up in her throat and she swallowed it back with difficulty. This violent veering from the extraordinary to the mundane was too much for her.

'If you like.' And then, seeing her face fall, she smiled and pressed his hand and said, 'Of course – that would be lovely!'

James scanned her face again, anxiously, it seemed to Emma, as if he was afraid she might be about to spring some other inexplicable change in her personality on him without warning. He seemed satisfied with what he saw, going to pour her a gin and tonic before they both went to change ready for the evening out.

Back in her room, Emma allowed her mind to empty, bathing and washing her hair, selecting seam-free underwear without straps to complement the close-cut black lace dress which was worn off the shoulders. She didn't want to think about what had happened downstairs, knowing there was no rational explanation for what she had heard, never mind to account for why she had responded to it as she did, she preferred to push all thought of Jago away. Sitting at her dressing table, she rummaged through her jewellery case for the jet earrings and velvet choker she always wore with the dress.

It was then that she knew that she was no longer alone. Slowly, she raised her eyes to the mirror again and her gaze met that of a man standing a few paces behind the dressing-table stool. She opened her mouth to scream for James, but somehow the sound caught in her throat so that, although her lips shaped the words, no sound came out at all.

The man was probably in his mid-thirties, of average height, with long, straight brown hair drawn back into a ponytail at the nape of his neck, and pale skin. His eyes were brown, flecked with hazel and he was wearing a small, manicured beard, not quite a goatee, but of a similar size, trimmed to a neat curve which followed the line of his chin beneath. It was a strong chin, a strong face, and Emma shivered.

As she watched, mesmerised by the compelling expression in his eyes, he approached her. Never taking his eyes from hers, he bent his head to press his lips against the exposed dip of her shoulder. Emma's eyelids drooped as she felt the warm, wet stamp of his lips against her bare skin coupled with the silky tickle of his moustache.

He smiled at her as he straightened, a smile of such tenderness that she felt her heart lurch in her chest. Then, with a small, almost courtly bow, he backed away.

'Don't go!' Emma whirled round to confront him, only to find that she was alone. A glance back at the mirror told her that his reflection was no longer there either and she felt his loss acutely.

'Jago?' she whispered, her eyes searching the shadowed corners of the room.

There was no reply and she realised that he was no longer in the room with her.

'Come on, honey – the table's booked for seven.'

Emma gave a guilty start as James appeared at the door.

'Almost done,' she said, offering him an apologetic smile. What would have happened if he had come in mere seconds before and found her relishing the touch of another man's lips against her skin?

Uncapping her lipstick, she drew it across the contours of her lips before blotting them with a tissue.

'All done,' she said brightly, standing up and giving him a twirl. 'Will I do?'

James grinned happily.

'Honey, I can't tell you what it does for me to see you so much more like your old self,' he told her.

Emma had to dip her head to hide her guilt that she could not be honest with him about the cause of her transformation. All the way to St Ives, she wrestled with the puzzle of the man in her bedroom. Rationally speaking, she supposed there had to be some logical explanation for his presence, yet deep down she knew that there was nothing rational about it at all. He did not act like an intruder. On the contrary, his demeanour was such that she might have thought it was *his* bedroom! That she was only using it because he was happy for her to do so.

Remembering how James had found the place so uninviting, Emma was forced to acknowledge that she was the catalyst, she was the one from whom the... what? Ghost? Presence?... drew his strength. Probably because he thought he knew her, believed her to be his Demelza.

Undoubtedly, there was something odd going on, but Emma was reluctant to think too hard about it. All she could think of was the possibility that he might come to her again that night. It shocked her to realise just how much she wanted it to happen.

The restaurant turned out to be not so much *ye olde Cornish Inne* as Cornish theme pub, with synthetic tasting pasties and warm white wine. James, whose idea it had been to order the local speciality, grew steadily more vocal in his complaints until in the end Emma got the impression that the staff were glad to see the back of them.

'That was the most godawful place I've ever taken you to – I'm sorry, Emma.'

Emma turned to look at him as he drove them back to Pengarron. Had he guessed that her attention hadn't been with him? The only thing she had been able to think about all evening was what would happen when she went to bed that night. Maybe her distraction had transmitted itself to James in subtler ways, making him tetchy with everything and everyone except the real cause of his discontent – her.

'It was all right,' she soothed. 'I've had worse. Maybe Mrs Helston will leave us one of her casseroles when she comes in tomorrow?'

James took his eyes off the narrow road long enough to shoot her a grateful smile before returning his attention to his driving. A picture flashed into his mind, like a photograph, of Mrs Helston's granddaughter in her tight denim shorts and halter-necked top and he pushed it away guiltily. For the rest of the drive he concentrated on transferring the desire he felt for Morgana to Emma.

Once back at the Folly, he followed her up to her room.

'James – why don't you use the same room you used last night?' she suggested as they reached the top of the stairs.

James's face registered shock and fury in quick succession. Her rejection was like a slap in the face after all his careful planning.

'But I thought—'

'I know, but you said yourself what a good night's sleep you had in there, and I've got to admit, I feel awful tired again.'

'You slept for four hours this afternoon!' James pointed out coldly.

'I-I know. I guess I must be sickening for something. I do feel exhausted for much of the time.'

That was enough for James. James wasn't good around sick people. Seeing his morbid dread of illness working in her favour, Emma was hard pressed not to smile.

'Well, if you're sure . . .?' he conceded grudgingly.

'Sure I'm sure,' she replied on cue.

'You'll be all right – I can't get you anything?'

'No – all I need is a few more nights' rest.'

'A few more!'

'Let's take one night at a time, James, shall we? After all, that was the idea of us coming here, wasn't it – for me to rest and try to get over what happened?'

James frowned, aware that he had been backed into a corner and not liking the feeling.

'Yeah, but I'd assumed we'd be together in the meantime.'

'I know,' Emma said, leaning over to place a chaste kiss against his cheek. 'Give me time.'

James pulled away from her with such violence that it made her wince.

'Time? Fucking hell, Emma – one minute you're all over me as if you can't get enough, the next you're asking me to give you time! What the hell's the matter with you?' He slammed his fist into the wooden panelling and glared at her as if he wished it had been her he had hit. 'You take all the time you want – just don't expect me to be available every time you fancy a quick screw.'

James stalked along the landing and slammed his bedroom door behind him and undressed ready for bed. His anger was suffocating him, sending the blood churning through his veins so that he couldn't stand still. Instead he paced the small room like a caged animal, up and down, wearing invisible tracks in the carpet as he fumed.

'Doesn't she know that I'm hurting too?' he said aloud. 'It was my child as well... my loss...'

'Aye, but it was not blood of your blood, flesh of your flesh, growing in your body.'

James whirled round as he heard the voice, female with a soft accent, but there was no one there. It was as if the sound had been generated in his own head, a thought implanted there without his noticing.

He stood in the centre of the room, listening intently. There was something different about the atmosphere in the room, a kind of thickening of the air that made the small hairs on the back of his neck prickle. He could smell lavender and the faint, sweet-sour smell of milk.

Peering into the darkest corner of the room, he saw the thickening of the shadows, watched with rising alarm as they seemed to shift and take form. It was a woman, of that much he was certain. As he watched, her face became clearer, as if lit from within. James sucked in his breath, recognising her at once as the woman he had dreamt about the night before.

There was an expression of such aching sadness on her lovely face that James felt his heart constrict. She didn't speak again, but she smiled sweetly. It was then that he realised that she was holding something in her arms, cradling it against her breast, but the shadows would not clear enough for him to make out what it was.

Then he heard the thin wail of a baby's cry and he knew.

'Who *are* you?' he whispered, trying to control the rising horror.

She did not answer, but, frowning, she closed her eyes, and before James's gaze she seemed to merge once again into the shadows.

James stood very still, even after the air cleared and he knew that he was alone again. His mind would not allow the evidence of his own eyes and ears. When at last his feet would move, he swore under his breath and wrenched his eyes away. It was nothing but a figment of his imagination. Maybe his anger had triggered it, maybe it was nothing more than a visualisation of his own emotions. Maybe Emma was right – he shouldn't keep his feelings on such a tight rein.

Crap! With a muttered curse, James went downstairs to fetch the bottle of good malt whisky he had left in the sitting room. No way was he going to go to bed alone – not without something to keep him warm!

Emma watched James as he stalked away from her across the landing, slamming the door to his bedroom, shutting her out. Turning away, she opened the door to her own room, closing it behind her with a gentle *'click'*. The moment she stepped through all thought of James and his anger fled her mind.

He was here, she was sure of it. It was warm in the room and the bed covers had been turned back to welcome her. They had been drawn up when she had left and, even if James could have come back upstairs without her noticing, which he couldn't have, it wasn't the sort of thing he would think of doing for her.

Emma hummed as she performed her bedtime routines with a minimum of fuss and changed into the voluminous cotton nightie. As it slipped over her skin she caught the scent of lavender, as if it had been put away in a drawer wrapped around a lavender sachet. Turning out the light, she folded back the covers so that they just touched her feet and lay back on the pillows to wait.

After a few moments she began to feel foolish, waiting for what was clearly a product of her overheated imagination. What had she expected – a dream lover waiting for her to conjure him up at will, whenever she desired him? Grimacing a little at the fancy, she sighed. There was obviously a perfectly rational explanation for everything that had happened so far. Perhaps in the morning, when she was less tired, she would be able to think of it. Closing her eyes, she practised emptying her mind of all thought. Gradually, she slipped into sleep.

As if by surrendering her conscious mind she had unlocked a door by which he could enter, Emma saw that he was standing at the end of the bed. His expression was tender, possessive even, only his eyes burned with the passion he was keeping in check.

She smiled at him, holding out her hands to beckon him forward. To her frustration, he did not oblige her, apparently content merely to look at her.

'Jago?' she whispered. 'It is you, isn't it?'

His eyes gently mocked her as he bowed low, never talking his gaze from hers.

'Aye, my lady – it is I.'

His voice was as clear as if James had spoken – this was no whispering voice of madness playing games inside her head. Emma felt her skin prickle with awareness as he gazed at her, the slow tendrils of sexual desire spreading through her as she lay, waiting. Hoping . . .

He did not attempt to come any closer, wanting, it seemed, only to feast his eyes on her, for they roamed her body with an intensity which made her tremble. His figure seemed almost insubstantial in the weak light of the moon, and Emma did not dare to reach for him in case he wasn't really there. Was she dreaming? If so she knew that she had never dreamed as vividly as this.

'Do not be afraid,' he whispered, as if he could divine the very thoughts running through her head. 'I wish only for your pleasure. Your pleasure is my pleasure.' He touched his fingertips briefly to his heart as he spoke and his gold rings caught a stray shaft of moonlight. Emma's eyes were drawn to them as he passed his hand back and forth across his chest. Her eyelids felt heavy as she stared at the rings, the blood buzzing in her ears.

Without really realising what she was doing, Emma began to stroke her own hair, which was spread across her shoulders. Jago's eyes followed the movement, his expression strangely approving. Somehow his gaze was as potently arousing as any touch could have been, and Emma found herself caressing the arch of her own neck, glad that the sight of it pleased him.

'Ah yes... so soft, so warm,' he crooned, and Emma fancied his eyes darkened in the gloom.

Her skin felt hot beneath the prim cotton nightdress and, without giving any thought to what she was doing, she rucked it up around her waist.

'Aye,' Jago murmured throatily, 'display yourself for me...'

It seemed so natural, so right to caress herself in front of him. Her nudity did not embarrass her in the least. Under his eyes she felt proud of her body in a way she had never felt proud before. It was a powerful feeling, one which she wanted to explore further. Encouraged by the approval she sensed in his gaze, Emma stroked the soft, velvety skin of her stomach with the palm of one hand in slow, circular movements.

Slowly, slowly, she allowed her heels to slip apart so that her most intimate flesh was exposed to the cool night air. She could feel the tension encircling her as she caressed her thighs, her fingers edging inexorably closer to the hot, moist centre of her arousal.

She sighed as the familiar languor seeped through her and she felt her breasts harden and her sex swell.

'Take off the nightgown,' Jago breathed before her fingers reached their goal.

Without any thought of questioning him, Emma did as he asked, pulling the heavy cotton garment over her head and allowing it to drop soundlessly to the floor. Holding his eye, she gathered up her full breasts in both hands and pointed the nipples at him, offering them to him. He made a small sound in the back of his throat, halfway between a groan and a curse, and Emma felt a surge of primeval triumph to have drawn it from him.

'Ah, such wanton needs,' he murmured. 'Such sport we shall have, you and I...'

'Now?' asked Emma boldly, knowing instinctively that, this time at least, he would deny her.

'Alas – tonight it is for me to watch you,' he replied, mock regret colouring each word.

'Watch me?' Emma frowned, slow to understand.

Jago did not reply, merely waiting at the foot of the bed for her to comply. A part of her rebelled at the thought of masturbating in front of someone else, especially a total stranger, but already her own desire was beginning to hurtle out of control and her body clamoured for release.

'I've never...' she whispered.

'You will have no need of other men once I am whole again. Do it for me... make me strong,' he said.

With a small whimper of submission, Emma lay back against the pillows and pressed the fingers of one hand into the soft, slippery folds of her sex. Ah, but it felt good, so good, the more so for the fact that she was watched. Closing her eyes, she bent her knees so that the soles of her feet were braced firmly on the sheet and her labia parted, the inner lips pouting as she trailed her fingertip around the entrance to her body.

The level of her arousal surprised her, the warm, heavy honey seeping from her body more copious than she would have thought possible in so short a time. Slowly, she brought it up, bathing the channels on either side of her labia with it so that her fingers moved easily across her skin.

Aware of Jago's heated gaze on her, Emma took care not to obscure his view as she swirled her finger around the stem of her clitoris, taking care not to touch it for fear that she would come too soon. Pressing the heel of her hand briefly onto the pelvic bone above it, she revelled in the sensations caused by the referred pressure on that sensitive nub.

It was so hot in the bedroom, so airless that she felt she could barely breathe. Taking shallow breaths through her nose, she murmured incoherently, tossing her head from side to side as the tension began to build. She felt restless, almost irritable as she climbed towards the peak, yet could not quite seem to reach it.

'Hush now,' Jago's soothing croon permeated the sensual fog which had befuddled her senses. 'Slowly... lightly... aye, 'tis better now.'

Emma responded to the note of understated authority in his voice, lengthening her strokes and caressing herself with a lighter touch. He was right, she had been trying to race too fast to the peak, to rush when there was no need. Already she could feel her jumpy nerves settling, the warmth coursing more smoothly through her veins.

Reaching down, she spread her sex with the outstretched fingers of one hand while with the other she rubbed rhythmically at the tender bundle of nerve endings at the apex of her labia.

'Aye – push it out, that's it! Give it to me, this gathering of your pleasure . . .'

Emma heard his voice as if through a fog, so engrossed was she in what she was doing. A part of her responded to his words even while she did not register them consciously, and she strove to do everything he asked of her.

'Open wider. By the stars but you are like a jewel! How I long to lose myself in that precious place. Would you take me inside you, Demelza? Would you draw the seed from my body?'

'Oh yes, yes!' she cried, responding to the urgency in his low-pitched voice as much as to the words he spoke.

It was coming now, the tension inside her building until there was no release for it but in climax. Emma cried out as a white heat seared through her body. Lifting her hips off the bed, she pressed her pelvis forwards, towards the man whose words of encouragement had pushed her over the edge.

On and on it went, wave after wave of heat, her clitoris throbbing beneath her fingers, her sex opening wider, more in hope than expectation. Never had she wanted to feel male flesh inside her more than she did at that moment. She felt incomplete, less than whole without the swift thrust of a lover's sex-flesh melding with her own.

At last the violent pulsings of her body began to ebb away and Emma stopped writhing on the sweat-soaked sheets. The hand she cupped over her sex now was more protective than arousing for her flesh felt tender and sore, the secretions of her body drying stickily on her inner thighs.

Exhausted, Emma rolled onto her side and brought her knees up to her chest. She could barely find the strength to stir as she felt the covers being drawn up around her chin. The sheets were cool against her heated skin, as were the fingers which smoothed the hair off her forehead.

'Sleep, little one,' he whispered close to her ear. 'Muster your strength, for this is but the beginning.'

Emma wanted to open her eyes, to question him, but they seemed to be welded together. And she was tired, so very, very tired. It wasn't long before she slept.

Five

James woke the following morning with a dull headache throbbing behind his temples and a sour taste coating his mouth. Unlike the first night, he had slept fitfully, plagued by the sound of someone singing. It was like a half-remembered song nagging at his consciousness, irritating but persistent. Yet it wasn't a song he could remember having heard before. It had sounded like a lullaby, a soothing, meaningless jumble of words that one might sing to a child.

This last thought reminded him of his hallucination of the night before and he pushed back the covers angrily. He had promised himself he wouldn't think of the woman in the shadows and what she had said. The half-empty whisky bottle on the bedside table bore testament to that.

Having identified the cause of the furring of his tongue, James hauled himself into the bathroom and set about repairing himself. Once he felt halfway human again, he strode along the corridor, intending to ask Emma if she would like to go into St Ives with him. She'd enjoy looking in the craft shops and browsing round the galleries while he staked out Andrew Joiner's hotel, then later, if the weather was fine, they could perhaps drive along the coast and find somewhere to eat.

Pleased with the idea, he went to open her bedroom door, only to find it locked against him. At first, he could barely believe that she had done it, and he tried the doorknob again. It moved round as it should, but the door itself would not budge.

James felt the fury mount as he saw his well-meant plans thwarted once again.

'To hell with you, Emma Lawrence!' he muttered through gritted teeth. Then, more quietly, 'To hell with you.'

The sunlight streaming through the half-drawn curtains woke Emma as the warming rays fell across the bed. She opened her eyes, disorientated, wondering where she was, and why James wasn't with her. As it came back to her, she lay back against the pillows and sighed. *Jago*.

Gradually she became aware that she was naked beneath the covers and her hand crept down between her legs. Her sex felt full and heavy, a residue of sex-juice coating the tender folds of flesh. As she pressed experimentally against her sleeping clitoris, she felt the unmistakable echo of an orgasm trickle through her body.

'Oh God!' she groaned, snatching her hand away and clasping the sheets up around her chin.

What was happening to her? After weeks of sex being the furthest thing from her mind, suddenly it seemed she couldn't get enough. And every time she came, it seemed that Jago grew stronger, more real. As if she was feeding on her desire. Was she losing her mind?'

No! Emma leapt up from the bed and ran naked into the bathroom. Thanking God that the owner of the Folly had installed modern plumbing, she stood underneath the needle-sharp spray of the shower and let the hot water cascade over her face and body.

She wouldn't think about what had happened yesterday, or last night, she wouldn't allow so much as a glimmer of memory to creep into her mind. Emma felt ashamed as she realised that since she had arrived at the Folly, thinking about her mysterious visitor had eaten into the time she had previously spent mourning the loss of her child. Before, that loss had filled her mind, overpowering everything else. Now it rarely displaced her growing obsession with Jago.

She was supposed to be spending her time this summer trying to make sense of what had happened to her, so she pushed away the uncomfortable thought that she was afraid to let go of her grief. It had become normal to her, as comfortable as an old coat. What would she be without it? Besides, was fixating on a dream lover any more healthy than clinging on to the pain of her loss?

Reminding herself that she was also supposed to be trying to patch up her seriously wavering marriage, Emma determined to switch her mind away from Jago and onto other things. James, for example, and their future together. He had been so angry when they had parted the night before, angrier than she had ever seen him, she mused, shuddering as she remembered his violence.

In the event, when she finally went downstairs, James

was nowhere to be seen. Emma stopped in her tracks as she walked through the kitchen door and found a broad-shouldered, grey-haired woman bending over the Aga.

'Oh good morning, my dear,' she said, beaming as Emma entered the room. 'You must be Mrs Lawrence. Sit yourself down and I'll make you a nice bit of breakfast.'

'Um, thank you. I'm afraid you have the advantage of me . . .?'

'Of course, you wouldn't know me from the devil's wife, would you?' She laughed as if she had said something witty, her round, finely lined face creasing up into deep lines of merriment. 'I'm Mary Helston from the village. I look after this place when it's empty, and I normally do for whoever rents it in the summer. Not that many do, of course.'

'Oh? Why is that?' Emma asked as she pulled out a chair and sat down.

'Hmm?' Mrs Helston turned from the sink and gave her a distracted smile.

'Why don't you get many visitors here?'

Perhaps it was her imagination, but Emma had the curious feeling that Mary Helston wished she hadn't made that last remark.

'Oh you don't want to be troubling yourself with silly rumours,' she said briskly. 'Now, what can I get you for breakfast? I've brought up eggs and bacon from the farm and fresh tomatoes from Mr Helston's garden. Then there's fresh bread from Mrs Jordan's place – she bakes her own you know, every Wednesday and Friday morning – and honey and butter from the big farm near St Ives. What would you like?'

Deciding that she had better turn her attention to her

breakfast or Mrs Helston would as soon cook her the whole lot as blink at her, Emma pushed away the disturbing thoughts and mustered her courage.

'Just toast, please,' she replied.

'Toast?'

Predictably, Mary Helston acted as though she had just asked for roast baby on rye.

'Yes. I'll try the butter . . .'

'Just toast on its own? I know, I'll poach you a couple of eggs to go on top—'

'No. Thank you, but I never eat anything other than toast for breakfast.'

Mrs Helston turned away, clearly scandalised.

'It's a good job that lovely husband of yours appreciates a good breakfast,' she said, cutting two doorstep-sized slices from the crusty bread.

'James? Did you cook him breakfast?'

'That I did – the full works!'

Traitor! Emma thought wryly. She had never known him eat anything more than toast at breakfast time either. Perhaps James had allowed himself to be charmed into accepting the whole shebang.

Emma realised then that Mrs Helston had seen James that morning and might know where he had gone. She asked her as she was larding rich yellow butter on the lightly toasted bread.

'Oh aye, I almost forgot – he asked me to give you a note. Over by the teapot. I'll leave you to it then, Mrs Lawrence, if that's all you want. I'll just have a quick whip round with me duster and the vacuum, then I'll see you again come Friday.'

'Right. Thanks.'

Mrs Helston waited, watching her until Emma bit into the toast. Presumably satisfied that she was going to eat it, she nodded to herself before going over to the door.

'Mrs Helston?' She paused as Emma called her. 'Maybe ... would you like to have a cup of coffee with me before you go? If you've time that is?'

She didn't know what had made her ask, she only knew that she suddenly felt awfully lonely with James already gone. Emma was glad she had asked when Mrs Helston's face lit up with a cheery smile.

'That'd be lovely,' she said, clearly pleased to have been asked. 'Only I'll have tea, if that's all right with you – never could get used to the taste of coffee.'

Emma returned her smile, waiting until the older woman had gone before picking up James's note.

I've gone into St Ives, she read, *a bit of business has cropped up. Came to see if you'd like to come along, but you'd locked your door. That's taking things a bit far, don't you think, Em? See you later.*

Emma put the letter down, frowning. Her door hadn't been locked, what was he talking about? *Jago*. Could he have barred her door when her husband came calling?

A hundred unanswerable questions swirled in Emma's mind as she drank her way steadily through the pot of coffee. By the time Mrs Helston came in for a break, she was ready to ask some of them.

'Mrs Helston,' she said as the older woman settled down to her tea and biscuits with a sigh of contentment. 'Do you know anyone locally called Jago?'

Mary Helston put her cup carefully onto its saucer and looked at Emma. Emma fancied that her skin had paled under the rosy complexion and she unconsciously held her breath as she waited for her to answer.

'Why do you ask? Where have you heard that name?'

Emma shrugged with feigned nonchalance.

'Oh, I can't remember exactly... I thought maybe it was the gardener's name?'

'Gardener? What gardener?'

Emma thought of the man she had seen from the bedroom window walking along the path away from the house that first morning.

'I thought I saw someone in the garden the other morning. Are you telling me that the Folly doesn't have a gardener?'

Mrs Helston smiled, though Emma gained the distinct impression that it was forced.

'D'you think it'd be in such a state if it had? No, me and Mr Helston, we do our best.'

'Perhaps it was Mr Helston I saw?'

'No, he's barely left the house the past few days.' She grinned suddenly. 'That'll be the ghost of old Jago Pengarron you saw, I reckon.'

It seemed to Emma that the air in the room stilled as she digested this.

'Jago Pengarron?' she echoed faintly.

'Yes. Just a silly rumour, but there are plenty who *know* someone who's seen him – none that have seen him themselves.' Mrs Helston snorted to show her scepticism. 'It was him that built the Folly, you see, when he married.'

'When was this?'

'A couple of hundred years ago.' Mary Helston leaned

forward in her seat as she warmed to her theme. 'Some said that he picked this spot because it's so far away from the village, up here on its own. Strange goings on, there were, and a lot of bad talk in the village.'

'What kind of things?' Emma asked, not sure whether she really wanted to know.

Mrs Helston's face closed and she shook her head.

'Best not to know, I always say. Drove his wife mad, it did, after she had the baby.'

'Mad? In what way, mad?'

'Threw herself off the cliff with the babe in her arms. And him no more than three months old. Shame.' Mary Helston shook her head and lifted herself heavily from her chair. Carrying their cups across to the sink, she rinsed them under the tap and set them to drain. 'It was a bad business by all accounts. Poor lass. And Jago Pengarron never got over the loss. Mad with grief he was, and guilt too I shouldn't wonder, if the stories are true. What that girl did for him! It was a scandal.'

Emma thought of the crying she had heard in the garden the day before and felt uncomfortable. Had it really been an unhappy echo from the past?

'Yet it's supposed to be Jago's ghost that haunts the Folly, not his wife's?' she said.

'That's right. They say he roams the cliffs looking for her – but you don't want to be listening to me! Mr Helston'd box my ears if he heard me telling you such nonsense!' Mary grinned in a way that told Emma that Mr Helston would dare to do no such thing.

'It's a good story, though, I guess,' she said, feigning a casualness she did not feel.

'Oh yes, it's a good story all right. Probably one made

up by the smugglers in the last century to keep curious folk away from these parts.'

'Effective, then.'

'True. If you're interested in the local history, you can find out more in the museum in St Ives. Lots of American tourists go there, I believe.'

Emma hid a smile at Mrs Helston's casual dismissal of her as an American tourist. 'Thanks, I might go in tomorrow with James.' She had to ask just one more thing about the story of Jago Pengarron. 'Mrs Pengarron – what was her name?' she asked, knowing the answer before Mary Helston replied.

'Demelza,' the older woman said, as Emma had known she would, 'that was it. Jago and Demelza.'

It was hot in St Ives, a heat haze shimmering across the ocean as James sat on the sea wall and watched the Meridian Guest House. A discreet enquiry with the chambermaid had revealed that this was where Andrew Joiner had run to ground. No one in their right mind who was trying to hide from the press used their own name.

He'd covered stories like this one before and had few feelings either way about his quarry. If he bothered to think about it, he supposed that if Andrew Joiner was genuinely trying to get away from it all, James staking out his hideaway was an infringement of his privacy. If, however, as James suspected, the whole thing was nothing more than a publicity stunt, then he was fair game. Besides, if James didn't cover the story, then someone else would.

James felt sticky even in his T-shirt and shorts and

his bad temper of the night before had spilled over into the day, making him feel prickly and irritable. He wished he knew what was going on with Emma. As it was he felt as though he was lost in a forest without a map, her behaviour was so unpredictable.

He felt himself harden as he thought of how she had taken him out of his pants and sucked him to a climax the day before. God, it had been good, but again he had gained the uncomfortable impression that she was using him, not really noticing him at all. It made him feel less, somehow, souring the experience for him and leaving him feeling vaguely resentful. Besides, Emma had never done anything that spontaneous before – he wished he knew what had come over her.

'Mr Lawrence!'

He looked up as he heard his name, his spirits lifting as he recognised the slight figure of Morgana Helston coming along the path towards him. With a brief wave of acknowledgement, he shielded his eyes from the sun and watched her approach.

She was wearing a dress today, in a muddy burgundy colour with shoestring straps. It fell straight from her chest, skimming her full breasts and ending midway between knee and crotch. Despite the heat, she was wearing a cream T-shirt underneath it and scarlet-coloured Doc Martens, without laces. The heavy boots made her legs look frail, the huge flapping tongues slapping against her shins as she walked.

James had a brief, vivid vision of how she would look naked. Her breasts were out of proportion to the rest of her body, but not freakishly so, just enough to excite him.

POSSESSION

As she came closer, he imagined himself gathering them up in his hands and burying his face in the warm, damp valley between them and his cock twitched in response.

'Hi!' she said as she reached him. 'God, it's hot!'

She flopped down on the wall beside him and James caught a waft of citrus-based perfume and fresh sweat. For some reason the combination made him even harder and he shifted uncomfortably on the wall.

'Is this where Andrew Joiner is hiding then?' she asked, her eyes dancing at him.

'Allegedly. What brings you here?'

Morgana looked at him steadily, her clear grey eyes unblinking.

'I was looking for you.'

James felt his own eyes widen as he was caught by her gaze. There was a frankness there that was unmistakable, a direct invitation that made him think that perhaps his fantasies abut her were not so very unattainable after all. Surely she didn't mean . . .?'

'Were you?' he managed feebly.

Morgana held his gaze for a moment longer, then she grinned.

'Yeah – I reckon you owe me a cup of coffee and a sticky cake for all that dusting I did for you the other day.'

James's eyebrows rose. Despite the now guileless expression in her eyes, James was sure she was playing with him, teasing him. Had his attraction towards her been so obvious? More to the point, could it really be that it was mutual?

Morgana wasn't giving any more away – she had

slipped off the wall and had bent to pick up the cream string shoulder bag which she had left at her feet.

'There's a terrific tea shop in a little village further along here – how about it?'

Now James was sure that there was a challenge in her direct grey gaze and he felt himself rise to it, both figuratively and literally. Feigning nonchalance, he shrugged. Tea was no big deal and he found that he didn't want her to go, not just yet.

'Sure. Looks like this turkey's staying in to roost for now, so I don't see why I shouldn't leave him to it. After all, I am supposed to be on holiday!'

Morgana laughed and, slipping her hand through his arm, they walked back to his hire car together. She directed him to a village which consisted of some two dozen houses clustered around a crossroads, overlooking the sea. Every now and then as he drove, he sensed her lean towards him a little more than was necessary and once or twice as he changed gear her fingertips brushed against his forearm, making him shiver.

Did she know how much he was attracted to her? James was finding it curiously difficult to breathe as the tension mounted in the little car. His prick felt as if it would burst through the denim of his jeans, his erection was almost painfully intense. It was a relief when they parked outside the little tea room at the top end of the village and he was able to get out of the car. As she came round to his side, Morgana's eyes lingered at his crotch and James felt himself flush, feeling like a youth again. To his relief, she didn't say anything, but the look she gave him was certainly not designed to deflate him.

Inside the tea shop it was all original beams and gingham-checked tablecloths. Morgana, who was apparently a regular, ordered them both a cream tea without consulting James. His eyes widened when it came and he saw the thick, pale yellow cream and blood-red jam which Morgana piled on the still-warm scones.

'Eat up,' she urged him. 'You can't come all the way to Cornwall and not have one of our famous cream teas.'

James was sure that the tea was as delicious as it looked, but truth was he hardly tasted it, he was too busy watching Morgana eat. For such a slender girl she clearly had a healthy appetite. James felt hot as he watched her small pink tongue lick the cream away which had stuck to her lips, imagining how her full, red lips would taste if he kissed her. Of strawberry jam and cream right now, he guessed, sticky and warm and—

'Penny for them?'

James started as Morgana cut into his thoughts, avoiding her eyes as he saw that she was looking at him as if she could read his mind.

'My thoughts aren't worth a penny,' he told her, refilling their tea cups. 'How long are you planning to spend with your grandmother?'

'I'm just here for the summer. You?'

James's face clouded over as he thought of Emma, locking the door against him up at the Folly. He supposed he didn't blame her really after his outburst the night before, but he was offended by it all the same.

'I don't know,' he admitted now. 'We came because I thought it would help Emma . . .'

Glancing at Morgana's face, he saw that she was

listening to him, *really* listening and he found himself telling her about the accident, and how Emma had reacted to it.

'I was driving, you see,' he concluded. 'It was my fault, and I don't think she's ever going to forgive me for it.'

He hadn't realised that he believed that until he said it aloud and a wave of desolation washed over him. Seeing it, Morgana reached across the table and covered his hand with hers.

'Had you been drinking?'

James nodded, ashamed.

'Not a lot, but enough.'

Chancing a glance at Morgana, he saw sympathy in her face rather than disgust and he felt a surge of feeling for her. She didn't say anything, no empty words of justification or condemnation, she simply seemed attuned to the way he felt – the shame, coupled with the knowledge that no amount of recrimination could make things different.

Her hand felt small and cool over his and James twisted his palm upward so that he could hold it. It was like a breath of fresh air, talking to Morgana. James sensed that she understood him, that she cared about how he felt. Her treatment of him was in such stark contrast to Emma's that at that moment he felt closer to Morgana than he did to his wife.

They sat like that for several minutes, then Morgana said, 'Let's go down to the beach and fuck.'

James was startled, though his body was quick to respond to the suggestion. Yes! it screamed. Yes, yes *yes!* Wordlessly, he nodded. Leaving enough money on the table to cover the bill, he followed Morgana out of the tea shop and along the path which led towards the sea. Whereas before, in the tea room, they had talked non-stop, now they were silent, each wrapped up in their own thoughts, the sexual tension increasing between them with every step.

Once they reached the top of the cliffs, they had to climb over a stile to reach the narrow coastal path which ran along the cliff top. Morgana walked quickly, casting frequent, mischievous glances over her shoulder at James who was more cautious as he trod the stony pathway. The sea seemed to be a long way down to his left, the path passing perilously close to the edge in places. None of this seemed to bother Morgana in the least, her step in the heavy boots was sure, her hips swinging enticingly beneath the flimsy dress.

Just as James was beginning to think that they'd never stop walking, the path began to descend steeply and he saw that they were heading for the beach below. It was no more than a little cove really, the firm, yellow sands totally deserted apart from the seagulls screeching overhead. The tide was out, the waves feeble, tired-looking as they sucked and hissed at the wet sand.

As they reached the bottom, Morgana caught hold of his hand and urged him to run with her across the sand. It was then that James saw for the first time the huge, black caves, gaping like open mouths on the side of the cliff. He hung back as Morgana headed for the entrance to one, earning himself a quizzical glance.

'Why don't we stay here in the sunshine?' he suggested, pulling her against him and trying to kiss her.

But Morgana evaded him, laughing.

'I know a better place – come on. Trust me!'

Dancing out of his reach, she ducked into the gloom of the cave and, reluctantly, James followed her. As he had known it would be, the interior of the cave was cold and dank, the walls slimed with wet seaweed, the sand soggy beneath his feet. He had to hurry to keep up with Morgana, for she was walking quickly along the tunnel made by the sea, clearly harbouring none of the childhood fears that James had suddenly remembered. He felt an instant's antipathy towards her – Christ, they'd come here to screw, not conduct an expedition into the heart of the cliffs – then he stopped in his tracks and let out his breath on a gasp.

Morgana was standing in a perfect circle of light, some six feet across. The sand beneath her feet was dry and powdery, the rocks gleaming in the sunlight which poured through the chimney hole in the rocks above their heads. James's sweeping gaze took in candle stubs in bottles lying on the flat rocks, saw a folded beach mat lying abandoned on one of the rocks, and he realised that this was a well-used hidey-hole, obviously popular with local lovers. He wondered how often Morgana had been here, then decided it didn't matter in the least. Bathed in warmth and light, Morgana smiled happily and held out her arms to him.

She felt fragile as he held her, her bones delicate, her flesh firm and springy beneath his fingertips. She smiled at him, a wide, open-mouthed smile and, stepping back, slipped the thin straps of her dress off her shoulders. It slithered down her slender body to land in a heap around her feet. Stepping out of it, Morgana kicked it away and faced him dressed in her cream-coloured T-shirt and bright red pants, the scarlet Doc Martens absurd on the end of her slender legs.

James felt the breath hurting in his chest as he forced himself to hold back. He wanted to leap on her, to ravish her on the powdery sand, to take and take until they were both exhausted. Something in the way Morgana was looking at him told him that she sensed this need and was not fazed by it. Holding his eye, she curled her fingers round the edge of her T-shirt and slowly, oh-so slowly, she peeled it upward, pulling it over her head and throwing it aside.

Her bare breasts were large and firm, the same butterscotch colour all over as the rest of her. Her delicate ribcage looked too fragile to support the generous globes of flesh and, unable to hold back for another moment, James stepped forward and gathered them up in his hands.

'Morgana . . .' he whispered, dipping his head to take one brown crest into his mouth.

Her skin tasted warm and sweet, the nipple puckering deliciously under his tongue and pressing against it. He lathed it lingeringly with his tongue before turning his attention to its twin, bringing that too to a bursting peak. Her nipple felt rubbery between his lips, springing back into shape as he pulled gently at it, making her gasp.

'Oh yes,' she said, laughing, 'let's do it now!'

James needed no more encouragement. Tugging at his shirt, he pulled it up, over his head, without bothering to unfasten the buttons. Morgana watched him, caressing herself lazily with the tip of her finger, drawing it up to the tip of her nipples as he stepped out of his jeans. Once he was naked, her cool grey eyes rested for a moment on his erect penis, and her lips curved into a smile.

'*Ver-ry* nice!' she said, her voice husky, at odds with the teasing expression in her eyes. James reached for her, but once more she evaded him. 'Wait . . .'

She reached into her bag and drew out a condom. James took it without comment, dispensing with the wrapper and unrolling it quickly along the length of his cock. He watched as Morgana lifted her arms and tilted her face up to the sun. Closing her eyes, she turned slowly in the circle of light, as if wanting to feel the warmth seep into her body from all sides.

The sight of her firm young body thus exposed was too much for James. With a decisive sweep of his arm, he pulled her against him and ran his hand impatiently over her flanks.

'You little witch!' he growled, pressing the hardness at his groin against the firm, full globes of her bottom. It sought and found the tender groove between her buttocks and nestled there hopefully.

Now that they were standing together, skin on skin, bone grinding against bone, Morgana seemed to cast aside her mischievous mood. With a muted cry, she turned in his arms and pressed herself into his embrace. Her nipples grazed against the hard planes of his chest and he felt the rasp of her pubic hair against the soft-skinned hardness of his shaft.

'God, I want you,' he murmured, his lips passing over the cropped hair above her ears.

Her hair was unexpectedly soft, the silky, dark strands tickling against his nose as he breathed in the musky, feminine perfume she was wearing. Everything about her excited his senses – the way she smelled, the springiness of her flesh beneath his fingers, the sounds she made in the back of her throat as he kissed her – all combined to drive him to the brink of losing control.

They kissed hungrily, tongues exploring, thrusting, expressing the strength of their desire far more eloquently than any words could. Morgana wound herself about him, her arms, her legs, the tender pressure of her lovely breasts, until James hardly knew where he ended and she began. He wanted to be inside her, to enter her so that they became one body, as close as any two people could get.

Together they sank onto the warm, finely grained sand. Moulding the tender dip at the base of her back with his palm, James traced the outline of her buttocks, running his fingernail lightly along the crease until he reached the puckered rose of her anus. He circled it lightly, stroking delicately at the sensitive skin before reaching lower, between her legs, encountering her vulva from behind.

She was wet, the slippery folds of her labia slick with the heavy dew of arousal. Just the feel of her feminine secretions was enough to make James's cock twitch against the soft swell of her belly. He felt himself begin to leak, the thin, sticky fluid smearing her skin, mingling with their perspiration.

He had reached her clitoris now, found it to be swollen and slippery as a small bead. Morgana sighed as he touched it, the slow expulsion of air swirling around his mouth as she continued to kiss him. The tip of her tongue was pointed and firm and as he flicked it with his own tongue he was overcome by the urge to taste the now throbbing button of flesh beneath his fingers.

Pressing her gently onto her back, James swept his tongue downwards, licking from the place where her collarbones met, between her breasts and across her stomach. The springy pubic hair on her mons tickled his chin as he delicately parted the labia with his tongue to reveal the small nub which was his goal.

'Ah! Oh, that's good!' she moaned as he lapped at the tiny mass of nerve endings.

He could see by the tension in her stomach and the way her thighs had begun to tremble that she was already close to coming and he slowed down, wanting to savour the experience. The salty-sweet secretions coated his lips and tongue. He couldn't get enough of her and he moved his lips further down to draw at the source of the slippery, honey-like juices.

Morgana moaned, and, knowing that he had frustrated her by breaking his rhythm, he reluctantly returned his attention to the true centre of her pleasure. She was hot, so hot that his fingers slipped easily over her skin as he caressed her stomach. It was stretched tight as a drum, her abdominal muscles clenched into a ball as she neared climax.

Sensing the impending release, James flicked his tongue more quickly back and forth over her quivering clitoris, grazing it gently with his teeth until she began to cry out. Judging his moment carefully, he enclosed the throbbing nub between his lips and sucked gently on it.

Morgana's legs scissored around his shoulders as the sensations exploded. She arched her back, lifting herself off the sand so that only her head and shoulders were balanced on the ground and her legs were braced around his shoulders.

James took her weight easily, burying his face in the wet, convulsing folds of her sex and entering her with his tongue.

'Oh-oh-oh!' she gasped, collapsing back down onto the powdery sand. 'Fuck me James – quickly, now!'

Only too happy to oblige, James flipped her over onto her front and lifted her buttocks up so that she was balancing on her knees and elbows. She had a beautiful arse, generous, but firm and round, her sex visible below the crease, open for him, waiting for the thrust of his penis. The over-stimulated flesh of her vulva was suffused with blood, the skin a deep pink, the labia plump and puffy, welcoming.

With a strangled groan of delight, James positioned himself at the entrance of her body and sank into her heated flesh. Once inside, he rested there for a moment, relishing the feel of her body enclosing him. God, but it felt good to be inside her! His cock felt as if it had been enveloped in warmth and moisture and as he began to withdraw, he felt the silky, cleated walls of her vagina ripple deliciously around the shaft, as if she did not want to let him go.

Easing back into her again, James reached round to where the generous breasts were hanging below her, their rosy brown tips brushing the powdery sand as the force of his body moving in and out of her made them swing. He kissed the damp skin at the nape of her neck and rested his cheek against her narrow back for an instant as he felt the gathering of pressure in his balls.

'Now,' Morgana whispered through gritted teeth, 'make it hard, James – come into me deeply.'

'Oh God . . .!'

His hips began to pump back and forth as he thrust into her, faster and faster, racing towards the moment when he would fill her with the seed now forcing its way into his cock. She seemed to be panting in time with him as he thrust and withdrew, going in deeper as she pushed her buttocks back against him.

Then it came, a rushing, gushing torrent, it seemed, of hot fluid, pumping from his body, prevented only by a thin skin of latex from flooding into hers.

Afterwards, James rested inside her, in no hurry to withdraw from the haven he had found there between her thighs. He felt like shouting, if he had had the energy, for with Morgana he felt restored, complete again. A man. He hadn't realised how much his trials with Emma had worn him down, made him doubt his own potency. There were no such doubts with Morgana. Smiling to himself, he kissed each individual vertebra on the curve of her back.

Morgana laughed, wriggling her bottom lewdly against him as she felt him begin to stiffen again inside her. James moved his hips experimentally, amazed to have recovered so quickly. Then he felt the lick of icy cold water over his toes and he drew back with a curse.

'Christ! Morgana – it's sea water! The fucking tide's coming in!'

She stood up and began to climb into her clothes. James, who was by now scrabbling into his, was fazed by her laid-back attitude.

'Hadn't we better get out of here?' he said, eyeing the entrance to the cave with trepidation. Visions of being trapped in this confined space as the tide overtook them danced in his mind and he felt slightly panicky.

'Yeah – we'd better not hang about,' she agreed.

Then she turned and smiled at him, and he saw the look in her eyes. Saw the slow-burning, feverish excitement that had little do with sex and everything to do with the adrenalin pumping through her veins. And he knew that she had known all along about the potential danger of coming into the caves. And that the possibility of danger had added to her excitement.

James felt a shiver run through him as he followed her out, not of fear this time, but of exhilaration. And he knew that this could not be a once only thing. He was going to have to have Morgana again. And again.

Six

Tossing and turning in the big four-poster, Emma dreamed she was visiting the house for the first time, when it was new, in the late eighteenth century. In her dream the fabric of the building was rough and unweathered, the beautiful furniture – made especially for the house by the Adam brothers and Thomas Chippendale with a few well-chosen pieces by Sheraton and Hepplewhite – were all new.

As her carriage had drawn up outside, she had watched as the great doors opened, and there stood Jago Pengarron on the threshold, his new wife by his side. They were smiling, welcoming her, but she hesitated before accepting her coachman's helping hand, for she sensed an exclusivity about them, an inviolable togetherness that left her feeling quite bereft.

Emma was wearing a long, full-skirted gown of silk and velvet in the deepest ruby red. The bodice of the dress was cut low to expose her cleavage and leave her shoulders bare, and her hair had been piled up on top of her head to accentuate the long sweep of her neck and shoulders. She felt attractive, feminine in a way she had never felt before. She even carried herself differently, her back straight, head up, her steps small and rapid on the stone steps.

They had greeted her and drawn her into the house, making her feel welcome, one on either side of her. Jago was dressed in a shirt of fine linen which clung to the musculature of his arms and chest. As she walked across the hall to the dining room, Emma was aware of the sheer maleness of him, distracting her from her hostess, making her limbs feel heavy.

Demelza was holding onto her arm, her fingertips stroking the delicate skin at the crook of Emma's elbow. The light but insistent caress served only to increase her sexual tension. Jago opened the door to the dining room and Emma saw that the table had been set for dinner. Three place settings, the silverware gleaming dully in the light of the numerous candles flickering in their holders placed around the room.

In her dream there was no conversation, nothing to distract her from the heady sensations trickling through her body as she took her seat between her hosts. The chairs were placed very closely together at one end of the oval-shaped table. Emma was supremely aware of Jago's leg pressing lightly against hers under the table. After a few minutes, Emma felt Demelza's slippered foot run softly up and down her calf.

Food was brought by a shadowy servant. Emma ate, though with no awareness of what she was putting between her lips. The wine moistened her dry throat and she drank freely, aware that the dimly lit room had taken on a kind of hazy shimmer. Her hosts' faces appeared to her as two pale ovals, lit by the flickering candlelight, their features indistinct. She was aware of the glitter of their eyes, of the flash of their teeth as they laughed and talked, but she could hear nothing. It was as if she was locked into a soundless, velvety cocoon in which sound had no place, only sight and smell and touch and the steadily increasing tempo of her own arousal.

Then the meal was over and Jago Pengarron was stroking his fingers along the curve of her neck, leaning towards her to allow his lips to brush against her hair. Emma shivered, glancing nervously towards her hostess, who merely smiled and nodded with a curious serenity, as if this was how it had been planned.

Like a puppet, Emma sat acquiescent as Demelza rose from her chair and moved to stand behind her. The other woman allowed her fingertips to play across the soft white skin of Emma's exposed neck and shoulders before they went to work on the fastenings of her dress.

Some small part of her wondered at the propriety of sitting at her hosts' table and allowing the mistress of the house to undress her while the master watched. She opened her mouth to make a half-hearted protest, but Jago silenced her by pressing his lips against hers.

It was a most effective method. Emma felt the delicate probe of his tongue against her teeth and she opened her mouth, welcoming him in. As he kissed her, she revelled in the way her body seemed to melt, a small knot of molten heat settling in the pit of her stomach. She could feel the soft lips of her hostess moving across her upper back, sending delicious little shivers up and down her spine.

When at last Jago gently pulled back, Emma thrilled at the expression in his eyes. They were like two luminous pools of desire, the pupils dilated to the point where they virtually covered the iris. Knowing that that desire was for her acted as a spur to her own arousal and she felt the tender, hidden flesh between her thighs swell and moisten in response.

A look passed between her host and hostess and Emma found herself being helped to her feet. As she rose, her unfastened bodice fell away from her body, exposing her naked breasts. Jago's appreciative gaze was hot on them, though his fingers were cool as he reached out and traced their shape.

Emma looked down and watched his strong, tanned fingers move across the milky whiteness of her skin. The soft rose tint of her areolae darkened as he circled them, the smooth skin puckering and hardening as the nipple grew and became taut. Jago seemed to be in no hurry as he explored the contours of her breasts, sweeping his fingertips from the sensitive crease beneath them up towards the pit of her arm.

Meanwhile, Emma could feel Demelza releasing her from her corset and peeling her skirts down, past her hips to her feet. Before long she was standing naked before them in the golden glow of the candles. Demelza came round to stand by Jago, her eyes assessing as she ran them over Emma's naked body.

Emma trembled under their gaze though she held herself perfectly still, waiting. The tension in her belly was growing to the point where it was almost unbearable and she felt the perspiration break through her pores as a dull pulse began to beat between her legs. Her mind felt numb, foggy, all rational process subjugated to the greater lure of desire.

Then Demelza smiled, a look of delight passing across her face as she glanced at her husband. The smile he gave her was one of indulgence and for a moment Emma felt excluded again. Seconds later, she was drawn into a three-way embrace that dispelled all such thoughts from her mind.

It was strange, to be completely naked in a room where everyone else was fully clothed. She felt deliciously vulnerable and the feeling only served to add to her mounting excitement. Jago and Demelza moved in unison, walking around her, and she turned with them, so that her back was to the table.

Looking from one to the other, she saw the affection they held for her and was reassured, though when they moved towards her, she took a step backwards. The cool mahogany of the dining table pressed against the soft, fleshy globes of her buttocks. In the light of the guttering candles, the couple's faces as they came closer seemed lit by strange sepulchral shapes and they moved in and out of focus as Emma lowered herself slowly onto her back.

The wood was smooth and cool against her heated skin, unyielding as she lay down on top of it. Jago leaned over her, a dark, beguiling shadow, and kissed her lips with teasing, butterfly kisses. Emma was aware of Demelza watching approvingly as his large hands smoothed a path down her body, stroking her, making the small hairs on her skin quiver against his palm.

Slowly, as if he had all the time in the world, Jago

began to kiss a meandering path down her throat to her breasts, where he lingered at the tumescent nipples. Licking each one, he ran his fingers lightly over the tips as his saliva dried on them and made them tighter still.

Emma felt a moan bubble deep in her throat, then Demelza's mouth was on hers. Emma's eyes widened in surprise as she felt the full, soft lips moving on her mouth. She had never kissed another woman before and for a split second her mind recognised the taboo, before her body swept it away.

Jago was at her knees now, kissing the soft skin of her inner thighs as she pressed them tightly together. His tongue probed the gap between them, coaxing her to allow them to fall apart. Emma's breathing became harsh as Demelza lifted one full breast and fed the nipple into her hot, sweet mouth. The sensation was exquisite, so much so that Emma's thighs parted of their own accord. She felt Jago's hands at her knees, easing them further apart, exposing her most private flesh to the cool kiss of the air.

His hand cupped her vulva, the middle finger entering her slowly, sinking into the wet, pulpy flesh and moving in a circular motion deeper and deeper inside her. Demelza's small hand was cool against the heated skin of her stomach as it rested there, as if measuring the tautness of her belly.

Emma felt hot, so hot that she moved her head from side to side, eager for the coldness of the silky wood against her cheeks. She sighed as Jago withdrew his finger from her body, gazing up at him pleadingly as he walked round to the head of the table and looked down at her. Passing his fingers across her lips, he coaxed them apart so that he could enter her mouth in the same way as he had entered her vagina.

With a small sigh of surrender, Emma drew in his moisture-slicked finger and sucked it clean of her juices. Jago gave her a small, approving smile. From her angle, seeing his face upside down, it looked like a sudden downturn of his mouth. Placing his hands on either side of her head, he raised it so that she could see Demelza caressing the insides of her thighs. The other woman gave Emma a small, catlike smile and licked her lips.

Emma could not take her eyes off that small, pink tongue which darted out and wetted Demelza's lips. It reminded her of a kitten's – sharp and pointed, glistening with moisture. She tensed as suddenly, without warning, Demelza dipped her head and burrowed her tongue into the warm, sticky folds of Emma's sex.

Everything in her told her to pull away, to put an end to this, but it was too good, and Jago was kissing her again, his tongue thrusting in unison with his wife's working diligently at those other, less public lips. Demelza licked delicately at the tender folds of skin, swirling her tongue around Emma's clitoris as if it was the greatest delicacy.

Emma's hips bucked involuntarily and Demelza reached up to hold her still. There was no escape from sensation, she was being held at her shoulders by Jago and at her hips by Demelza. Between them Emma found all her senses were stretched to their limit. She could hear the laboured sound of her own breathing and fancied she heard the erratic thud of her heartbeat echoing in her skull. From between her legs she could hear the wet, lapping sounds caused by Demelza's tongue and her own copious juices.

Jago was kneading her breasts now, his hands less gentle, his nails scratching slightly at the over-sensitised flesh. He rolled her nipples between his finger and thumb, pressing down on them with his thumbpads as Emma made a small sound of protest. It was if he had found a switch, a means by which to transmit sensation from her breasts to her womb. Emma felt a fresh rush of moisture seep from her and Demelza lapped at it greedily with her tongue, clearly enjoying herself.

Emma could feel the hot, jagged waves of orgasm gathering in her womb ready to break over her. As if sensing this, Demelza centred her attention on her clitoris, moving it with her tongue, rolling the tip over the slippery skin which covered the hard little bead. Then she closed her teeth, oh-so-gently over it, and nibbled.

At the same moment, Jago leant over her and sucked one nipple into his mouth, while pinching the other between finger and thumb. Emma's mouth opened in a startled 'o' as the room seemed to splinter and disintegrate before her eyes, the candlelight flaring as if each little flame was about to become one blazing inferno.

'Oh God!'

She sat up in bed, her clitoris pulsing wildly as the climax woke her, wrenching her cruelly back to reality. The bedclothes were twisted around her, damp with her sweat, and her vulva pulsed still.

Slowly, Emma lay back on the pillows. How could she have dreamt such a thing? So vividly that she actually came. And as a result of another woman sucking her . . .

Emma groaned, filled with shame and an undeniable excitement which remained long after the last echoes of her climax faded away.

Emma was on edge at breakfast the following morning. James had not yet emerged from his bedroom, where he had retreated the moment he had arrived home the previous evening, but that was the least of her worries. The worst thing was that Jago had not appeared to her since she had spoken with Mrs Helston about him.

After discovering who he was, and for whom he had mistaken her, she had waited for him to come to her with eagerness, hoping to talk with him and find out more about him. The minutes of the night had ticked on, more onerous as her eyelids had drooped and, eventually, she had given up her vigil and fallen into a restless sleep.

The dream had affected her mood on waking and Emma could not seem to shake it off. She wasn't one to attach importance to dreams, or to believe that they held any meaning, but she could not shake off the feeling that this dream had been different. It seemed silly to allow it to affect her in such a way, but she couldn't seem to pull herself together. By the time James walked into the kitchen she was feeling thoroughly scratchy.

'I want to go into St Ives today,' she told him without preamble.

James, who had been struggling with his own nocturnal fantasies which invariably had Morgana Helston as their star, looked at her in surprise.

'Shall we check the weather forecast first – the sky looks very grey.'

Emma made an impatient gesture.

'I don't care about the weather. I won't dissolve if it rains. You don't seem very keen on my coming with you – are you still angry about yesterday?'

'Yesterday?' James looked at her blankly, having completely forgotten how she had locked her door against him the previous day.

'Well, I've barely seen you since, I thought you must be sulking,' she told him.

Feeling that she was deliberately trying to provoke him for some reason, James refused to rise to it.

'No,' he said. 'It's just that I'm going to be working on a story – it could get boring for you.'

Emma looked at him oddly.

'I won't get under your feet. I thought we'd travel in together, then meet up later on.'

James couldn't think of any reason why he could refuse. Besides he was probably being paranoid – he hadn't made any plans to meet up with Morgana in St Ives today. He had simply been hoping that she might appear again as she had yesterday.

'Okay,' he said grudgingly. 'Can you be ready in half an hour?'

'Sure. I'll go get my bag.'

There was no doubt about it, James's behaviour was decidedly odd, Emma mused as she packed a notepad and pencil in her shoulder bag and ran a brush through her hair. He still seemed impatient with her, but there was a subtle change in his attitude. *Impersonal* was the only word she could think of. No matter – he'd been altogether too emotional lately for her liking. She shrugged her shoulders and with a last glance around the room she ran down the stairs to meet him.

St Ives delighted her with its narrow streets paved with granite and its bustling harbour front. She barely noticed that James was so eager to be off that he didn't bother to kill the engine when he dropped her, her goal was to find the public library and spend the morning in the local history section.

A sense of being on the verge of something exciting made her walk faster, the adrenalin pumping steadily through her veins as she walked away from the more touristy areas and towards the civic part of the town.

Pausing to admire the 'Dual Form' sculpture presented to the town by the artist, Barbara Hepworth, Emma asked a local newspaper vendor for directions.

'If it's local history you be wanting, you'd be best to browse through some of the galleries as well,' the man told her once he'd given her directions. 'There's one down the alley apace which might interest you.'

Thanking him, Emma made a mental note to do as he suggested before moving on to the library. It didn't take long, with the assistance of a helpful librarian, to locate the contemporary documents of the time. Jago Pengarron had evidently been a prominent citizen, a well-respected merchant. His fortune, it seemed, came from his interests in the then thriving pilchard industry, the centre of which was in St Ives.

'They say he used to pose as a simple fisherman so that he could spy on his men and keep them on their toes,' the librarian told Emma.

Emma glanced at the girl. She was in her early twenties with thin blonde hair tied back in a ponytail. Her face was unremarkable, apart from her eyes which shone with intelligence and a lively interest in everything around her.

'Are there many tales about Jago Pengarron told in these parts?' Emma asked her, carefully refolding the old newspaper she had been reading.

The girl smiled and, with a quick glance around to check that her supervisor wasn't around, she drew out the chair beside Emma and sat down.

'They say he wasn't really a merchant at all, that the fishing was just a front.'

'Really? For what?'

'Well, he had two ships, you see, which he used to export the fish all over the known world. On the return voyage he would pick up goods to sell in England – and not all of them would be legal imports.'

'You mean he was a smuggler?' Emma was incredulous. The more she found out about him, the more intriguing Jago Pengarron sounded.

The girl shrugged.

'So they say. And if you think about it, it all makes a kind of sense, doesn't it? He built that weird house, miles away from anywhere with its own beach. There are huge caves along that stretch of the coast – there could easily have been a tunnel built leading from the beach right up to the house itself.'

Emma, who hadn't even realised that there was a beach below the cliffs on which the Folly stood, sat very still. She had assumed that the scandalous goings-on that Mary Helston had hinted at had involved Demelza Pengarron – could it be that she was only indirectly involved, that the real scandal concerned Jago's business interests?

'I heard that his wife went mad and threw herself off the cliffs.'

The librarian nodded.

'It's awful, isn't it? That poor girl. They'd only been married for a year.'

'Why did she do it?' Emma asked, fascinated.

'Goodness knows. It was all a long time ago, wasn't it?'

Not to Jago Pengarron it isn't, Emma thought sadly. To him it could all have taken place only yesterday. Realising that the librarian was watching her closely, she forced a smile. There was one more question she had to ask her.

'And what of Jago himself – what happened to him?'

'No one knows. Apparently, after his wife died he was mad with grief. The locals used to see him walking along the cliff path at night to the point where she had jumped, calling for her.' She shuddered. 'It gives you the willies, just the thought of it, doesn't it? Then, suddenly, he disappeared.'

'Disappeared?' Emma echoed, aware that her heart had skipped a beat.

'Yeah. Some said he must have jumped, others that he was killed by pirates, or someone he had fiddled. It was a mystery. His body was never discovered.'

Emma felt as if something was crawling over her skin. She felt sick, a horrible sense of foreboding threatening to overwhelm her. Suddenly, all she wanted was to be outside in the sunlight.

'Thank you for all your help,' she said politely. 'It's been real interesting.'

She stood up, but the girl's curiosity had clearly been pricked by Emma's interest in the Pengarron family.

'Is there any particular reason why you're finding out about all this? I don't mean to sound rude, but...'

Emma smiled tightly.

'My husband has rented Pengarron's Folly for the summer. It's a fascinating place,' she said, gathering up her things.

She paused as she saw that the girl's eyes had grown round and she was no longer bothering to hide her curiosity.

'Ooh, you're not *staying* there, are you?'

'Yes – for the rest of the summer. Why do you ask?'

The younger woman seemed to shake herself and she grinned.

'No reason. It's just that they say that the ghost of Jago Pengarron still walks the cliffs at night. Spooky stuff, eh?'

Emma smiled.

'Not really. He's there all the time, actually, not just at night. He and I have become quite good friends.'

She turned and walked away, leaving the librarian staring after her as if she had gone mad.

Perhaps she had, she mused as she wandered along the narrow streets, deep in thought. Surely it was not sane to become obsessed with a man who had been dead for two hundred years? Searching through her mind for her scant knowledge of European history, Emma worked out that Jago would have died at the beginning of Britain's long struggle with Napoleonic France. He might have read Jane Austen when her books were first published, or the poetry of Blake. He and Demelza might have heard Handel performed or danced at one of the great balls of the time.

These thoughts gradually made her realise how wide was the gulf between them, wider even than death itself, for that condition seemed to be a barrier which Jago could transcend. What did he make of the modern world which he seemed to be able to visit at will?

Pausing outside a gallery window, more because her thoughts had disturbed her than out of interest in the paintings exhibited there, Emma gradually came to realise that this was probably the gallery the newspaper vendor had suggested she browse through. On an impulse, she stepped through the door.

An old-fashioned bell jangled as she entered and a white-haired woman glanced up at her over her bifocals. Emma saw that there was paint staining the gnarled old fingers which curled around the ebony handle of her walking stick.

'Good afternoon,' she said, her voice unexpectedly strong given that her body was so frail. 'You'll have come looking for Demelza, I don't doubt.'

Emma stood and stared, wondering if she was seeing another ghost, or, at the very least, a fortune teller. The old lady chuckled at her expression and beckoned her towards the stairs at the back of the shop.

'Don't look so alarmed – never mind me. Go up the

stairs to the old part of the gallery. There are many old portraits there which I keep in the hope that one day they might be wanted again. There's one of a local girl who married into the gentry – when you see it, you'll understand my fancy.'

She sat down on the padded chair behind the desk on which the till stood, as if the little speech had exhausted her. Emma smiled faintly and walked towards the stairs. They were old and narrow, curving in a spiral to the upper floor. Upstairs, the light was poor in stark contrast to the large, airy gallery downstairs and she waited for a moment for her eyes to adjust to the gloom. Coughing a little at the accumulated dust, she ran her eyes along the rows of paintings hung haphazardly around the room.

Suddenly she was very aware of the erratic thud of her heart, supremely conscious of the tightening of her chest. For there was Jago, captured in oils, staring directly at her from the far corner of the room. He was wearing the white-powdered wig which was fashionable for the gentlemen of the day and his tall, muscular figure was clothed in tight, cream-coloured breeches and a long, dark blue coat. The shoes on his feet were black and shiny with silver buckles which gleamed dully even through the film of dirt which had dulled the portrait over the years.

Next to him, dressed in an exquisite lace gown of cream silk, was his bride. Emma's mouth turned dry and she felt quite faint in the dusty heat of the room as she stared at Demelza. For it was as if she was looking at a portrait of herself.

Seven

When she had recovered from the shock, Emma moved forward and studied the picture more closely. The pose was stiffly formal, the young couple – she much younger than him – standing slightly apart, their expressions bland. Yet the artist had managed to capture their happiness in the luminous glow of Demelza's eyes, the pride in Jago's demeanour as he posed with his bride.

The unknown painter had even managed to convey the sense that, though they were standing apart, as soon as the sitting was over they would move together, to embrace perhaps, or maybe simply for one to touch the other's hand. There was a definite togetherness about the way they were standing, as if they were attached by an invisible cord.

Gazing into Demelza's eyes, Emma decided that the dead girl was far more beautiful than she could ever be. The similarities which had struck her at once were mere superficialities: the wayward, red-gold hair, the pale skin, the slanting green eyes. They were probably the same height and build, but there was a delicacy to Demelza's frame which Emma knew she lacked, a sense of fragility which was probably considered fashionable at the time. Emma was made of stronger stuff.

She smiled, knowing that she had to have the painting. Turning her back on it reluctantly, she returned downstairs.

'How much do you want for the portrait?' she asked the elderly woman.

'It's not for sale, my dear.'

'Why ever not?'

The other woman shook her head.

'It's been in this shop since the first day it opened. The artist lived here and used that top room as his storeroom. It's too gloomy up there to be a studio – he did the actual painting in a rented hut near the harbour.' Glancing at Emma she saw the incomprehension on her face and smiled. 'I do ramble on a bit, don't I? You see, my great-grandfather painted that portrait for Jago Pengarron himself.'

Emma shook her head, puzzled.

'Then why isn't it hanging in the Folly? I'm staying there,' she explained as she intercepted the gallery owner's quizzical arch of the eyebrows.

'Ah. Well, by the time it was ready poor Demelza was already dead. Jago Pengarron never claimed the picture and so it was put into storage.'

Emma thought of the picture hanging, unseen and unappreciated, in this tiny shop for two hundred years. Had Jago and Demelza ever seen it? The fact that they had probably never seen the finished work hardened her resolve to buy it. She named a price which made the old woman's eyebrows rise in surprise, though still she shook her head. Emma leaned forward on the desk.

'Let me hire it then. I'll hang it in the Folly all summer long, then return it to you when I go back to London.'

The shopkeeper thought for a moment.

'All right. You can borrow it, so long as it's properly insured, until the autumn. It was meant to hang in Pengarron's Folly – it will give me pleasure to think that it will hang there at last, if only for a little while.'

The two women smiled at each other, and Emma emerged, blinking, in the bright sunlight, feeling triumphant.

'Hello, Mrs Lawrence.'

She blinked as she turned around to see who had spoken to her, smiling when she recognised Mrs Helston's granddaughter.

'Hello – Morgana, isn't it?'

'That's right. Been looking round the galleries?'

Emma nodded and fell into step beside the young woman as she strolled along the street.

'I've been finding out about the original inhabitants of the house – Jago and Demelza. It's a fascinating story isn't it?'

Morgana shrugged her shoulders.

'Sounds pretty familiar to me,' she said cheerily.

'Familiar? What do you mean?'

'Well, you know – young girl marries older man, he overdoes the jealousy, wants to possess her. It's enough to drive any girl mad, isn't it? Only in those days there's no way out, so she jumps off a cliff. Pretty final solution that.'

Emma hardly heard her, she was too busy replaying

what Morgana had said earlier. He wanted to *possess* her. Was possession by the man one loved really so bad? Perhaps it was, if he was insanely jealous at the same time. Recalling the atmosphere of rage she had felt in the room the last time she had been intimate with James, Emma felt a tremor of alarm.

She was about to ask Morgana what else she knew of the story when both women's attention was caught by a shout.

James hurried along the street, his stomach churning as he saw who Emma was talking to. Surely she couldn't have met Morgana by chance – what if the other girl had sought her out, had told her about yesterday... Conveniently forgetting that he had spent the morning hoping to see Morgana himself, he reached the two women and positioned himself beside Emma.

'What are you two up to?' he asked, sounding slightly out of breath.

Emma looked quite startled, while Morgana, the little witch, merely looked amused.

'I just came out of the art gallery over there and bumped into Morgana. Oh, James, I must tell you what I've found!'

James only half listened as Emma told them both briefly about the picture. His eyes roved Morgana's face, resting wistfully on her full, red lips and remembering the feel of them against his skin.

'I'd best be getting on,' Morgana said when Emma finished.

James felt a flutter of panic as she smiled politely at Emma and turned away.

'Wait!'

He glanced guiltily at Emma as he felt her surprised gaze on him.

'I was just wondering when your . . . your grandmother was coming to the Folly again?' he asked, feeling foolish.

Morgana grinned widely at him and fiddled with the strap of her shoulder bag. He couldn't take his eyes off her long, white fingers as they played with the strip of canvas.

'Tomorrow, I should think,' she said. Then, incredibly, she took pity on him and said the words he longed to hear. 'Of course, it might be me instead – if you don't mind, Mrs Lawrence?'

She looked at Emma all wide-eyed and Emma waved a hand at her.

'Whatever. We'll perhaps see you tomorrow, then. Come along, James – Morgana must have better things to do than stand talking in the street with us. James?'

He pulled himself together with an effort and said goodbye.

'Really, James, since when have you taken any interest in when the house gets cleaned?' Emma teased him as they walked back to where he had parked the car.

'I was just trying to be friendly,' he muttered defensively.

'Well, she *is* very attractive,' Emma said.

James shot her a wary glance. Had Morgana said something to her? Could she have guessed? But Emma's expression was unconcerned and he breathed a sigh of relief.

'Not my type,' he said lightly, putting his arm around Emma's shoulders.

For once she didn't pull away, so he left his arm there as they walked along. The sexual tension which had been building in him all morning formed a tight knot in his stomach and he found himself responding to the familiar stimulus of his wife's perfume and the softness of her breast pressing against the side of his body as they walked.

Would he really want to lose her all for the sake of a meaningless fling? Deciding that no, he would probably not, he kissed her briefly on the top of her head, earning himself a surprised glance.

James was very moody just lately, Emma thought as they reached the car. One minute she was lucky to get two words out of him, the next he was hugging her and whistling under his breath, like now. She gave a mental shrug as thoughts of Jago crept back into her mind. Finding the portrait had excited her, but elements of his story had left her feeling uneasy. No one seemed to know what had ultimately been his fate.

At least she had some kind of explanation for why he had mistaken her for Demelza. Yet that too worried her. By all accounts he was a possessive husband, jealous to an extreme that might well have driven his wife to suicide.

And yet, and yet... the memory of his hands on her body, his voice in her ear, his warm breath wafting across her cheek obliterated everything else. Emma could not deny that, even knowing that he was from another time, she wanted him with a hunger that would not easily be satisfied.

Glancing across at James, she noticed how the sunlight lit up his light brown hair and gilded the tanned skin of his hands as they rested on the wheel. He was an attractive man too. She had seen the way Morgana Helston had looked at him. And he was alive, so very much alive.

Looking at James, she experienced a trickle of fear. What would happen to her if she allowed the ghost of Jago Pengarron to possess her as he had possessed Demelza in life?

Suddenly she wanted James with an intensity that astounded her. More than anything she wanted to feel the solidity of his body covering hers, to feel the reassuring thud of his heart against hers, to smell and taste the unique flavour of his skin.

'Pull over, James,' she said, her voice sufficiently throaty to attract his attention and cause him to glance at her in surprise.

Her desire for him must have been apparent on her face for she saw his eyes darken and he transferred his foot from the accelerator to the brake pedal. There was a lay-by several yards ahead, screened from the road by a small island of trees. As soon as he killed the engine, Emma reached for her seat adjuster and pushed it back as far as it would go. James watched her, his hands still holding the steering wheel, his expression wary.

'What is it, Emma?' he asked at last.

Emma didn't say anything. Holding his eye, she began to unfasten the buttons of her blouse. James's eyes narrowed and she felt the tension in him. A small pulse began to beat in his jaw and his knuckles showed white on the steering wheel.

'Em—'

'Ssh! Please, James . . . let's make love.'

'Here?' he said, incredulously, glancing around them.

'Yes.'

'Why don't we go back to the house and—'

'No!' His eyes widened at her vehemence and she shook her head. She couldn't make love to him in the house, not knowing that Jago was watching them, knowing that it would hurt him to see her making love with another man . . .

'I don't want to go back to the house,' she said more calmly. 'I don't want to think about it, I just want you to love me, like you used to. Please?'

James closed his eyes for an instant and swallowed. Emma watched the contraction of his throat and felt the heat spreading slowly through her. Surely he wouldn't reject her now?

At last he turned and reached for her and it was as if that moment of hesitation had never been.

'Oh Emma,' he whispered, his lips against her hair, one warm hand slipping beneath her hair at the nape of her neck, the other edging inside her blouse.

Emma sighed and opened her mouth under his. She welcomed the thrust of his tongue, meeting it with her own as he sought the sweetness of her mouth. His fingers were already easing up her skirt, tracing the elastic line of her panties at the top of her thigh. Restlessly, she parted her legs so that he could cup the damp, cotton-covered mound with generated so much heat he commented upon it.

'God, Emma, you're so hot . . . so wet . . .'

POSSESSION

His fingers slipped underneath the flimsy barrier of her knicker elastic and eased into the slippery folds of her sex. Emma clenched her thighs so that his hand was trapped inside, moving her bottom feverishly until he pressed on the aching nub of her clitoris.

'Yes!' she whispered as he began to stroke it, lightly at first as he knew she liked it, then more firmly, more quickly, always in perfect rhythm.

Emma clung to the breadth of his shoulders, pressing the upper half of her body against his and absorbing the heat of his skin. He was perspiring, the sweat breaking out all over his body as her excitement transmitted itself to him and he matched it with a tension of his own. Emma sensed his impatience, knew that he wanted her to come quickly so that he could get on with what, to him, was the real business of sex.

Bearing down on his fingertips, she concentrated on letting go, knowing that the end was in sight as she felt the sensations melting through her, flowing outward from the tiny bundle of nerve endings which formed the centre of her pleasure.

She cried out as she came, revelling in the momentary release from tension orgasm brought her, eager to feel the swift thrust of James's body into hers. He did not disappoint her. He managed to hold back just long enough to eke out every last tremor from her climax, then he wriggled out of his jeans and climbed over the centre console so that he was straddling her.

Dispensing with Emma's sodden panties, he parted her labia almost tenderly with his fingers then, with a small sound of satisfaction, he sank into her molten flesh.

This was what she had wanted: the hard thrust of a real, flesh-and-blood man, filling her, using her as she had used him. The aftershocks of her orgasm rippled along the silky, cleated walls of her vagina, milking him, drawing him in ever deeper.

He seemed to swell and harden still more inside her. Reaching beneath them, she cupped his balls in her hand, feeling the fullness of the hairy sacs, the skin stretched tight over their hardness. Opening herself still wider, she fed them into her hungry sex, coating them in the thick slippery fluid of her body and making James groan with pleasure.

Knowing it would be too much for him, Emma tickled gently along the tender line of his perineum with her fingernail, gradually edging towards his anus. Before she reached that forbidden orifice, he cried out and she pressed firmly against the base of his scrotum with her fingertip as he began to ejaculate.

The cords in his neck stood out, his expression halfway between agony and ecstasy as he spilled his seed into her. Emma dug her fingers into the firm pads of his buttocks, holding him close to her as if she never wanted him to withdraw. When at last he collapsed over her, panting, she ran her palms feverishly over his neck, his shoulders, his head, as if to reassure herself that he was real.

Only gradually did she realise that the handbrake was sticking painfully into the soft flesh of her thigh and that the angle of the car's seat incline had given her an unpleasant kink in her back. They peeled apart far more self-consciously than they had come together. Emma avoided James's eye as she straightened her clothes.

After a few minutes, he broke the uncomfortable silence that had fallen between them.

'Shall we go back?' he asked her.

Emma nodded. Now that the sudden, burning desire had been assuaged, she felt empty, completely numb. For some reason it seemed that James felt the same way. It occurred to her that they should be celebrating what had happened, should regard it as a new beginning for them, but instead they were acting like strangers. Slightly embarrassed strangers at that. It was almost as if she felt she had been unfaithful. Absurd! she told herself angrily, James was her husband, Jago merely ... what?

Suddenly she could not wait to get home, to be alone in the bedroom so that she could try once more to call Jago to her. There was so much she wanted to tell him, so many questions she wanted to ask. And, if the truth be known, her brief interlude of lust with James had merely whetted her appetite for more.

She realised then why she felt so alienated from James, even after they had shared such an intimate interlude. It was because her arousal had stemmed from thinking about Jago, James was no more than a convenient stand-in. For only Jago Pengarron could satisfy her as she needed to be satisfied.

James made no attempt to detain her when she went early to her bedroom that evening. Emma was so focused on what she intended to do that she did not stop to consider that his behaviour was out of character, she was merely glad that he did not stand in her way.

The portrait had arrived from the gallery at tea time and Emma had watched as the men hung it over the stairs. It looked so right there, with the young couple overlooking the hall, that Emma knew this was where Demelza had always intended it to hang.

She noticed James's eyes widen when he saw the portrait of Demelza, as if he had seen her before, but he said nothing, merely looking from the portrait to Emma and back again, a strangely closed expression on his face.

In her room, Emma changed into her nightdress then moved restlessly about, opening and closing drawers, wondering how she could call Jago to her. Supposing he stayed away tonight as he had the night before?

'Oh Jago!' she whispered into the silent room. 'Where are you?'

There was no answer, no subtle change in the atmosphere that normally signalled his arrival. Going over to the dressing table, Emma began to brush her hair. Her own face stared back at her, pale, with shadowed hollows which shocked her. When had she become so drawn, so tired-looking? Studying her reflection more closely, she realised that her eyes had an unnatural brightness about them, a feverishness that she had never noticed before. Beneath them there were bluish-grey smudges, like two thumbprints on her skin.

Beside the dressing table there was a large blanket box, covered by a lace-trimmed cloth. Without thinking, Emma pulled at the edge of the cloth and brought it up to her face, dabbing at the dark circles beneath her eyes with it, as if to reassure herself that it wasn't something that could be wiped away.

The cloth smelled musty with age, though Emma could detect the lingering trace of lavender. Her eyes fell on the blanket box and she frowned as she noticed that the small clasp which had secured it was hanging loose. She stared at the box for several long minutes, conscious suddenly of the ebb and flow of the blood through her veins, the dull thud of her heartbeat echoing in her skull. It was an unremarkable-looking piece of furniture, though clearly as old as the house. There was no outward sign that it would contain anything of significance. Yet Emma found herself strangely reluctant to open it.

Eventually, she slipped from the dressing table stool onto her knees beside the chest. Her fingers caressed the clasp lightly, hesitating before grasping it. The hinges creaked with age as she slowly raised the lid. She coughed at the musty, ancient odour released, aware that her heart raced now with something close to fear.

At first she thought there was nothing inside and disappointment swamped her. She had been so sure, so certain. Then a glimmer at the bottom of the chest caught her eye. Reaching inside, her fingers encountered the stiffness of silk and lace. The garment was heavy, but delicate-looking and Emma lifted it out almost reverently and shook out the folds.

She recognised it at once as the dress Demelza had worn on her wedding day. Yet this was not the pristine confection captured by the artist for the portrait. Emma felt little waves of alarm travel along her spine as she realised that the beautiful gown had been ripped apart from neck to hem. There were mud and grass stains smearing the fabric and a few spots on the inner back of what looked like rust ... or blood.

'Oh Demelza!' she whispered. 'What happened?'

'Tis no more than the violence of passion – it is not what you think.'

Emma whirled round as Jago's voice reached her. She had been so engrossed with examining the dress that she had failed to notice his arrival and she wondered now how long he had been standing there, watching her. She held the ruined dress against her breast, as if in defence.

'Jago!' she whispered, unable to stop the unruly leap of her heart at the sight of him.

He was standing in the corner of the room, half in shadow, so she could not see his expression, though she knew that he smiled at her.

'You have hung the portrait in the hallway,' he said unexpectedly.

'Yes. I am not Demelza, Jago, though there is a likeness, I think.'

He shook his head.

'In truth I always knew it,' he said sadly. 'I knew it could not be. But I hoped ... forgive me.'

'Oh no – don't go!' Emma cried out in alarm as he began to fade. 'Please ... stay.'

Jago looked at her steadily and gradually the shadows cleared so that she could see his face. The sadness which marked it made her heart ache for him and she made an involuntary move towards him.

'Do not try to touch me!' he warned her as she came closer.

'But you were able to touch me ...'

He smiled grimly.

'A little. But you cannot know me unless you meet me in the world between my time and this.'

'How? How do I do that?' Emma asked him eagerly. Could it really be possible that they could meet as equals?

Jago regarded her steadily, his eyes intent on her face.

'You are like her, 'tis true,' he said suddenly. 'And you are sad, as she was. It was that which drew me to you, the sense that you suffer as she suffered. If I could help you it might atone for my failure to save Demelza.'

He seemed to be talking to himself, making little sense to Emma. She thought of the Demelza who had made love to her in her dream and thought that she had seemed more than happy then. But that was just a dream, she reminded herself, a product of her imagination. It might not be how it was with Jago and his Demelza.

Looking at Jago, her consciousness focused on the sheer sexual energy which she could feel emanating from him. How could a ghost be so intrinsically *physical*?

All she knew, all she really cared about, was the fact that she wanted him. To feel his hands on her body, to touch and kiss him – she knew it would be good, so good. Demelza's dress slipped unnoticed from her nerveless fingers as she moved closer.

'Take me with you,' she whispered urgently, 'take me to this place where we can be together. Where you can make love to me properly . . .'

Jago's eyelids drooped slightly as he ran his gaze over her face and down her figure. There was something so inherently masculine about that appraisal, so thrillingly sexual, that Emma felt the heat spread rapidly through her body, lighting a touchpaper to her senses.

'No mortal has ever tried to cross over before... it could be dangerous,' he said, but the timbre of his voice belied the seriousness of his words and Emma chose to ignore the warning.

'I want to... oh, Jago, I want *you*!'

He was fading, she could see the energy slipping away from him even as they spoke.

'Wait... I will come for you,' he said, his voice growing faint as he stepped back into the enveloping shadows in the corner of the room. 'Wait for me.'

Emma stared at the place where he had stood for a long time after he had gone. She was trembling, consumed by a mixture of fear and sexual tension. Her throat was dry, the delicate flesh of her sex throbbing dully in thwarted anticipation.

Slowly, she sank down onto the bed, still staring at the place where Jago had been, large as life, only moments before. The ruined bridal gown lay in a crumpled heap at her feet and she bent down to pick it up. Without thinking about what she was doing, she buried her face in the extravagant folds and breathed in deeply, imagining she could smell the intimate scents of the passion Jago had said took place on it.

Closing her eyes, she imagined Jago and Demelza rolling together on the grass near the Folly, their mutual desire overwhelming them, causing him to rip the gown from her body. What frenzy of lust had spurred them on? What recklessness had encouraged Demelza to open her body to him with such wild abandonment...?

With a small groan of frustration, Emma pulled her nightdress over her head and wrapped herself in the tattered remnants of the gown. The lace scratched against her over-sensitized skin, the stiff silk feeling cool against her overheated flesh. Imagining the healthy, energetic coupling of Jago and his new bride, she masturbated against the stained silk, straddling it and moving her hips back and forth, rubbing her burning flesh faster and faster against the fabric.

Would he take her with such animalistic ferocity? God, she hoped so! Never had she wanted anyone so intensely, so desperately as she wanted Jago Pengarron. It was on that thought that she came, her body jerking and twisting as the strength of her climax rocked through her, taking her breath away with its intensity.

Emma fell asleep with Demelza's dress twisted around her body, her mind full of anticipation of how it would be when Jago returned.

Eight

James woke early the following morning. Opening his eyes, he had that kind of anticipation of something good about to happen that he used to have when he was a boy and he woke up on his birthday and didn't immediately remember what special day it was.

When he remembered the source of his excitement today he grinned. Of course – he would see Morgana later. Frowning at his reflection as he shaved, James marvelled at the way he felt. Like a lovesick youth who'd just discovered sex. He grimaced. *Play it cool, Lawrence*, he told his mirror image sternly. *Don't let her see how keen you are.*

He frowned when he thought of Emma. Sex in the car with her yesterday had been fantastic, exciting in a way it hadn't been for a long, long time. Yet afterwards she had acted as if she couldn't wait to see the back of him, almost as if she had regretted what had happened.

It occurred to James that he had never been this obsessed with sex before they came to Cornwall. Sure, it had been an important part of his life, but not the axis on which his world spun, which was rapidly becoming the case now. Of course, Morgana Helston had to be a greater part of the reason. Could it be an early middle age creeping up on him, taking him unawares?

The uncomfortable thought made him stare at his reflection in the mirror with unmitigated horror. It was a sobering thought and thoroughly unwelcome. After all, she was a good ten years younger than him, they had nothing in common as far as he could see except their mutual attraction. 'Pull yourself together man!' he said aloud, rinsing his face and rubbing it dry with a towel. 'You're twenty-nine – nowhere near middle-aged!'

Thinking about it was useless, there was no rationalising a relationship which, on his part at least, was fast running out of control. He couldn't wait to see her, to arrange a meeting. He thought of the way she had propositioned him, so directly that the mere words had almost made him come there and then in the café. *Let's fuck*. God, there was music in those words!

Closing his eyes, James remembered how he had watched as she pulled off her clothes, standing unselfconsciously in front of him, naked save for those ridiculous boots. His memory was so vivid, so immediate, that he could almost feel the silky slip of the sweat over her skin as he caressed her, could see the delicious symmetry of her buttocks as she raised them in front of him.

His penis had slipped inside the hot, moist channel of her sex so easily. He grew hard now just thinking of it. Reaching down he touched himself, running his hand along the hardening length of his shaft. Glancing at the shower, he considered stepping in for a quick wank, but decided against wasting his energy. He'd save it all for

Morgana. On that thought, he decided that he couldn't wait for another day to have her again, he would have to invent some excuse for Emma's benefit so that he could get out of the house today.

Emma wasn't in the kitchen. After he'd eaten, James went upstairs to tap on her door, but there was no answer. Concerned, he tried the handle, only to find that once again it was locked.

'Emma! Emma – can you hear me? Are you all right?'

Still there was no reply. Supposing she was ill, or had slipped in the shower... A litany of *what-ifs* went through his mind, all of which he dismissed as being melodramatic. She was probably just sleeping, he told himself, no need to worry.

Pushing away the guilty thought that he was glad she wouldn't be around when Morgana arrived, James turned away and went downstairs.

Emma lay on the bed and listened to James's knocking. She knew she ought to reply, that it was childish of her not to, but she couldn't seem to summon up enough energy. So she lay, quite still, until she heard his footsteps retreating along the landing.

She was glad he hadn't tried to come in, for she didn't want to talk to him. She didn't want to talk to anyone, for she was waiting. Waiting for Jago.

It was like a waking dream, this crushing, enervating lethargy encasing her. She had woken to find her naked limbs still entwined with the remnants of Demelza's wedding dress, her skin salty with dried perspiration. There was nothing in her head except the knowledge that soon she would find the gateway between her time and his that Jago had spoken of and that when she found it, she would be with him. What happened before, or after, did not interest her one iota. All that mattered was that she would soon be with him. Possessed.

Emma smiled at the word, realising that it had stayed, hovering at the edges of her mind, ever since Morgana had used it. Tantalising her. So many things about Jago tantalised her. So many half-truths and rumours, unresolved conflicts and mysteries. He beguiled her, not just physically, but emotionally and mentally too, using up all of her energy, feeding on it.

As she waited, neither patiently nor impatiently, Emma reviewed what she had found out about him so far. That he had once ostensibly been a merchant who sometimes posed as a fisherman. But who might have been a smuggler ... He had been a jealous husband, and yet she sensed that her dream the other night had been rooted somehow in real events. That he was a highly sexual man she had no doubt.

The atmosphere thickened and became tainted with the now familiar smell of cinnamon and tobacco. Emma smiled as she felt his presence, coming closer, moving about in the very air.

'Who *are* you Jago Pengarron?' she whispered aloud.

There was no answer, though she felt his fingers brush across her shoulder and linger against the swell of her exposed breast. A dart of lust, sharp and piquant, arrowed through her, making her stomach muscles clench. Slowly, she rose from the bed and picked up her cotton robe. Slipping her arms into the sleeves, she scanned the room anxiously for a glimpse of him.

'Why don't you appear?' she said aloud, her voice shimmering with desire.

Narrowing her eyes, she fancied she saw a thickening of the shadows, no more than an increased density of the air, and she guessed that that was Jago, or whatever it was of him that lingered in this world. As she watched, the shadow moved towards the door. Emma stepped forward and opened it, treading carefully so as not to alert James to the fact that she was up and about.

She paused at the top of the stairs. The door to the living room was ajar and she could hear James moving about inside. Hesitating, she realised that Jago had moved on, that he was already halfway down the stairs. Pulling her robe tightly around her, she ran softly down the steps and into the hall.

For a moment she couldn't see him and she panicked. Then she saw the way the sunlight that was streaming through the window beside the main doors was interrupted as it hit the panelling at the far end of the hall, to one side of the central staircase. There was nothing in the hallway to create that patch of shadow, no rational explanation for its presence at all, so she moved towards it, puzzled.

As soon as Emma reached out to touch the rapidly fading shadow patterning the wood panels, it vanished, leaving her with a churning stomach and the acidic taste of fearful excitement on her tongue.

She didn't understand – why had he brought her here? It was then that she remembered what the librarian in St Ives had said about how many of these old houses had their own secret access to the beaches below the cliffs. Her heart rate quickened. Supposing there was just such a passageway here at Pengarron... Could Jago have been trying to show her where it was?

Narrowing her eyes, Emma studied the panelling carefully, tracing the path of the intricate carving with her fingertips. She snatched her hand back as suddenly, without warning, the panel gave way. Reaching out, she pushed tentatively and the panel moved as if on hinges, revealing stone steps leading downwards.

Emma felt as if she couldn't breathe; a tight band of apprehension seemed to have tightened around the upper part of her chest. It took her a few seconds to gather the courage to poke her head through the gap and peer down the steps. It was pitch black, so dark that it was impossible to see beyond the small triangle of light just inside. The air smelt stale and dank. Straining her ears, she could hear the faint *drip, drip, drip* of water a short distance away then, suddenly, the scurry of what sounded like rodent feet. With a muffled gasp, Emma pulled the panelling to and stepped back. No way was she going in there without light!

Yet this was obviously where Jago intended for her to go, or why would he have brought her here to this spot? Perhaps if she could find a flashlight...?

Padding softly into the kitchen, Emma searched the drawers until she found what she wanted. Holding her breath, she checked that the large torch had batteries intact, a broad grin spreading over her face as the strong beam of light fell across the kitchen table.

She jumped guiltily as she heard the front door open

and the brisk clump of boots coming across the flagstones. Shoving the torch back in the drawer, she smiled at Morgana Helston as she walked into the kitchen.

'Good morning,' she greeted her, amazed that her voice sounded so steady, so *normal*.

'Morning.'

Morgana's gaze took in Emma's robe and her bare feet, and her eyes registered surprise. Glancing at the clock above the Aga, Emma saw that it was almost ten o'clock.

'I overslept,' she offered, wondering as she did so why on earth she felt obliged to explain herself to the young girl who was busy filling the kettle.

'Heavy night?' she asked conversationally.

Emma thought of how she had pleasured herself and smiled.

'You could say that,' she replied lightly. 'Well, if you'll excuse me . . .'

Deciding that she really didn't have to answer to anybody, she opened the drawer and retrieved the torch. Ignoring Morgana's curious glance, she smiled serenely and walked across to the kitchen door.

'I'll leave you to get on, Morgana. Um . . . if you see my husband, would you tell him I've gone back to bed?'

'Are you not feeling very well, Mrs Lawrence?'

'No. I just need to sleep, that's all. Ask him not to disturb me.'

She didn't know what Morgana made of that, but neither did she care. All she knew was that if she was going to find out what was behind the panelling, she was going to have to move fast, before James or Morgana saw what she was doing. Something told her that it was necessary to keep the existence of the secret passage to herself, that Jago had revealed it to her and her alone for a reason, though what that reason could be she had yet to fathom.

Closing the kitchen door behind her, she ran silently across the hallway and pushed open the secret door. Hearing James's footsteps in the living room across the hall, she stepped inside quickly and pulled the panelling shut behind her. The darkness enveloped her, bearing down on her from all sides like a thick, suffocating blanket. Emma fumbled with the torch until she found the 'on' button and yellow light flooded the passageway.

She found herself inside a narrow tunnel, lined with slate. The ground was cold and slippery under her bare feet and Emma cursed her lack of foresight for not taking the trouble to dress in proper clothes and sturdy shoes. It had only been her eagerness to follow Jago which had made her grab her robe.

It was too late to go back now for she could hear James and Morgana's voices in the hall. How could she explain leaping out at them from the panelling, never mind manage to come back inside without their noticing? Putting all thought of going back to dress from her mind, Emma clutched the robe more tightly across her naked breasts and began to walk.

The passage seemed to have been designed to run between the rooms of the house. It twisted and turned so that she didn't know what she might find around the next corner. In reality, there was simply more passageway, though she was intrigued to discover that spy holes had been cut into the slate so that she could see into each room that she passed.

By pressing her eye against the first hole she came to, she saw the kitchen. The kettle was boiling merrily and Morgana was setting two mugs on a tray. As Emma watched, James walked into the room and began to make coffee. He turned and said something to Morgana that she couldn't quite catch and the younger girl laughed. There was a flirtatiousness in that laughter, an intimacy which set warning bells ringing in her mind and she hesitated before moving on.

It was like looking into one of those Victorian seafront attractions labelled *What the Butler Saw*. Emma felt oddly removed from what was happening in the room beyond, as if there was a screen between them and her which was far more substantial than the physical barrier of the passageway.

As she watched, she saw James reach for Morgana and kiss her. Emma felt something kick in her stomach and the bile rose in her throat. So that was why James had been acting so strangely. He was busy trying to seduce Morgana Helston. Summoning an emotional detachment she had never realised she possessed, Emma wondered if he had succeeded yet.

More pertinently, did she care? Emma frowned as the rogue thought popped into her mind. Of course she cared! she told herself angrily. Enough to abandon her search for Jago and go to confront them? Ah, now that was something else. Grimacing wryly, Emma acknowledged that she had no right to sit in judgement on James for actually doing something that she herself was desperately trying to achieve. The fact that Morgana was very much alive while her potential lover was not should not come into the debate. Should it?

Shaking her head in confusion, Emma dragged her eyes away from the kitchen where Morgana had evaded James and was now making coffee. It occurred to her that there could be some advantage to the situation. For if James was having an affair with Morgana, at least it kept him occupied, less likely to notice her.

Moving on, she realised that the passageway zigzagged through the house, taking in each room from the study to the bedrooms. Disappointment flooded through her as she began to wonder if it in fact led anywhere, or whether it was merely a means by which the master of Pengarron had spied on his guests. Or his wife? Then, just as she felt she would have to try to find her way back to the hallway, the passage dipped down sharply.

Emma was disorientated after following the passage through the house, walking backwards and forwards, up and down, but she realised that this section was different. For a start, it didn't smell the same. Inside the house there were the lingering odours of wood and dust and human occupation. Now that scent was replaced by a heavy, musty smell.

Beneath her feet, Emma felt a trickle of icy water. She gasped as a drop dripped from the slate roof onto her neck. The quality of the darkness was different too, it was less heavy, somehow, though no less oppressive. The torch which had seemed so powerful in the familiarity of the kitchen now only managed a faint yellow light, defeated by the thickness of the dark.

Emma clutched the torch tightly and tried not to think of the rats and insects that could be watching her from the blackness. Just as long as none decided to run across her bare feet, she could cope.

The passageway was descending more steeply now and Emma guessed she was walking through the very cliff itself. The mix of terror and excitement that kept her walking steadily downwards was curiously close to sexual. Even while she cursed herself for undertaking such a venture, Emma was aware of a deep, primitive excitement that made her mouth run dry.

Soon the passageway must surely come to end and then what would she find? Gradually, she became aware that the air was becoming fresher and her step quickened at the thought of reaching the end of the tunnel. The sound of water was closer now, the continual *hiss* of the sea becoming more distinct. She could even smell the salt air and hear the cries of the seagulls.

At last she saw a sliver of light at the end of the tunnel and her steps slowed. Now that she was there she was almost afraid.

'Don't be such a wimp!' she admonished herself. The sound of her own voice bounced off the walls eerily, adding to her apprehension.

Gradually the narrow passageway began to open out into a cave until, at last, Emma felt the softness of cold, wet sand beneath her feet. A few more metres and the cave opened out so that there was sufficient light for her to shut off the torch.

Emma paid no more than passing attention to the interior of the cave, she was too keen to go out onto the beach and see if Jago was waiting for her. One sweeping glance though was all it took for her to take in the 'shelves' hewn into the rockface by those who had used the caves long ago and the iron candle sconces which still hung haphazardly where they had been embedded in the rock.

As she came out onto the beach she gasped at the sheer beauty of it. A small cove of firm, golden sand, littered with clusters of rocks that were washed by the sea at each high tide so that they shone dully in the bright sunlight now beating down on them, clothed in a layer of seaweed, impossibly green.

A seagull wheeled and screeched overhead and Emma shielded her eyes against the sun as she tracked its progress across the peerless blue sky. Her eyes took a while to become accustomed to the brightness after what must have been a good half an hour underground.

The cove opened out to give an unmatchable view of the ocean. Emma gasped, blinking as if she could not believe her eyes. For there was a ship at anchor in the bay, a ship made of fine English oak with broad, solid bulwarks and towering masts. The sails were furled while the great merchant ship rested, bobbing lazily on the tide.

It was then that Emma realised she was not alone on the beach. A little way off to her left a lone fisherman sat tending to his nets. He was naked from the waist up and barefooted and he seemed not to have noticed her approach.

There was something about the way in which he held himself, something about the angle of his head that made her heart skip a beat.

'Jago?' she breathed.

As she drew nearer she saw that it *was* him. Only he was alive, truly alive. His sun-bronzed skin glowed with vitality and good health. His hair, loose about his shoulders, was streaked with salt and sand. His square jaw was clean shaven with an endearing cleft in the centre of his chin that made Emma's fingers itch to touch it.

He was younger than his spirit manifestation, perhaps in his early twenties. But no, surely that was one of his vessels at anchor in the bay beyond? Would such a young man be so wealthy? Glancing up, Emma saw that the cliff top was desolate, no sign of the Folly at all. Yet surely he would not be here mending his nets with his ship out at anchor if he hadn't already built the house for Demelza, if he wasn't a good ten years older than the man sitting on the beach?

It didn't matter. Chronology seemed confused in this curious pocket of time, as if the years were as nothing, melting into one as do the waters of the ocean despite the ebb and flow of the tides. It was a curiously liberating notion, that the boundaries of time could be blurred, setting Jago free to meet her here, on the beach.

Emma felt a leaping, juddering excitement, her arousal so strong she imagined that she could taste it.

He looked up as if he hadn't expected to see anyone else on the beach. Emma saw that he didn't know her, at least not yet. Trusting that this was how it should be, Emma smiled and went forward.

The young fisherman stopped what he was doing as she approached, his eyes widening as he caught her heated, direct glance. Emma could smell the heat of his skin, could see the sheen of fresh sweat pearling the sculpted muscles of his shoulders and arms as he straightened. She held up a hand as he would have spoken.

'Don't talk,' she cautioned. She let the robe slip from her shoulders so that she stood naked before him on the deserted beach. 'Make love to me.'

The nets slipped through his fingers, landing soundlessly on the damp sand as he moved towards her. He lifted his hand and stroked her breeze-whipped hair away from her cheek. Emma noticed that his fingertip was calloused, as if he did more than merely play at being a fisherman. A thousand questions clamoured in her mind, but she pushed them all away. She didn't really want to know about his life as it was at that moment, she only wanted to be possessed by her dream lover at last.

The sunlight slanted across the sands, lighting up his face. Emma could feel its warmth across her back, gilding her naked skin. Apart from that one gesture when he had caressed her cheek, Jago made no further move to touch her. He merely looked at her, running his eyes slowly from her face down her body to her toes, lingering on her breasts and the gentle mound of her sex on the way.

Emma stood very still and bore his scrutiny without flinching. She knew she looked good, her lithe body tanned and firm, the skin soft and well cared for. Yet Jago gave no sign of whether her appearance pleased him or otherwise, his expression was inscrutable. Emma could feel the muscles in her calves protesting at being kept standing in one position for so long and she began to tremble. Just as the tension became unbearable, he touched the tip of one nipple lightly with his fingertip.

Sucking in her breath on a gasp, Emma swayed slightly towards him. The small caress sent shockwaves right through her body and a melting, liquid warmth seeped through her veins. Without realising what she was doing, Emma moistened her suddenly dry lips with the tip of her tongue. Jago's eyes darkened as he watched the movement and his mouth tightened. Emma could sense the tension in him, knew he was battling with himself.

It empowered her, this knowledge that he was holding himself in check, subject to forces that, at that moment, only she could release. A seductive smile spread across her face and she reached for him, placing the palm of one hand against his heart. She could feel the slow, steady thud of it, beating against her hand, could feel the heat and softness of his skin over the muscular planes of his pectorals. A shiver went through her, starting at the point where their two bodies met.

'Please . . .?' she breathed, hardly aware that she had spoken.

He slipped his hand underneath her hair, to the back of her neck, and pulled her to him. Not roughly, but firmly, taking control away from her and establishing his greater strength. Emma acknowledged this, and submitted. She felt too weak, too compliant to even think of protesting.

Bending her back, over the iron-hard bar of his arm, he looked deeply into her eyes for several seconds. Then he spoke.

'I know you.'

That was all. Three words, uttered in a low, wondering voice, vibrating with a bridled passion. *I know you.*

'Yes,' Emma whispered.

Then he lowered his mouth onto hers and the need for words became past, obsolete, totally irrelevant.

Her head spun as the kiss went on and on. With his free hand, Jago moulded the shape of her breast, smoothing it to a cone and stroking the tumescent nipple with the pad of his thumb. His skin was slightly rough, creating a pleasurable friction against the sensitive bud. Emma moaned, deep in her throat, and clutched at his shoulders to stop herself from overbalancing.

There was a heady sense of surrender in allowing herself to be swept up in his arms so that he could carry her over to the rocks nearby. She wondered for an instant what he was doing, then he broke his stride for long enough to kiss her again and she immediately stopped thinking. His tongue was insistent, probing at the soft recesses of her mouth, as if by kissing her more deeply he might find something else about her that was hidden.

He lowered her gently until her feet touched the sand and her back was against the satiny surface of the rock. The sun was directly behind him now, casting his features in shadow and creating a nebula of light around his head. Emma was finding it difficult to breathe, her desire was so strong that it made her chest tight and her lungs hurt.

Why didn't he just take her?

'Jago—'

'Ssh!'

He laid a finger against her lips. Emma darted out her tongue and licked at it, drawing the tip into her mouth in a blatant expression of need. Jago eased his finger out of her mouth and traced a path across her cheek to her jaw. Turning her face against his palm, Emma closed her eyes for an instant, revelling in the scent of his skin.

'A mermaid,' he whispered gruffly, 'daughter of the sea...'

As he leaned forward to press his lips against the soft skin of her neck, Emma felt the entire length of his body against hers. It was lean and firm, wholly masculine with well-developed muscles and a smattering of body hair that tickled her tender nipples. She cried out as he pulled away, shocked to have his presence so abruptly removed.

Though she could not see his eyes, she suspected that they were mocking her, though not unkindly. He could not help but be flattered by her desire for him. Emma could see from the enticing bulge in his bleached, half-length trousers that he was as highly aroused as she and she leaned towards him as if to encourage him, pushing out her breasts and lifting her hips away from the slippery rock.

He chuckled softly.

'Aye, but you're a wanton piece,' he said good-naturedly.

Emma laughed and moved her feet further apart so that his eyes were drawn to the tender pink line of flesh which glistened between her thighs. Jago sucked in his breath and unexpectedly dropped down onto his haunches. His eyes were now on a level with her sex, and Emma gave in to the instinctive urge to bend her knees slightly, to open herself and invite his gaze.

At first she thought he would touch her, perhaps even bury his face in her mound and service her with his tongue. She certainly did not expect him to scoop up two large handfuls of damp sand and run them up her legs to her waist.

She gasped as the cold, slightly abrasive sand was smeared across her quivering belly and up towards her breasts. Jago looked into her widened eyes and she caught the flash of his teeth as he grinned.

'I could shaft you now, my mermaid, but that wouldn't be enough for 'ee, would it?'

'But—'

'Don't fret – I'll have you soon enough. But first . . .'

He ground the wet sand against her breasts, grazing against her nipples so that she cried out, more in surprise than in pain, though it was not a comfortable experience. And yet, as he kneaded the besmirched globes of flesh, Emma felt a raw, dark pleasure creep beneath her shock. Her body responded to it at once, her nipples cresting into two round stones, as hard as the rock on which she rested. Of their own volition, her hips pressed forward towards his, yearning for the imprint of his hard body upon the softness of hers.

''Tis good, is it not?' he whispered against her hair. 'There can be pleasure in pain?'

'Oh . . . yes . . . yes!' Emma moaned, incoherent with need.

'Turn around,' he whispered suddenly.

She moved at once to obey him, pressing herself against the unyielding rock. It felt smooth and cool against her cheek, in direct counterpoint to the heat of her skin. Twisting her head, Emma watched as Jago scooped up more sand and spread it over her back and buttocks. He lingered there, his fingers slipping into the crease and probing the dip of her anus while he kissed a path from one shoulder, across the back of her neck to the other side.

'Open your legs,' he whispered.

Emma felt his lips curve into a smile against her cheek as she complied. Anticipation made her tremble, shuddering through her as she tried to imagine what he would do next. The thought skittered through her mind that when she entered the secret passage in search of Jago she had not quite known what it was she sought, what she hoped he could give her. Now she knew that this was exactly what she needed: pure, uncomplicated sex, unmitigated excitement.

She watched as he searched for something on the beach, her eyes widening in surprise as he picked up a long string of seaweed. As he wound the end around his hand and slapped the dangling fronds experimentally against his thigh, Emma bit her lip. Was she really ready for this?

He smiled as he saw she was watching, a predatory grin that caused a trickle of alarm to run through her. Then he leaned forward and kissed her again and all the anxiety seemed to be sucked out of her.

'Let it come,' he whispered throatily.

Emma held every muscle tense as she waited for the whip of the seaweed across her body. Her buttock muscles clenched and she held her breath. Closing her eyes she imagined that Jago was all around her, his ghostly voice sounding in the screech of the gulls and the whispering of the gentle breeze. The smell of the salt spray was strong, the crash of the waves against the cliffs an echo of the blood coursing violently through Emma's veins as she waited for him to make a move.

She cried out as the wet seaweed slapped across her naked thighs and she pressed herself into the cold, unyielding rock, raising her buttocks in an unspoken plea for more. He did not disappoint her. The seaweed was heavy with sea water. There was no pain, only a tingling where it touched her skin.

Emma felt hot all over, the pressure building in the core of her, making her toss her head from side to side. Seeing her restlessness, Jago struck her harder and faster, patterning her buttocks and thighs with a pink flush that made her feel as if she was on fire.

Grinding her hips against the slippery rocks, Emma tried to gain some relief by rubbing herself against them, but Jago did not stop, whipping her into a frenzy.

'Stop! Please.... please.... no more!' she gasped at last, throwing herself round so that she was lying, spread-eagled against the rock in the full glare of the merciless sun.

She was panting and the sweat was pouring down her body in rivulets which cut a path through the wet sand that plastered her. Jago shucked off his trousers, setting free the cock that reared up against his belly, straining towards her.

Emma gasped as he covered her body with his, knocking the air out of her as he pushed against her. Lifting her by the hips, he lowered her open sex onto his cock, ensuring that her clitoris scraped slowly across the coarse hair which arrowed downward from his belly.

After waiting for so long, that slight stimulation was enough to push Emma over the edge into orgasm. It rippled through her with a violence that took her breath away. Wrapping her body around him, she felt him thrust inside her convulsing body and she dug her nails into his shoulders, trying to hang onto reality by the tips of her fingers.

His seed spilled from his body into hers like a rush of the tides, flooding her, marking her as his in the most primitive way possible. And as her ghost lover made her his, Emma let out her breath on a low, shuddering sigh.

Nine

James watched as Morgana flitted about the living room, occasionally taking a desultory swipe with the duster at each surface she passed. She was wearing a short, black jersey dress that ended mid-thigh and made her look like a child. No, not a child, he corrected himself at once as he watched the shape of her body moving inside the loose confines of the dress. He was pretty sure she wasn't wearing anything underneath it for there were no telltale ridges, no unsightly interruptions to the smooth line of the clinging fabric.

Every now and then she glanced over to where James was making a pretence of writing notes for the Andrew Joiner story, and flashed him a small, mischievous smile.

'Why can't we go to the beach today?' he said eventually, scoring through the gibberish he had written with exasperation.

Morgana looked at him with mock coyness and he knew that she was enjoying herself.

'I told you – I don't like routines,' she said infuriatingly.

'Twice doesn't make a routine!' he protested, but she merely laughed and carried on with what she was doing.

James stopped pretending to work and watched her openly now. When he'd walked into the kitchen and seen her there that morning he had an instant erection and it hadn't subsided since. He shuffled discreetly on his seat by the small desk under the window, but there was no relief to be had. And Morgana seemed disinclined to help him.

That she was deliberately teasing him, leading him on, he had no doubt. He could tell that the little witch was conscious of his eyes on her as she moved about the room. All he had to do was stand up and he could be across the room in half a dozen strides and...

'Jesus!' he whispered.

Morgana was bending over to pick something up off the floor, straight-legged so that her short skirt rose up at the back to expose her bottom. Her perfect, *naked* bottom. James stared at the smooth caramel-coloured skin and the darker crease between the two rounded globes. Below, he could see the oval purse of her sex, dark and inviting and glistening with moisture.

Morgana squealed as he came up behind her and slipped his hand between her legs, feeling the sticky-soft folds of skin open greedily beneath his fingers.

'Let's go somewhere,' he growled in her ear, his hand working at the hardening bud of her clitoris.

'No,' she said, twisting her head so that she could nibble at the lobe of his ear. 'I want to do it here.'

He swore as her small white teeth bit painfully into his flesh.

'Ow – that hurt!'

He pinched her clitoris in retaliation and she moaned,

her voice low and rich with promise.

'Oh yes! Do it again.'

James obliged, storing the knowledge away for future reference. So she liked to play rough did she? He'd show her rough if he could just get her out of the house!

'We could go back to the beach—'

'No!'

She began to pull at the fastening to his jeans, distracting him for a moment.

'Your place then?' God, he wasn't going to be able to wait much longer!

Morgana moaned and shook her head, grinding her pelvis against his moving fingers.

'Uh, that's *so-o* good! Don't stop . . . don't ever stop!'

'Morgana . . . baby, we can't do it here!' James pleaded, his voice rising on a note of desperation.

Morgana's cool hand was edging closer to the heated flesh at his groin and she had manoeuvred them somehow so that her bare bottom was leaning against the edge of the table. One leg was bent double, her foot balancing flat on the surface, giving him easier access to the hot, silky flesh inside her.

'Fuck me, James,' she breathed.

'Oh yes, I'll fuck you all right, I'll fuck you senseless – but not here!'

Morgana thrust her tongue into his ear and swirled it around, sending shivers down his spine. She was rubbing her pelvis against him now and the friction against his cock sent messages of imminent disgrace directly to his brain. Pushing her away slightly, he stared down into her eyes.

He recognised the expression in them with a jolt. It was the same expression she had worn at the cave. Her pupils were dilated and they shone with a feverish excitement that made his stomach lurch in response. And he knew that she was excited by the thought of screwing with him here, in a place where his wife could walk in at any moment and find them. Danger was as big a stimulant to Morgana Helston as the sight of her luscious, sexy body was to him.

As before, James was excited by the knowledge of what had turned her on. He didn't want Emma to walk in and find them like this. He felt sick with guilt even thinking about Emma. But he couldn't stop himself, not now.

Morgana grasped him by the hair at the back of his neck and pulled him roughly to her as she sensed his capitulation. James kissed her savagely, spurred on by her rapidly spiralling arousal. Helping her up onto the table, he pushed her onto her back and lifted her legs by the knees, opening her.

She stared up at him almost defiantly, proud of her exposed body, happy to let him enjoy the sight of her opened sex. And he did enjoy it. Breathing hard, he took the time to admire the intimate topography of her body, marvelling at the intricacy of the many folds of flesh. The skin grew darker as it reached the shadowed passage, graduating from a deep flush pink to a colour which was almost purple. He could see her clitoris protruding from its hood, a small, slippery bead.

Time seemed to stand still for a moment as he met her eyes. Then James bent his head and fastened his mouth over the wet, open lips of her sex, kissing them as he would the lips of her mouth. Morgana cried out as he probed her opening with his tongue, swirling it round and round her entrance before plunging inside. Thrusting in and out, he used his thumbs to stroke the stretched membranes of her labia, pressing lightly on the sensitive area around her clitoris with every upward stroke.

Morgana's fingers tangled in his hair, pressing his face closer to her as she neared climax. James ground the tip of his nose against her quivering bud, lapping at the sweet-salt stickiness which now flowed freely, coating his lips and tongue and running down his chin.

She came noisily and James straightened so that he could muffle her cries by covering her mouth with his. At the same time he pulled his jeans down to his knees and thrust into her. The table was just the right height to hold her sex on a level with his groin. With his feet planted squarely on the ground, he was able to piston in and out, slamming into her welcoming body with savage, urgent thrusts.

He could see by her face that she was enjoying his lack of finesse. Her mouth was stretched wide over her teeth and her eyes were tightly shut as she concentrated on the sensations running through her body. Pushing his hands underneath her dress, James kneaded her breasts, then slipped down to her waist so that he could hold her still as he came.

Morgana had her second orgasm at the same time as he had his first so that their pelvises mashed together in a brief, savage climax which left them both panting for breath.

James allowed himself only seconds to recover before

pulling out of her. Morgana laughed as he glanced guiltily behind him.

'It's all right,' she drawled, 'she's not there. What a considerate little husband you are!'

James glanced at her with a sudden sharp dislike, but Morgana merely laughed again.

'It was good though, wasn't it?' she said after a minute or two.

Pulling down her dress, she ran a hand through her short, spiky hair. James watched as she licked her forefinger and passed it once over each eyebrow, smoothing them into place. Then she stepped forward and kissed him, quite tenderly, on the lips.

'Don't worry – *Mrs* Lawrence is safely tucked up in bed.'

James's eyes widened.

'You knew she wasn't likely to see us?'

Morgana merely smiled.

'Give me an hour to do what I'm supposed to be doing here, then come and join me in the kitchen,' she said coolly.

'I don't think—'

'That's right, James, you *don't* think,' she interrupted him sharply. He was so taken aback that he merely stared at her. He blinked as her mood changed yet again and, smiling seductively, she came close to him. 'Except perhaps with this,' she added, brushing her hand over his now flaccid cock.

'See you later!'

James watched her as she sashayed out of the room. Incredibly, he had responded to the light caress and was hardening again. An hour? Everything reasonable in him said he should stay out of Morgana's way for the rest of the day. He closed his eyes for a brief moment, trying to marshal some shred of decency, of loyalty to the marriage he was supposed to be trying to save.

It was no good. It might not be right to join Morgana in the kitchen in an hour's time, nor was it honourable, or any of the other things he liked to think he applied to his character, but he knew that he'd be there.

Emma nuzzled her face into the warm cup of Jago's shoulder and breathed in deeply. She could smell the faint trace of cinnamon and tobacco that had become so familiar to her. Against her lips she could feel the steady pumping of his blood through his veins and she knew she hadn't been mistaken, and that this was no dream. In this place, at this time, Jago was very much alive.

They were lying on the sand at the water's edge, she on her back, he between her legs, moving inside her. After they had made love against the rock, Jago had picked her up and walked with her into the freezing water. Emma had gasped as he stood her up and splashed her, her skin taking on a bluish tinge and her teeth chattering as the icy water ran down her skin.

Jago had laughed and, taking her by the hand, had pulled her along after him as he ran back to the water's edge. With the warmth of his body pressing against her Emma soon forgot she was cold and slowly, inexorably, they had sunk down onto the wet sand.

He slipped inside her at once, sinking into the hot, sticky passage as if he were coming home. Now he moved slowly, no more than a gentle rocking of his hips, stimulating her from the inside.

Emma no longer noticed the coldness of the water that lapped at their prostrate bodies and was only vaguely aware that the tide was creeping closer, the waves becoming bigger, more relentless. She could feel tiny tendrils of pleasure rippling through her, radiating out towards the point where their two bodies were joined.

From the expression on his face, Emma was sure that Jago felt the same way. His skin was smooth and warm beneath her hands, his legs, entangled now with hers, were hot. As he kissed her, she tasted the sweat on his upper lip and felt the erratic thump of his heart against her flattened breasts.

Her clitoris seemed to throb in time with his pulse, a tiny heartbeat that grew stronger with each passing moment. As if sensing the deepening of her response, Jago began to thrust into her more urgently. Emma folded her arms around him and they rolled on the wet sand so that she was on top.

Panting slightly, Emma peeled her upper body away from his so that she could look down into his face. His long hair fanned out from his head on the wet sand in serpentine coils and his eyes glittered darkly as they watched her. Emma ran her eyes over his face, committing every detail to memory, for she knew she would want to relive these precious moments again and again.

Breathing raggedly, she raised her pelvis so that his shaft withdrew from her body, right to the very tip. Then, slowly, she sat back down on him, watching how the ecstasy chased across his face.

He reached up and clasped her round the waist, as if trying to control her movements. Emma smiled wickedly and demonstrated how easily she could outmanoeuvre him. A slow grin spread across Jago's face, a grin she didn't quite trust. She squealed as he suddenly reared up and flipped her over onto her back.

'So, my little sea nymph – think you that you could better me, eh?' he growled, his eyes flashing amusement at her and something else, something indefinable that made her pulse race and her mouth grow dry.

Emma thrilled at the sensations provoked by her submission, giving a little cry of surprise as Jago lifted her arms above her head and pinned them there with one large hand. Now she was effectively pinioned under him, imprisoned at her wrists and her pelvis. She tried an experimental wriggle and Jago laughed.

'Ah no, my fine beauty – now you are subject to my pleasure.'

He chuckled at the apprehensive expression that passed across her face, lifting himself up slightly so that he could run his eyes over her exposed neck and breasts.

'Now let me see – do you like this?' He dipped his head and sucked one tumescent nipple into a shiny, wanton cone.

'Ah yes, I see that you do,' he mocked her gently.

Unsure whether she liked the sensation of being completely at his mercy, Emma tried to twist her body away from him. He laughed at her and she quickly gave up, succumbing to his superior strength. A wave of panic washed over her, icier even than the sea water.

'Let me go,' she said through gritted teeth.

Jago ran his tongue quickly along the join of her lips, making her gasp.

'I don't think you want me to. Do you?'

He planted a series of little kisses down her throat and across her heaving breasts and Emma's panic swiftly dissolved into pleasure.

'Do you want me to stop now?' he asked her, his voice gruff with suppressed passion. 'Tell me.'

Emma sighed, aware of a new sensation building in her womb.

'No,' she whispered. 'Jago – God, no, I don't want you to stop!'

Jago kissed her, tenderly on the lips, then nuzzled the dip beneath one arm.

'What do you want me to do?' he asked her, rocking his hips with unbearable lightness so that he sent a tremor all along the cleated walls of her sex.

'I want you to possess me,' Emma moaned, barely conscious of what she was saying.

'Possess you?' Jago repeated, puzzlement colouring his tone. 'Aye, my mermaid, I'll do that. I'll possess you and make you mine, for all time.'

'Centuries?' Emma whispered.

He let go of her arms and she brought them round his shoulders, kneading the strong muscles in his neck with her fingers.

'Aye,' he said, his voice low and husky, 'for centuries.'

Emma wrapped her legs around his hips and drew him further into her as they began to roll into the sea. The waves crashed over them, the surf pulling at their bodies, hissing as the waves rolled back.

Neither noticed the cold or the wet. Between them they created a furnace, an all-consuming, nascent heat that made the elements surrounding them an irrelevance. They rolled, as one, over and over in the surf, conscious only of the tides that flowed within them, the intimate waves that crashed against their inner shores. And when she came, Emma felt as though she were drowning, sinking below the water.

For an instant Emma blacked out, her climax was so intense that she could not bear it. When she opened her eyes, she was lying at the water's edge, alone save for a solitary seagull pecking desultorily at the sand.

Gradually she became conscious that she was sitting naked in freezing-cold sea water. Pushing her wet hair out of her eyes, she scanned the beach for Jago. Deep down, she knew she would not see him, he had vanished into the ether. So had the ship which had been at anchor in the bay.

Slowly, Emma hauled herself to her feet. She slipped several times as she tried to gain a foothold on the wet sand which sucked greedily at her toes. Feeling groggy and disorientated, she searched the beach for her robe. There was no sign of the nets that Jago had been working on when she arrived.

Shivering, Emma pushed her arms into the sleeves of her robe and, picking up her torch from where she had dropped it, walked slowly back to the mouth of the cave. The path to normality was dark and forbidding after the bright sunlight which had bathed the moments she had spent out of her time. Slowly, almost hesitantly, Emma walked towards the back of the cave and searched for the entrance to the secret tunnel which would lead back to the house. Back to the twentieth century and the concerns of her own time.

She frowned as she realised that she hadn't reached the narrowing of the cave which signalled the beginning of the man-made tunnel as expected. Perhaps she had lost her bearings? Dampening down her rising unease, Emma shone the torch slowly across the back wall of the cave. It was solid, with no sign that there had ever been a passageway cut into the rock.

Emma felt a band of pressure tightening around her chest, squeezing her lungs. She felt dizzy, pressing her fingertips to her temples as she fought down the panic which threatened to rise up and overwhelm her. Could it be that she was trapped here, forever stuck in a pocket of time which bore so little relation to the time she knew? Could she never go back?

Casting her eyes frantically around the cave, she gasped. For there on the wet sand, illuminated by the yellowing light of the torch, were footprints.

That they were her own footprints she had no doubt, but she could not understand their position. For they led directly from the solid wall at the back of the cave.

It occurred to Emma then that the disappearance of the tunnel through which she had come held a certain logic. She had come, taken what she was looking for – why should the way back be via the same route as she had come in? Turning, she half ran out of the cave. Running over the firm, golden sands to the water's edge, Emma did not pause to look back until she reached the sea. Relief surged through her as she saw the solid, reassuring bulk of Pengarron's Folly towering over the cliff top.

Of course! Why hadn't she considered the possibility that time had shifted onto its normal course in those few seconds when she had blacked out?

Emma's relief was tempered by the prospect of the long trek up the cliff path which was the only route to the Folly. Glancing ruefully at her bare feet, she headed towards the bottom of the steps cut into the cliff face, presumably by Jago Pengarron two hundred years before.

Half an hour later, Emma reached the top. She was drenched in sweat and her leg muscles felt as if they had been stretched beyond endurance. She was so tired she could barely put one foot before the other. Her head ached, sending purple strobes of pain through her temples and into her limbs and she shook as if with fever.

Past caring what anyone would think if they should see her, Emma could think of nothing but her desire to reach her bedroom and fall into bed. Realising she was probably coming down with flu, she mentally thanked her lucky stars that she had managed to walk safely up the side of the cliff. Was this the spot where Demelza Pengarron had jumped to her death? She shivered, pushing the unpleasant thought away.

The hallway was quiet as she pushed the door open. A drink of water seemed like an attractive idea, so she made for the kitchen, only to be brought to an abrupt halt as she heard voices. The kitchen door was standing slightly ajar, so Emma moved forward quietly so that she could see into the room without being seen. The sight that greeted her made her hand fly to her mouth to suppress her gasp of surprise.

James was standing in the middle of the room, naked except for his T-shirt. His feet were planted four-square on the flagstones and he was facing the scrubbed deal table, thus Emma could see him in profile. It wouldn't have mattered if he had been facing the door anyway, for Emma doubted if he would have seen her, he was so engrossed in what he was doing.

The expression on his face was intent, familiar to Emma. From where she stood, she saw that a pulse was beating steadily at his jaw, and he was breathing hard. Morgana Helston was lying on her back on the table, her short dress pulled up, beneath her arms. Emma could see her large breasts with their brown-tipped nipples, her smooth, caramel-coloured skin stretched taut across her stomach and her outspread thighs.

She was masturbating with the handle of a wooden spoon, working it slowly in and out of her body. As Emma watched, she saw the thin handle, slick with the secretions from Morgana's body, slide up, then move slowly back inside her. As it did so, Morgana uttered a muffled, sighing sound, deep in her throat. The sound was strangled by the fact that her head was thrown back, exposing the tender line of her arched neck as she tipped her head backwards, over the edge of the table.

Emma's eyes fastened on the steady slip and slide of James's cock over Morgana's tongue.

The atmosphere in the room was intense, almost claustrophobically so. A dark, all-embracing eroticism cloaked the couple, both of whom were too wrapped up in their own pleasures to notice Emma watching at the door.

In spite of her own recent exertions, and the encroaching fever, Emma felt her own sex-flesh stir in response. Somehow the fact that her husband was a participant in the scene unfolding before her eyes seemed not to penetrate the fog of lust which had clouded her mind.

James was close to coming. Emma recognised the increased urgency in his movements, the almost-glazed look in his eyes as he pumped his hips back and forth into Morgana's eager mouth. Morgana had inserted a good four inches of the handle of the wooden spoon into her body and was turning it slowly, round and round. Beads of sweat broke out on James's forehead as he watched her and Emma understood that the visual stimulation was acting as a spur to his own impending orgasm.

Emma slipped her hand into the folds of her robe and pressed the heel of her hand against her pubis. Her over-sensitised flesh stirred and tingled, springing to life beneath her fingers. As she rubbed herself slowly with her fingertips, Morgana's hips began to buck and she withdrew the spoon, tossing it to one side and cupping her vulva with her hand as her climax broke.

With a muffled cry, James ejaculated into Morgana's mouth. Emma watched wide-eyed as the girl sucked greedily on his shaft. Emma closed her eyes momentarily as her own climax shivered through her.

It was very quick, and she was able to pull her robe about her body just before James opened his eyes and saw her standing there. Emma saw shock, horror and guilt chase rapidly across his face.

'Jesus Christ!' he shouted, pulling abruptly out of

Morgana's mouth and spilling what was left of his semen onto the floor.

Morgana twisted round, her face a picture of dismay as she saw Emma standing in the doorway. Emma looked from her to James to the spreading white stain of his ejaculate on the flagstones. A wave of dizziness overcame her and she swayed, putting out a hand to steady herself and encountering the wooden doorframe.

Glancing at the frozen tableau before her, Emma thought of her own recent adventures, and she laughed aloud.

Ten

'Stop that!' James's voice was harsher than he'd intended, but the sound of Emma's laughter had unnerved him. It was unexpected and he thought there was a slightly hysterical edge to it that made him feel panicky.

Hastily climbing into his trousers, he glanced at Morgana and motioned for her to get dressed. Morgana, for whom, he knew, the danger of discovery was half the thrill, seemed subdued. Obviously, the possibility was far more exciting than the actual event.

'Mrs Lawrence ...' her voice trailed away as Emma stopped laughing and met her gaze.

Morgana was the first to look away. James wondered what she had been about to say. As if there was anything, really, that could have been appropriate.

He noticed then that Emma was wet, her hair plastered against her head as if she'd been swimming. Her feet had left wet prints on the flagstones. She moved slightly and he saw that she was naked under the thin cotton robe. Resorting to outrage in the face of her silence, he said, 'Where the hell have you been? You're soaking wet!'

Emma gave him a look that withered him, and turned away without a word. With a helpless glance at Morgana, James hurried after her.

'I can explain, Emma – it's not what you think...' Despising himself for his weakness, he nevertheless trotted out a string of appropriate clichés, none of which seemed to make the slightest impression on Emma. Her face was flushed, her skin, when he reached for her hand, felt clammy to the touch. She looked down at James's hand as if it were trespassing and he hastily snatched it back.

'I feel awful, James – let me get to bed.'

That was all she would say. James watched her undress and slip between the covers. To his consternation, within minutes she was asleep.

'Is she all right?' Morgana accosted him the minute he walked back into the kitchen.

James scanned her face quickly and saw that her concern was genuine.

'She's asleep, would you believe? Went out like a light. She doesn't seem well – she's burning up.'

'Here, let me give you the telephone number of the doctor who covers Pengarron.' Morgana scribbled the number down on a piece of paper. 'He's a good bloke, one of a dying breed who still makes house calls.'

James took the scrap of paper from her and stared down into her eyes.

'You're going then?'

'I think that's best, don't you?'

James looked away.

'Yes. But, God help me, I want to see you again.'

He looked at her then and saw that she hadn't expected that. Her small, white teeth worried at her lower lip as she thought about it.

'All right,' she said at last, 'but you'd better wait until the fuss dies down here. Call me.'

'All right. Christ, Morgana – what's happening to us?'

'What do you mean?' she asked him gently.

James made a small, helpless gesture with his hands.

'It's something to do with this house, I swear it is! Ever since we arrived Emma's been acting strangely. She's been . . . distant.' He thought briefly of her sudden sexual aggression and his eyes slid away from Morgana's searching gaze.

'And you?' she prompted when he did not go on.

'Me?' James gave a short, harsh laugh. 'I hardly know myself. I thought at first it was purely because I find you so bloody sexy, but now I wonder if it isn't as simple as that.'

'Well, thanks a lot!'

'No – Morgana, I didn't mean . . .'

He pulled her into his arms and kissed her hard on the mouth. She wriggled sensuously against him and he groaned, setting her away from him.

'You see – you only have to kiss me and I want to bend you over the table and fuck you senseless!'

Morgana laughed and he realised that he was forgiven.

'It's just that this isn't me, not really. It's as if I've suddenly become some kind of maniac, insatiable.'

'Suits me,' Morgana told him with a shrug, and James realised she didn't understand what he was trying to say at all. But then, why should she? After all, he couldn't even begin to understand himself.

'I'll get going now,' she said, picking up her bag and swinging it over her shoulder. 'You'll call me?'

James nodded, pushing his hands deep into his pockets as he listened to her swift footsteps crossing the hallway. Once he had heard the click of the front door closing, he ran back upstairs to check on Emma. She seemed to him to be hotter still. She was tossing and turning restlessly in the big four-poster which she had made her own exclusive territory.

Watching her from the doorway, James tried to make sense of her mutterings, but he could only make out one word with any certainty, and that was a name. *Jago*.

Telling himself that he had no need to feel guilty when it was obvious that Emma's attention was also being directed to someone else, he went downstairs to telephone the doctor.

Oblivious to James and her surroundings, Emma watched as Jago paced the room she knew as the drawing room downstairs. She could sense his anger and she shrank from it, glad she was only an observer and not a participant in the scene unfolding before her eyes.

It was evening and the heavy damask curtains had been drawn across the windows, keeping out the chill. A fire burned merrily in the grate, casting a reddish glow over the room. Emma could smell soot and candle grease and the sickly sweet aroma of freesias. There was no other light, save for a single candle burning in a holder placed on a table to one side of the window.

There was a woman sitting on the window seat, and

Emma knew at once that it was Demelza. She was dressed in a heavy, winter-weight dress of the deepest sapphire blue which set off the tendrils of red hair which had escaped the top knot fastened to the top of her head and lay in wisps on her shoulders. Every now and again, she absently pushed at the errant wisps of hair, seeming not to notice that she was displacing the arrangement still further every time she touched it.

Her eyes followed her husband warily as he paced back and forth, though her bottom lip protruded slightly in an expression of stubbornness. Emma's eyes were drawn to her long, elegant fingers which kept folding and unfolding over a small rectangle of white card.

'But why can't we go, Jago?' she said suddenly.

To Emma, Demelza's voice was as clear as a bell, as if she was actually sitting in the room with them. It was obvious from its tone that the argument had been raging back and forth for some time. Emma's attention switched to Jago. His expression was dark, his eyes stormy as he turned them on his wife.

'Why would you wish to go?' he snapped, his voice low and reverberating with a barely suppressed anger that made Emma shiver. 'To draw the eyes of all the young men at the ball? Is not your husband's regard enough for you?'

'Of *course* it is, how could you think otherwise?' Demelza cried. 'You know my eyes, my heart, all of myself is only for you . . .'

'So why torment me with your pleas?'

Demelza's hands fluttered in her lap in an expression of helplessness.

'I only thought it would be a happy jaunt... We see so few people here.'

It seemed to Emma that it was the romantic heart of a very young girl which spoke, of one who loved to laugh and be gay. Her heart squeezed in her chest as she caught the note of wistfulness in Demelza's voice. Jago had caught it too, but his response was very different to Emma's.

'And who is it my lady would wish to see?' he said, his voice icy cold.

Demelza's face registered dismay, but it seemed that Jago was not moved by her obvious distress.

'Am I not enough for you? Do I not fulfil your every need? Speak now, my lady, for if it is so I would wish to know it!'

Emma's heart went out to him as she saw his jealousy, and the deep-rooted insecurity that was its cause. She sensed that Demelza understood this too, for the other girl leapt to her feet and, with a passionate cry of denial, she tore the invitation into pieces. The scraps of card fluttered to the ground around her feet and, as she watched them fall, so Demelza opened her arms to her husband.

'I would not wish to go if it causes you distress,' she told him. 'It was no more than a foolish woman's fancy that made me think to reply to Lady Jeavons that we would attend her ball. Please – wipe that frown from your brow, my own love, and show me that I am forgiven.'

Jago crossed the room in three strides and enfolded Demelza in his arms. Her hair gave up the unequal fight to stay in the top knot and tumbled around her shoulders in a glossy shawl.

'Forgive me,' Jago muttered, his voice muffled by her hair. 'It is as if my mind is enclosed by the thickest fog when I think of you with others. It is only that I love you so, you know that, do you not?'

He leaned back to scan her face and Emma saw Demelza nod.

'I know,' she murmured, 'I know.'

Their mouths fused in a kiss that made Emma's own lips ache. After a moment, the spark which had ignited between them seemed to blaze into an inferno. Jago pulled Demelza's dress down over her shoulders, lifting her breasts free from her undergarments and bringing them to his lips. They were small, but perfectly formed with tiny, pale pink nipples set within a perfectly circular areola which puckered before Emma's eyes.

She felt as if she was intruding on this most private of moments between them, but she was unable to rise from the seat in which she was sitting. Instead, she found herself growing warm, the soft, secret flesh of her sex throbbing in empathy with the young couple who were now feverishly undressing each other.

Emma's breathing quickened as she saw how beautiful Jago was, running her eyes down the golden sweep of his back and across the paler globes of his firm, muscular buttocks. Those buttocks clenched now as Demelza took him into her hand and began to stroke the hardening shaft which reared up to meet her touch.

'No man could give you what I can give you,' Jago whispered urgently.

'There is no other for me but you,' Demelza whispered in reply as she sank to her knees before him.

It sounded like a benediction, a ritualised exchange

of words which both had repeated often before, almost religious in intensity. Demelza closed her eyes for a moment as she dabbed at the bulb of his penis with her tongue, running the tip along the tiny slit at its end.

Emma was reminded, uncomfortably, of the scene she had witnessed in the kitchen earlier. But that was nothing to this. Demelza took him into her mouth so lovingly, so tenderly, her soft pink lips opening slowly to enclose him. Emma knew at once that this was an act of love as well as lust, and in comparison the sexual athletics she had witnessed between James and Morgana faded into insignificance.

Yet, strangely, she felt no jealousy towards the girl now kneeling at her own dream lover's feet. Rather she felt a tenderness, a yearning sisterliness. Remembering the dream she had had when the soft lips now enclosing Jago's penis had pleasured her, Emma accepted the way she felt and enjoyed the sight.

After a few moments, Jago reached down and drew Demelza to her feet. Staring into her eyes, he lifted her up, from the waist, and lowered her onto his cock. Demelza's eyes widened as he embedded himself within her and her arms came about his neck to steady herself.

Emma recognised the flush staining the other girl's pale skin and realised that, though Jago had not touched her, she was close to orgasm. The couple moved together as if this was a scene they had played out between them many times. The tension which held them both in thrall seemed orchestrated, as if familiarity had honed their responses so that one look, one touch was enough to trigger the desired response.

Jago's legs were planted firmly apart, his knees slightly bent as he supported all of Demelza's slight weight. It was impossible to move much in this position though, so he gradually bent his knees and lowered them both to the floor.

His large, tanned hands covered the paleness of Demelza's breasts, kneading and stroking the pliable flesh until she cried out and moved her head from side to side. As if this was a signal for which he had been waiting, Jago slipped his finger to the point where their bodies joined and moved it delicately across the sensitive, stretched membranes of her sex.

Demelza cried out again, her legs scissoring wildly round Jago's waist. Emma caught the fleeting expression of triumph which passed across Jago's face before he pushed harder into his wife's convulsing body.

'You're mine, Demelza,' he said urgently as he quickened the pace of his thrusts. 'Mine . . .'

'And you are mine, my only love,' Demelza responded, her voice cracking with emotion.

Curling her fingers into the hair at his nape, she held him close to her. There was no doubting her sincerity as she welcomed the sudden rush of his seed into her body, but Emma saw the anguish which momentarily darkened Demelza's lovely green eyes and she felt a shiver of apprehension for her. For how, she reasoned, could anyone remain sane in the face of such possessiveness?

And Emma knew, at that moment, the true extent of the danger that Demelza faced. For it was not Jago who imprisoned her, but the strength of her own love for him.

She wanted to speak out, to try to warn the young

couple now lying entwined on the carpet that their love was too intense, too stifling for it to survive. For she knew that the bright flame of love she had witnessed would be snuffed out if it was starved of oxygen.

They'd listen to her, they'd have to, all she had to do was get up from this chair and go over to them . . .

'Emma! Emma!'

She fought against opening her eyes, but the voice was insistent. She was being pulled back, physically restrained, and she knew she could not fight against it. Reluctantly, she turned her back on Jago and Demelza and turned her attention to the here and now. Opening her eyes, she saw that James was leaning over the bed. He was not alone, for standing to one side was a dark-haired man in middle age whom Emma did not recognise.

'What—'

'This is Doctor Abbott,' James interrupted her, anticipating her question. 'I was worried because your temperature was so high. You've been raving – I asked the doctor to come over and take a look at you.'

Emma bit her lip in case her instinct to tell them both to go away and leave her alone overwhelmed her.

'I'm not sick,' she croaked, aware as she did so that her tongue felt as though it had swollen in her mouth and her head throbbed as if she'd been up all night having hit the bottle with a vengeance.

'Perhaps you should let me be the judge of that,' the doctor said cheerily, waving James aside and sitting down on the edge of the bed.

Emma regarded him warily. He was handsome in a kind of restrained, almost patrician way and he looked at Emma steadily, as if measuring her thoughts.

'Now let's see, shall we?' he said after a few moments.

'I'll wait downstairs, doctor,' James interjected hurriedly. 'You'll be all right, Emma?'

Knowing he would be desperate to absent himself from a scene of illness, Emma nodded, then wished she hadn't. Her head felt as though it had been kicked repeatedly on the inside.

'Tender head?' the doctor asked, laying his palm against her forehead.

His hand was cool and dry and Emma found herself responding to his professional touch – hardly surprising after the scene she had just witnessed in her dreams. She defended herself at once. 'Yes – but that's all. That and a slight chill, I'm afraid. My husband shouldn't have called you out, it's a complete waste of your time,' she told him with a sudden burst of irritability.

'Ah well, poor chap was worried,' the doctor said as he slipped a thermometer under her tongue, effectively silencing her.

Emma watched him as he opened his case and took out his stethoscope. Could he feel the thickening of the air as she could? She smiled to herself as she realised that Jago had joined them. She couldn't see him, but she knew he was there, hovering in the shadows.

The doctor took the thermometer out of her mouth and held it up to the light. Frowning, he gave it a shake and slipped it back into his case.

'Have you been like this for long?' he asked her, making a note on his pad.

Only since walking from one world into another and

back again, Emma answered him in her head.

'No,' she said aloud. 'I think I might have caught a chill when I went swimming this morning.'

'In the sea?' he asked her, raising his eyebrows.

'Yes. It was very cold.'

'Hmm. It's a common misconception that becoming cold and wet causes chills. More likely you'll have swallowed some sea water and ingested some unpleasant bacteria with it. The sea might look clean around these parts, but I can assure you it probably isn't. Besides, the currents are treacherous below these cliffs – I'd think twice if I were you before going swimming alone again.'

Emma wanted to ask him what made him think she was alone? but instead she merely smiled meekly.

'Yes, doctor,' she murmured.

The doctor glanced at her sharply as if he was aware that she was mocking him. Emma thought for a moment that he would say something else, but all he said was, 'If you'd loosen your nightdress, I'll just check your breathing.'

Emma could feel Jago's presence growing stronger, pressing closer as she unbuttoned the front of her nightdress. She frowned, noticing the tension building up in the air of the room, not understanding its cause, but knowing that it came from Jago.

Doctor Abbott rubbed the disc of the stethoscope between his palms to warm it before pressing it against the upper curve of Emma's breast.

'Deep breaths, please,' he said, listening intently as she complied.

Emma hardly noticed what he was doing for the atmosphere in the room had thickened. She could smell the thin, pervasive scent of tobacco curling round her, could sense the anger which striped the air.

The doctor nodded and tapped her lightly on the shoulder to indicate that he wanted her to lean forward. Emma held the fabric of the nightdress against her naked breasts as she did so, her eyes falling on the dressing table across the room.

Jago was watching her through the glass of the mirror. Their eyes met and Emma recoiled from the fury she could see in his. This was the same expression he had worn during his altercation with Demelza earlier, only now his possessiveness, his jealousy, was directed at Emma.

Emma felt sure that the doctor must have been able to detect the acceleration of her heartbeat, yet he said nothing as he put his stethoscope away. Emma caught the faint frown though between his eyes as she lay back against the pillows.

'What's the verdict, doctor?' she asked him with a lightness she was far from feeling, more because she wanted to stop him from turning and possibly seeing Jago's image in the mirror than because she wanted to hear what he had to say.

'You'll live,' he replied. 'I'd like to feel your abdomen though, if you'd just pull up your nightdress.'

He looked away discreetly as Emma modestly folded the sheets to her waist and pulled up her nightie. The doctor's hands were cold as he gently palpated her flesh and Emma shivered. At once a vibration seemed to take over the room, a disturbance in the air that made

Emma's eyes widen in alarm. Then, suddenly, a cut-crystal perfume bottle which sat on the dressing table fell to the floor with an almighty crash.

'Good God! What was that?' the doctor said, abandoning his examination and turning round.

Emma was shaking, for she understood at once that the incident was merely an expression of Jago's impotent rage. The sound of the crash brought James bursting into the room.

'What happened?'

He stopped in his tracks as he saw the shards of glass glittering on the floor, looking from Emma to the doctor with raised eyebrows.

'The thing just fell off the dressing table,' the doctor said, the tone of his voice shaky.

It occurred to Emma that perhaps the doctor was concerned that allegations of misconduct could be made against him, that he was belatedly considering the folly of having allowed James to leave the room while his wife was examined.

'Could you find a dustpan and brush or something, James?' she said quietly to distract him.

'Yeah, right,' he said, clearly nonplussed.

'I'll come with you,' Doctor Abbott said with alacrity, adding rather lamely, 'I've finished here.'

Emma watched as the two men left the room, then sank back on the pillows. She felt ill and groggy, yet she knew that she needed to muster the strength to talk to Jago. She called him, softly.

'Jago? Jago, speak to me. I know you're still here.'

She sensed him appear beside her, but could not

summon the energy to turn her head.

'Why did you do that?' she whispered.

'You ask me why?' he said bitterly.

Emma frowned.

'You frightened the doctor.'

'Doctor? He was a physician? How so?'

'I've caught some kind of virus – a sickness.'

She sensed Jago struggling with himself, concern and anger jostling for a place in his consciousness. Anger, it seemed, had won.

'Think you that I would stand by and watch you lift your skirts for the physician? A pox on him! His hands were all over your body!'

'He was examining me,' she explained, exasperation colouring her tone. 'Trying to find out what was wrong.'

'Do you think me a fool?' Jago hissed. He was so close to her she felt his cinnamon-scented breath brush across her cheek. 'I saw the way you shivered and sighed as he touched you!'

Emma drew the breath in through her nose and tried to hang onto her temper. Had she not witnessed his jealousy before, she would have lashed out at him in anger; now she tried to think of a way to reassure him, as she had seen Demelza try to do. That thought made her stop and think again. For what had Demelza gained from appeasement?

'Jago, do you not trust me?' she asked, as calmly as she could manage. 'Do you not think that I would be true to you?'

'I saw you—'

'His hands were cold, Jago, that's why I shivered at

his touch. Honestly, think – even if you believe that I am capable of betraying you with another man, which I am not, would I really respond to him when I knew you were watching us? It doesn't make sense.'

Jago was silent, though she could hear him breathing. Slowly, Emma turned her head and her gaze collided with his. He was resting his head beside hers on the pillow and his dark eyes were thoughtful. Sensing that she had successfully arrested his anger, she reached out to touch his face. It was cold as the grave, the skin waxy and slippery beneath her fingers. Jago pulled back as if she had burned him.

'Do not touch me, not here!' he told her.

Emma frowned.

'I don't understand – why is it that you can touch me, yet I can't touch you?'

Jago looked at her, his expression sorrowful as he rubbed at the place where she had touched him.

'I know not why, only that it is so. Will you come to my world again?' he asked her.

'Yes,' she breathed, forgetting at once how ill she felt and thinking only of the sensual promise in his glance.

'I am glad.' He appeared to hesitate, then he said, 'I know not why I am this way, it is how I am made. I could never stand the thought of another man's hands on the body of the woman I love.'

Emma's breath caught in her chest and she stared at him. Was he saying that he loved her?

'You loved Demelza,' she said softly.

A look of such intense pain passed across Jago's features that she almost wished she hadn't asked him.

'Aye,' he whispered. 'But my love was evil, twisted... It killed her.'

'No! Jago, you must not think that!'

He shook his head sadly.

"Tis the truth. She chose death rather than to live with my love.' Spitting the word as if it was a blasphemy, he looked directly at Emma and his gaze was intense, piercing. 'And now I see her in you and it seems I have learned nothing. I wait for you in the time between my world and this. I yearn for the sweetness of your body, yet a part of me prays that you will not come.'

'But why?' Emma cried, not understanding.

'Because my love is a sickness that will possess you – aye, possess you,' he said passionately as he saw her recognition of the word. 'What redemption can there be for me if you follow the path of my Demelza?'

'But I won't!' Emma said desperately, seeing that he was fading from her, his strength used up by emotion. 'Jago, I am *not* Demelza – I won't leave you...'

'I will wait for you, I will live again for you. I will live for the sweet lure of your body, for the sound of your cries as I pleasure you and for your submission as I possess you...'

'Oh yes – wait for me, Jago!'

Emma held out her hand to him as he seemed to merge into the shadows, growing fainter, weaker in the half-light. His words had aroused her, clouding her judgement, making her dismiss the warning he had given her before. For how could she not go to him when his mere words were enough to set a pulse throbbing insistently between her thighs, her stomach cramping with need?

'Wait for me,' she whispered as he faded.

Then he was gone, leaving the faintest trace of cinnamon hanging in the air.

'Who were you talking to?'

Emma spun round as she heard James's voice. How long had he been standing there? How much had he heard? By the look on his face, Emma guessed he had heard enough, of her side of the conversation at least. His face was ashen, the dustpan and brush hanging forgotten from his fingers.

'Who is Jago, Emma?'

'The man who built the Folly, James. Jago Pengarron.'

'A dead man?'

Their eyes locked for a moment, then Emma nodded. James's jaw tightened.

'I see.'

He went to clear up the broken glass at the foot of the bed. Emma watched him, aware that there was a dam waiting to burst inside him. When eventually he straightened, he put the dustpan full of glass onto the dressing table quietly and turned to face her.

'So now you're deluding yourself that you have a hot-line to heaven are you? I guess that's a natural enough progression.'

Emma flinched from his cutting sarcasm.

'James, please listen. Ever since we came here I've been conscious of something... something not quite right. You've been aware of it too, I know you have! Look how you wouldn't sleep in this room with me, how you complained of the cold... and look – I found this.'

Ignoring the banging in her head, Emma scrambled

out of bed and went to lift Demelza's wedding dress from the trunk.

'What is it?'

'It's a dress—'

'I can see that.'

'A dress,' she continued, ignoring the interruption, 'that belonged to Demelza Pengarron. She's the woman in the portrait I've had hung in the hall, the wife of Jago Pengarron. I found out that she died when she jumped off the cliffs with her baby in her arms – oh James, it's such a tragic story!'

'I'm sure it is,' James said, refusing to think about the hallucination he had had of a woman and child in his room when they first came to the Folly. 'But I don't see what it has to do with us.'

'I keep having these dreams... only they're not dreams, not really. It's as if I'm watching events that happened here in this house two hundred years ago. And sometimes... sometimes I seem to take part in those events myself.'

Glancing at James, Emma saw that he didn't believe a word of what she was telling him. Why would he? It sounded completely crazy.

'James, please listen. Jago Pengarron has been visiting me. He's shown me a way of walking between this world and his to a place where he lives and breathes—'

'So you're telling me that you were talking to a ghost?'

'Yes. I know it sounds screwy, but—'

'Damn right it sounds screwy! Screwier still when you consider that you've just walked in on Morgana and me, and you've barely even bothered to react. You're too wrapped up in your fantasies about a supposed ghost. So I guess that tells me just how much you care about me and our marriage.'

'Hang on a minute,' Emma countered, sitting down on the edge of the bed. 'I catch you *in flagrante* with the cleaner, and it's my fault?'

James had the grace to flush slightly.

'It's your fault that you don't damn well care,' he grated. 'You don't care, do you?'

Emma stared at him, trying to make sense of her feelings.

'I'm not happy that you're having an affair—'

'But you don't care enough to let it distract you from your ghost, do you?'

He swore viciously as he saw the guilty agreement written on her features.

'Christ, Em, I don't think I know you any more!'

Emma's mind raced as she tried to think of some way she could convince him that Jago did exist, that he wasn't some phantom she had dreamt up as an excuse not to care about James. If only she could take him to the cove, show him . . . She thought of the secret passage and leaped up.

'I can show you the secret place. That's where I was this morning – down on the beach, only it wasn't nineteen ninety-five, it was sometime in the eighteenth century. *I can show you.*'

James shook his head, exasperated, but he followed Emma down the stairs to the place where she had found the concealed door in the panelling. Running her hands over the carving, she located the trigger and the panelling swung open a few inches.

'There!' she turned to him, triumphant. 'Look for yourself. If you follow the passage to its end, you'll walk through the cliffs and come out on the beach.'

James poked his head around the door and peered in. It looked as though there might well have been the kind of passage Emma described – once. However, this particular passage had been bricked up long before.

'Nice try, Em,' he said dryly, standing back so that she could see the blocked entrance for herself.

The look of astonishment on her face could not be anything but genuine and James felt a pinprick of sympathy for her. It was clear to him that when they got back to London he would have to organise some serious therapy for her. He'd wanted her to have counselling after the accident, but she had refused. Convinced then that to shun help was a mistake, now he knew his instincts had been correct. If only she had talked about her loss, brought everything out into the open instead of bottling it all up inside, maybe things wouldn't have come to this.

He knew they couldn't stay here in Cornwall for much longer, just until he'd completed his assignment for the paper.

'But it was there only this morning. Truly, James, it was – I walked along it myself...'

James sighed heavily.

'Come on – the doctor said you should stay in bed for the rest of the day.'

They walked up the stairs in silence. Emma's bewilderment was palpable. She climbed into bed and allowed James to tuck the covers up around her chin.

'I don't understand,' she whispered.

Feeling the emotion kick in his chest, James reached out and stroked her forehead.

'There's nothing *to* understand, Em,' he said softly. 'You're overwrought, that's all – and my behaviour hasn't exactly helped.'

'No, it hasn't,' she replied coldly.

James stared at her, Snatching his hand away, he clenched his fists by his side. The affection he had felt towards Emma a few moments ago had been dispelled by those three words of condemnation.

He'd behaved like a heel, he wasn't denying that. But the rest, that wasn't his fault and he wasn't having Emma blame it all on him. He wanted to take her by the shoulders and shake her until her teeth rattled. All she seemed to care about was that her preposterous story about ghosts and dreams and illusions had been shown to be the result of self-delusion. James seriously doubted if the crisis between them had even entered her head.

'Do you want to know *why* I'm screwing Morgana?' he asked her furiously.

'James, I—'

'I'll tell you why. I'm fucking her because she makes me feel like a king. Not a piece of shit she accidentally stepped in.'

'James! I don't treat you like that!'

'Don't you?'

An expression of weariness passed across his face. Emma knew she should go to him, cross the enormous chasm which had opened up between them without her even noticing it. She cared, of course she did! But she couldn't honestly say at that moment that she cared enough.

Dropping her eyes from his, she said, 'I'm sorry you feel that way, James.'

The silence lay heavily between them for a few moments. It was James who broke it.

'The doctor says you should be okay in twenty-four hours or so. I think it might be a good idea if I move into a hotel for a few days, give us both time to think things through.'

He didn't mean a word of it, had made the threat only to try to shock a reaction from her. His heart seemed to somersault in his chest as Emma nodded.

'All right.'

She could see from the expression on his face that James had been bluffing. She only had to say the word and she could still stop the chain of events which were grinding into motion. Truth was she *wanted* him to go. She wanted to be alone at the Folly.

James's face was a picture of misery. Remembering how she had found him with Morgana, Emma hardened her heart against him and turned her head away.

'I'll leave you a telephone number where you can contact me. I'm leaving now, Emma.'

She wondered what he expected from her. Last minute histrionics? Pleading? She held her breath, willing him to go and get it over with. From the corner of her eye she saw a rogue muscle twitch in his jaw.

'Right. I think it's time we thought about going home.'

Panic clutched at Emma's insides and she shook her head. How could she leave here now?

'I don't want to go back. I have to find out—'
'Look, I'll call you, say, at the weekend? We'll talk then.'
'All right,' she replied, her voice small.
'You'll be okay?'
'Yes, I just need to sleep a little.'
'Goodbye then.'
'Goodbye, James.'
Emma sat bolt upright in bed and listened as he crossed the landing. It didn't take him long to throw a few clothes into a suitcase. As he passed her door, he paused, as if debating whether or not to come in. Emma let out a sigh of relief when he moved on. She heard his footsteps running down the stairs and across the hall. The front door creaked on its hinges, then slammed shut. As he started up the car and drew away, the headlights lit up the bedroom for a moment, raking across the shadows.

When at last she was alone, Emma lay back on the pillows and hugged herself.

'Well, Jago,' she whispered into the velvety darkness, 'wherever you are, now you really have got me all to yourself.'

Eleven

James drove straight to St Ives and checked into the Meridian Guest House. If he was going to spend time away from Pengarron's Folly, he reasoned that he might as well complete the assignment his editor had given him when he first arrived. And an exclusive interview with Andrew Joiner, the high-profile, West End producer whose disappearance had led to the collapse of one of the newest, brightest production companies in West London would significantly improve his career profile.

'How long will you be staying, sir?' the receptionist asked him, eyeing his single small suitcase pointedly.

'Book me in until the weekend and we'll review the situation then,' James said curtly.

The receptionist, a sour-looking blonde with large breasts crammed into a blouse that was too tight for her, pursed her thin lips and nodded.

'Very well, sir.'

James took his case up to his room and, without bothering to look around him, made straight for the ensuite bathroom. It had hardly hit him yet that he had actually walked out on Emma. He felt a twinge of conscience.

Should he have left her when the balance of her mind was so obviously disturbed?

The details of her story swirled in his head, making it ache. What she had told him, fantastic though it was, had struck a reluctant chord in him. He thought of the flame-haired woman who had haunted his dreams and of the sounds of singing. But it wasn't possible, he knew that. He didn't *want* it to be possible.

Standing under the stinging spray he told himself that tonight he wouldn't even think about what had happened. Tonight he would go down to the hotel bar and get very, very drunk, then in the morning he'd consider his options.

For a small hotel the bar area was singularly impersonal. The furnishings – black and red sofas with stingy cushions and glass and chrome coffee tables interspersed between them – looked strangely dated. A bored-looking youth in a black dinner jacket with shiny seams stood behind the bar, one eye on a TV set which played soundlessly in the corner. Every now and again he took a languid swipe at the bar surface with a damp cloth that looked none too clean.

He glanced without interest at James as he approached.

'Scotch,' James said. 'Leave the bottle.'

The youth served him sullenly, plainly resentful that he had been dragged away from the television. As soon as he'd paid for the Scotch and had coaxed a tumbler with ice from the barman, James looked around him. Sitting on one of the sofas by the window was Andrew Joiner, the producer James was supposed to have tracked down. He looked up and nodded politely as he felt James's eyes on him. James reciprocated, then turned away. He could keep.

At the far end of the bar, a bottle blonde of indeterminate age tapped her foot restlessly in time to the Muzak piped through the lower floor of the hotel. She smiled when she caught James's eye, perceptibly straightening in her seat and flicking her long, curly hair over one shoulder.

Marking her down as a prostitute, James smiled tightly, then turned away. There were a selection of newspapers lying on one of the coffee tables and he began to work his way through them as he drank his way steadily through the Scotch. It wasn't long before he felt sufficiently mellow to relax back into his seat.

It was then that the woman made her move.

'Do you mind if I sit here?' she asked him, sliding onto the sofa opposite.

'It's a public bar,' James muttered, not wanting to encourage her.

The woman smiled and signalled to the barman for another martini. As she waited for it, she reached into her capacious shoulder bag and rummaged around for some cigarettes. James shook his head when she offered him one and she shrugged.

'Suit yourself.'

Close to, James saw that she wasn't as old as he had first thought, probably no more than thirty-eight or nine. She had clear, unlined skin, only lightly dusted with make-up, though the silver-grey eyeshadow lay heavily on her lids, making her look a little desperate. Her lips were painted a bright, brave red to match the tight tube of a dress which showed off her black-stockinged legs.

'Have you just checked in?' she asked him conversationally when her drink arrived.

'Yes. And you?'

She smiled, confirming James's suspicions about her.

'Monica,' she introduced herself, holding out a hand. James took it briefly in his.

'James.'

Monica regarded him thoughtfully for a moment, drawing the smoke into her lungs and blowing it out in a long, slow stream.

'Hi, James,' she said softly. She smiled again and it occurred to James that it made her look much younger, more approachable.

'You should smile more often,' he said impulsively.

'Well, James, you might be able to help me out on that score actually.'

James regarded her warily.

'Oh? In what way?'

Monica smiled seductively and leaned towards him.

'You see that guy over there by the window?' She nodded her head at Andrew Joiner who, James could see, was trying hard to mask the fact that he was watching them closely.

'Yes.'

'He's waiting for me to find someone willing to have sex with me while he watches. There's no need to worry – he's paying,' she added hastily, misinterpreting his silence.

James stared at her and, despite his reservations, his

cock stirred at his groin. So Andrew Joiner was a voyeur was he? The journalist in him framed the headlines and he smiled. Monica was certainly not unattractive and she was offering him sex on a plate. Why turn her down?

'All right,' he said calmly. 'Where do you want to go?'

'It's all set up in his room. You don't mind, performing in front of another man?'

James shook his head, realising that he was secretly thrilled at the idea.

'Lead on, Monica!'

James hung back so that Monica walked up the stairs in front of him. Her dress was so tight that every ripple of muscle, every shiver of flesh was accentuated as she walked. The skirt ended about two inches below the crease between buttock and thigh, so that from below James could see an enticing, intriguing shadow where her legs joined.

At the top of the stairs Monica turned and smiled at him and he knew that she had known he was watching her, had maybe even enjoyed it. His spirits lifted as his interest was pricked. Suddenly he was glad that he hadn't finished the bottle of Scotch. He'd drunk enough to rid him of any inhibitions which might have modified his behaviour, but not so much that his performance would be affected.

He'd never been with a prostitute before, and he had to admit that the idea excited him. Knowing that it was a common enough fantasy to pay a woman for sex did not diminish its potency one iota. Though the reasonable, everyday part of him recoiled from the thought that by exchanging cash for services rendered the normal rules of behaviour need not apply, a deeper, more primitive side of his personality got a thrill from it. The woman now opening the door of the hotel bedroom was bought and paid for – all he had to do was give the word and she would do anything he wanted. *Je-sus*!

Andrew Joiner's room was slightly bigger than James's, but the furnishings were virtually identical. Once inside, Monica went over to draw the curtains before smoothing the duvet over the bed. Then she switched on a single bedside lamp which had been draped by a red silk scarf so that the room was flooded by a diffuse, reddish light.

They looked at each other over the short distance separating them.

'What happens now?' James asked when Monica did not immediately make a move towards him.

She held up her forefinger and pressed it lightly against her lips. Her fingernails were long and sharp and painted a virulent shade of scarlet. She pointed towards the door and James heard Joiner's footsteps coming up the stairs. The door opened and he turned.

Andrew Joiner, apparently oblivious to the risk of exposure to which he was subjecting himself, went to sit in an armchair which had been placed in the far corner of the room. He avoided James's eye and James immediately understood that he wanted no contact between himself and the players he had chosen; his role as watcher was to be absolute.

That suited James. Until that moment he had been worried that Joiner might want to live up to his name and join in, maybe even make a pass at James himself. He had nothing against gay men, but he was old enough and experienced enough to know that he had no leanings in that direction whatsoever.

Monica motioned him to a chair and moved across the room to where a shiny black cassette player stood ready on the chest of drawers. The raw, aggressive voice of Robert Palmer filled the room and, finding a space at the end of the bed, Monica began to dance.

She was good, James noted with surprise. Her arms and legs moved in a constant, fluid motion, her torso undulating suggestively as she writhed and shimmied for their delight. Sitting in the shadowed corners of the bedroom, James felt as if he and Joiner were an audience in a strip joint. The lighting gave the room the air of a brothel and the atmosphere grew thick with sexual tension.

The raucous rock song came to an end and was followed by a slow, haunting ballad. As he watched, Monica ran the palms of her hands slowly down her body from her breasts to her thighs. She was sweating, her face shiny in the muted light, her dress sticking damply to the skin between her breasts and beneath her arms.

James imagined licking the little pearls of sweat from her top lip, running the tip of his tongue along her lipsticky lips and pushing into her mouth. He felt his own mouth run dry and his cock stiffen at the idea.

Monica smiled at him, as if she could read his mind. Her eyes fell on the telltale bulge at his crotch and he saw her pupils dilate. She seemed not to notice Joiner sitting in the far corner of the room, she had eyes only for James. Glancing swiftly at the other man, James saw that he was breathing heavily. Sweat stood out on his brow and his eyes were glazed, fixed on Monica as she reached for the zip at the back of her dress.

James's attention was drawn back to her as he heard the gentle rasp of the zip being drawn down. Monica swayed in time to the music, bending her knees slightly so that she could balance on her ridiculously high heels. James loved her sandals – the heels were thin and spindly. They made her look helpless, shackled. He hoped she would leave them on while he fucked her.

Her shoulders, when she peeled the dress away from them, were narrow, her arms shapely and well toned. James held his breath as he saw the black bra strap against the white skin. He almost came in his pants when she peeled the dress down to reveal the tackiest, sexiest push-up bra he had ever seen. Made of cheap black lace, it forced her breasts unnaturally high and pushed up her nipples so that they lay, like two ripe cherries, just above the line of the bra.

There was something intensely erotic about the red dress rolled to Monica's waist, revealing her breasts in the tacky bra. It added to the anticipation, heightening James's arousal until he felt like leaping up from his seat and pulling the dress off himself.

Could she be wearing stockings and a garter belt? The thought made his breath catch in his chest. It might be a fairly pedestrian fantasy, but James had never met a woman who was willing to indulge him in it. Dragging his gaze from her breasts, he looked at her legs. They were encased in black nylon . . .

He held his breath as Monica slowly, teasingly, rolled the dress down over her hips. James closed his eyes momentarily and swallowed hard as he saw the wisp of black lace around her slender waist and the elasticated vertical straps stretched taut from belt to lacy stocking top.

'Jesus!' he whispered.

The music had stopped now, leaving only a faint, static hiss. James could hear Andrew Joiner's heavy breathing. Glancing swiftly at him, he saw that he was stroking himself slowly through his trousers, his eyes fixed firmly on Monica.

Stepping out of the skirt as it fell to her ankles, Monica kicked it aside. James ran his eyes over her body, taking in the long legs in the sheer black stockings, the shapely calves elongated by the position of her feet in the high-heeled sandals.

Beneath the suspenders she was wearing a pair of sheer black panties which fitted snugly over her mound. Turning round slowly, she raised her arms up above her head, as if wanting to show the watching men how she looked from all angles. James admired the firm, rounded globes of her buttocks beneath the almost transparent fabric.

Once she had her back to them, Monica brought her arms back down to her sides. Then slowly, with almost theatrical timing, she bent from the waist, keeping her legs straight, but apart, her hands on her hips.

James sucked in his breath as her buttocks parted and the dark channel of her sex came into view. It was then that he saw that she was wearing crotchless panties. As she bent further, thrusting her bottom up towards him, the two sides pulled apart to reveal the wet, pink folds of her most intimate flesh.

The air in the room seemed thick with anticipation.

James felt as though he couldn't breathe. The outfit was cheap and tacky, a parody of Everyman's idea of what a whore would wear. As an aphrodisiac it was first class.

Straightening, Monica turned and smiled at him. With her hands on her hips she shimmied slightly, making her breasts shake.

'Well? What do you think?' she said.

James stood up slowly and, completely ignoring the other man, he approached her. When they were standing toe to toe, he ran his hands down the sides of her body, coming to rest at her hips. As he had expected, the lace she was wearing was cheap and scratchy, setting his teeth on edge as he stroked it, yet sending signals of pure lust to his brain.

'I think you're wasted on all this,' he said, his voice gruff.

Monica threw back her head and laughed. It was a pleasant sound, light and musical. Impulsively, James bent to kiss her. Her lips tasted sweet, like ripe cherries. After a few seconds, Monica pulled away.

'Not on the mouth,' she said, shaking her head.

James saw in her eyes that she would have liked to go on kissing him, but he understood that kissing was not in her brief. Giving a small, cynical smile, he decided that it didn't matter, she'd turned him on so much thus far he'd do whatever he had to do to fuck her.

'What now?' he asked her.

Monica smiled approvingly at him.

'It goes like this – you take off your clothes, then you rub me all over with oil. Once you've got me good and slippery, I get to suck you while you bring me off with this.'

Going over to the bedside table, Monica opened the drawer and took out the biggest, pinkest dildo James had ever seen.

'Jesus Christ!' he breathed.

Monica held his eyes as she wrapped her lips around the bulbous, latex head of the vibrator. Her cheeks bulged as she eased it to the back of her throat, her eyes half closing as she allowed her head to fall back on her shoulders. As she drew it out again, James saw that it was slippery with her saliva. It left a shining, silvery trail on her skin as she rolled the dildo down between her breasts, stroking it across the tip of each nipple.

'Where's the oil?' he croaked.

Monica flicked her head towards the drawer and James went to get it out. Undressing quickly, he watched as Monica arranged herself face down on the bed. It was a relief to release his erection from the confines of his trousers. His only worry was that he might not be able to hold off for long enough to play the role as written.

The red glow of the covered lamp shone eerily on Monica's skin. Climbing onto the bed, James straddled her at the thighs, sensing Joiner moving round to the chair he had recently vacated so as to get a better view.

Monica's skin was smooth and flawless. Sliding his fingers over it gave James an unexpectedly sensual satisfaction. Within minutes he had her back slathered in oil, so he moved down the bed to anoint the gap between her panties and her stocking tops.

'Turn over.'

Starting at the tops of her thighs, James let his fingers linger at the edge of her knicker elastic. He could feel the heat of her vulva, see where the edge of the split-crotch panties was darkened by the secretions of her body.

Sensing the tension in her, he felt a surge of masculine pride that he could move a battle-hardened pro like Monica to shivering at his touch. He smiled at her as he rubbed the oil into the taut flesh of her stomach, spilling it into the well of her navel until it overflowed and ran in shiny rivulets onto the covers below.

Teasing her, he turned his attention to her arms, caressing each one with studied concentration. By the time he was ready to oil her neck and breasts, she was breathing heavily, her breasts rising up to meet his touch.

'O-oh!' she moaned.

James smiled as the first cool, oily drops dripped onto her nipples from a height. He watched as the already puckered flesh of her areolae swelled, glistening in the dim light. Then, slowly, he covered them with his palms and began to move his hands in a circular pattern, massaging each breast in an outward movement.

Monica moaned again and James saw that she was having difficulty in holding onto her control. It gave him a rush of pleasure to know that, far from being a mere puppet in this game, he was now dictating the direction which it would take.

Pinching her nipples lightly, James rose up on his knees and nudged at Monica's lips with the tip of his cock. A thin thread of clear fluid smeared her lips and she put out the tip of her tongue to lick it away.

James felt hot, the adrenalin buzzing through his veins as he fought to stay in control. Monica held his eye as she slowly opened her mouth and enclosed the head of his cock. James sighed raggedly. The inside of her mouth was hot and wet and welcoming. Leaving her breasts, he braced his hands on the pillows either side of her head and gently eased himself in.

It would have been easy to simply keep on moving in and out of her accommodating mouth until he came, but James remembered the dildo and several possibilities for what he might do with it passed across his mind's eye. It took a great deal of self-control to withdraw completely from her mouth and sit back on his heels. His cock stood proud, rising up between his thighs like an angry baton.

'Get up on all fours,' he said huskily.

He reached for the dildo as Monica complied. Weighing it in his hand, James switched it on and watched as it began to vibrate. From the corner of his eye, he saw Monica begin to tremble and his pulse quickened. Holding the vibrator against his cheek, he felt its action. Turning it off again, he smiled.

'So – you want me to use this on you,' he said conversationally. 'Interesting. Very interesting. I wonder how you'd like it best. Here, perhaps?'

He stroked the tip of the dildo across the peaks of her nipples as they dangled below her body. Monica shivered, a little moan of disappointment escaping through her lips as he moved it away again.

'I see you like that.'

Glancing across at Joiner, James saw that he liked it too. In fact the other man had unzipped his flies and was slowly stroking his naked penis. There was a line of perspiration on his upper lip and he seemed to have fallen into some kind of a trance.

James turned his attention back to Monica, leaving Joiner to his own private pleasures. Switching the vibrator to its slowest speed, he ran it slowly along Monica's spine, from the base of her skull to her coccyx. He liked the way she undulated as the latex-covered mock penis passed over each vertebra, so he repeated the action, more slowly.

'Mm, I like the way you do that,' he told her softly. 'Do you know how you open yourself when you push your ass up into the air like that? That's what you might call easy access . . .'

He ran the gently buzzing instrument from her clitoris backwards, along the split of her vulva and up to her anus, which contracted as it was touched. James chuckled softly.

'I do believe I've found the place you like best, Monica,' he drawled softly. 'Now let's get down to business.'

Turning the dildo up a notch, he stroked it across her tight nipples again, watching her face closely as he moved from one to the other. It was clear she had responsive breasts for, judging by the look on her face, he could have brought her to orgasm just by stimulating her nipples.

Wanting to take things further than that, James passed the vibrator down between her breasts and across her belly. Monica sucked her stomach in as it moved over it, shuddering as it reached the nylon-covered mound of her mons.

The dildo slipped easily between the moisture-slick folds of her vulva, nestling between her inner labia and vibrating gently. Monica sighed, and a fine film of perspiration pushed through her pores, gilding her skin. James swirled the end of the instrument around the entrance to her body, drawing the moisture along its length and running it slowly back to her clitoris where he held it still.

Watching Monica's face, he gradually increased the speed of the vibration until her jaw slackened and her breathing became short. Panting, Monica bore down on the vibrating head, grunting slightly as she came.

James let her rest for a few moments. Monica took the weight off her elbows and knees and lay face down on the bed. After a minute or two, James picked up the bottle of oil and trickled it slowly over her buttocks. The black nylon of her panties grew wet and oily as he massaged the thick fluid into the crease of her behind.

'That's it, Monica,' James crooned, 'time to go back to work! Lift up your ass.'

She lifted her head and caught his eye. James saw a brief struggle take place in their depths, then with a small moan which sent a shiver down his spine, Monica pushed her buttocks up high.

'That's it, baby,' James glanced across to where Joiner was now masturbating himself in earnest. 'Hey, you – come and take a look at this – this will make you come for sure.'

The other man looked startled and James saw at once

that he did not like being drawn into the scene being enacted on the bed. His pleasure came from watching, not from taking part. Switching his attention back to Monica, James turned on the latex dildo and began to play its head up and down the shadowed cleft between her buttocks.

Monica moaned and swivelled her hips, leaving James in no doubt that she was enjoying this encounter as much as he. Encouraged, he ran his penis along her back, revelling in the oily slip of her skin against his.

There was a resistance at first to the nudge of the vibrator against the entrance to her anus, but once past that first sphincter of muscle, it slipped in easily. Monica gasped as James turned up the speed and twisted it round and round.

'Oh God! Oh God I'm coming again!' she cried.

As he watched her body convulse once more, James knew he was near to climax himself. With a muffled cry, he pulled the dildo out of Monica's body and flipped her over onto her back. Monica pulled her knees up to her chest, opening herself to him as if she expected him to thrust into her, but James had other ideas.

Bringing himself quickly to crisis point by hand, he shot his sperm all over her breasts. He gasped as he watched the white globules landing on the soft skin of her chest, spraying her nipples and staining the black lace of her bra.

Monica reached up and ran her hand up and down his shaft, milking him of the last few droplets. Then, incredibly, she sat up and slipped him into her mouth. She sucked him gently as he grew flaccid, licking the tip of his penis clean.

POSSESSION

From the sounds coming from the corner, James knew that Andrew Joiner had finally climaxed too. The show was over.

After a few minutes, James climbed off the bed and into his clothes. Monica watched him without comment from the bed. When he was ready to leave, James leaned over and kissed her briefly on the lips.

'I hope he gives you a bonus,' he said.

Monica smiled.

'I'll make sure of it,' she assured him.

The following morning James got up early and showered. His plan, which he had thought out when he got back to his own room the night before, was to confront Andrew Joiner over breakfast and trade him an exclusive interview against scandal. He doubted that *Mrs* Joiner would like to read about her husband and a prostitute named Monica over the breakfast cornflakes!

James was whistling as he came down the stairs. The receptionist who had booked him in the night before peered suspiciously at him and he gave her a grin.

'Good morning! Another lovely day – makes you feel good to be alive, doesn't it?' He chuckled as the receptionist's habitual scowl became blacker. 'Could you tell me what time Mr Joiner normally comes down for breakfast? We're old friends, you see, and I thought it would be good to surprise him by being at his table when he comes into the dining room.'

'Old friends? Oh, what a shame!' The girl smiled coldly at him. 'Mr and Mrs Joiner have just left.'

'Mrs Joiner is here?' he asked, bewildered.

'No. She was, of course, but as I said – they've left.'

'Left?' James felt the colour drain out of his face as he saw his juicy story slip away. 'You mean they went out early?'

'No, sir, they've checked out. It was only a few minutes ago – you might just catch them.'

James hurried outside, just in time to see Andrew Joiner getting into a taxi. There was a woman with him, dark-haired, chic, a woman he vaguely recognised from press functions in the past. Mrs Andrew Joiner.

He frowned, sure he must have made a mistake. If his wife had been with him in the hotel then how had Andrew Joiner managed to procure a prostitute to indulge him in his kinky games last night?

The taxi drew away from the kerb and executed a neat three-point turn in the road. As it passed him, James bent down to get a good look at the woman. When he saw her face, he knew at once that he had been duped. There but for the blonde wig and heavy make-up was Monica.

As she passed, Monica/Mrs Joiner turned her head and caught his eye. At first James thought she wasn't going to acknowledge him for she seemed to be looking straight through him, as if she didn't know him from Adam. Then, just as they swept past, he swore that she winked.

James stood at the kerbside and watched as the taxicab disappeared round the bend.

'Sonofabitch!' he murmured.

He'd thought he had the Andrew Joiner story stitched up, watertight. Instead the tables had been turned on him. Had they known who he was when 'Monica' propositioned him? Or was it sheer coincidence that he was selected for their game?

It didn't matter, not really. If he was honest with himself, James knew that he didn't really care whether he was able to turn in the story or not. Shaking his head at his own gullibility, he laughed and went back inside.

Twelve

Emma walked, disconsolate, along the shoreline. She was barefoot and the tiny waves tickled over her toes as they approached and then receded.

Last night she had slept badly, not because James had walked out, although that gnawed at the corners of her mind, insisting that at some point she would have to face it. Not yet. At the moment she was more concerned that her gateway into Jago's world seemed to have closed.

The brick wall was still in place when she'd opened the panel that morning. So she had walked down the path up which she had climbed the day before and gone into the cave. The shelves cut by smugglers of old into the rocks were still in evidence, as were the iron sconces that hung from walls as she remembered. But there was no tunnel at the back of the cave.

On closer inspection, Emma realised that the entrance had been blocked deliberately by means of fitting loose rocks into place to form a wall. It had looked solid to her the day before, but then she hadn't known what to look for. At least now she knew that there had indeed once been a secret tunnel, and that it had been opened for her. She wasn't going mad, as James obviously thought she was.

That didn't solve the mystery of how she was going to find Jago's world again. Sighing, Emma turned away from the sea and started back to the house.

She felt much better this morning; her temperature had reduced and a bout of sickness seemed to have purged her body of any lingering poison. Even so, she felt slightly out of breath as she reached the top of the cliff.

As soon as she opened the front door of the Folly, Emma sensed that there was someone else there. Not a ghostly presence, but a real flesh-and-blood person, moving around in the kitchen. Emma's first thought was that it was James. She frowned. She wasn't ready to see him yet. Reluctantly, she moved towards the kitchen and pushed open the door.

It wasn't James who turned as she entered. It was Morgana Helston.

'You! I didn't think you'd have the nerve to come back!'

Morgana bit her lip and shrugged. She had her back to the Aga and seemed to be hugging it, as if for protection.

'I came to apologise, Mrs Lawrence.'

Emma stared at her. Morgana was wearing black jeans today and a faded pink T-shirt, slashed at the waist to show off her flat, caramel-coloured midriff. Her Doc Martens were laceless, and Emma saw that she didn't wear socks with them. She wondered, irrelevantly, if they gave her blisters.

'Well,' she said at last, 'I appreciate your front, coming to face me like this, but "sorry" is a pretty empty word after the event.'

Morgana's face flushed.,

'I told Gran I'd see to what needs doing. Grandad is badly again so she couldn't come herself.'

'Ah, I see. You had to come, so you thought you'd try apologising to see if that would smooth the way.'

'It isn't like that...' Morgana trailed off as she saw Emma's disbelieving expression. 'All right, maybe that's how it is. But I *am* sorry, for what it's worth. I never meant for you to get hurt.'

'Really? It was all right then, was it, having it off with a married man just so long as the wife didn't find out?' Emma laughed bitterly. 'Get on with your dusting Morgana and spare me your warped philosophy of life.'

The younger girl looked thoroughly uncomfortable as Emma turned away.

'I just wanted you to know that I feel like a right bitch.'

Emma glanced cynically at her over her shoulder.

'Good,' she said, closing the door quietly behind her.

James pounded along the beach, pushing himself as he neared the rocks. The urge to get out of the guest house and run had been too overwhelming to ignore and now he revelled in the sheer physical exercise. The sweat ran down his face and lay, salty wet, along his upper lip.

There was nothing like running to help clear the mind, he told himself as he splashed through the water to get to the next bay. And boy, did his mind need clearing! Since he had seen Andrew Joiner and his wife drive off that morning, he'd spent time reflecting on the events that had overtaken him and Emma since they arrived in Cornwall.

Maybe he had been hasty, leaving Emma alone. After all, she was obviously ill and the hallucinations she had been having were worrying. It was just that he had sensed that she wanted him to go, that she really didn't care about his dalliance with Morgana. After her violent mood swings which had left him feeling as if he didn't know whether he was coming or going, it had been too much.

Realising he was heading towards the cove beneath the Folly, James decided to run up the steep cliff path and head back towards St Ives. He was still too confused to face Emma, though he promised himself he would ring her the minute he got back to the guest house. When he actually saw her he wanted to be clear in his own mind of what he wanted to say, and what he wanted the outcome of their meeting to be. The issues had been too confused for too long.

Running along the edge of the road, James almost jumped out of his skin when a car horn sounded behind him. Turning to give the driver a two-fingered salute, he faltered as he saw who was behind the wheel of the 2CV drawing up at the roadside.

'Hi – need a lift back into town?' Morgana had to dip her head to catch his eye and he saw that she was laughing.

'Hi. I could easily run it,' James said, piqued by the disbelieving look she gave him.

'But you'll accept the lift anyway since I'm going your way,' she finished for him.

James opened the passenger door and crammed himself inside the confined space. Morgana's glance took in his red face and sweaty torso and she jerked a thumb towards the back seat.

'There's a towel back there,' she told him.

James picked it up and wiped himself down with some relief. He would go to hell and back rather than admit to Morgana how glad he was to see her – or, more specifically, her car – but he grinned at her now.

'Have you been to the Folly?'

'Yeah,' she confirmed, drawing away from the roadside. 'Gran couldn't make it so I was drafted in as substitute. I don't know what they'll do when I go back to uni – caretaking that place is too much for them both now.'

'Are you leaving soon?' James asked her, trying to ignore the pang that the idea gave him. After deciding he wanted to work things out with Emma he didn't want the clearer waters of his feelings muddied again by his lust for the girl sitting next to him.

'Not until September. Why did you walk out on her, James?'

Taken aback by the suddenness of the question, James answered honestly.

'A touch of injured pride coupled with frustration, I guess.'

Morgana glanced at him from the corner of her eye.

'Don't you want to work things out?'

'I think so, yeah. But whether Emma does too, well, that's another story.'

'You're not going to find out while you're skulking in St Ives though, are you?' she said baldly.

James ran a hand through his sweat-damp hair.

'I know. Turn left on the main road – I'm staying at

the Meridian. Morgana, do you have time for a coffee?' he asked impulsively.

'A coffee? I don't know, James, Emma—'

'I want to talk about Emma. I thought maybe you could give me the female view on things, you know?'

Morgana glanced at him incredulously.

'Do you really think that *I'm* the right person to ask?'

James grimaced.

'You're the only friend I've got in this place.'

Morgana sighed heavily.

'Okay. But coffee and a chat is as far as it goes this morning, all right?'

'All right.' James smiled at her. 'You're what you English call a "good sort", aren't you, Morgana?' he said, touching her cheek affectionately.

Morgana laughed.

'I've been called a few things in my time, but never that!' she said, deftly pulling into a parking space and killing the engine.

Inside the guest house, James ordered coffee and took Morgana through to the bar-cum-lounge. She smiled knowingly at him and then sat down on one of the sofas.

'Is this to show your intentions are honourable, James?' she teased him.

'I guess. Morgana – how did Emma seem to you this morning?'

She shrugged her narrow shoulders, but James noticed she looked uncomfortable at the question.

'Pissed off with me,' she replied, 'but I expected that. We *were* a bit out of order, weren't we?'

'Just a bit. She wasn't still feverish then?'

'Not that I noticed. Did you call the doctor?'

'Yes, he came and saw Emma shortly after you left. He seemed to think she might have swallowed contaminated sea water and that whatever it was she'd caught, it would clear up in twenty-four hours.'

'And you left with the doctor, did you?'

James nodded, avoiding her eye.

'More or less. She didn't want me to stay. It seemed to be the best thing at the time.'

Morgana made an impatient sound at the back of her throat and James rushed on hastily.

'She's been acting very oddly – seeing things and having these vivid dreams which she thinks aren't dreams at all.'

'What does she think they are?'

James shrugged, at a loss.

'I'm not sure exactly. She called them scenes from the past, as if she really believed she was experiencing some kind of flashback.'

James glanced up as he realised that Morgana's interest had been pricked.

'And what are they about, these "dreams" that aren't dreams?' she asked him.

'About the original owners of the house.'

'Jago and Demelza?'

'That's right – do you know about them?'

'I'm not an expert on local history, but all the kids who live round here grew up hearing stories about the ghost of Jago Pengarron.'

'Ghost?'

'Yeah. He's supposed to roam the cliffs at night searching for his long-lost love.'

'Demelza?'

Morgana nodded.

'Yes. She came to a sticky end – apparently she jumped off the cliffs on the headland, killing both herself and her baby.'

'Yeah, Emma told me the story. Trouble is, she thinks she's struck up some kind of relationship with this Pengarron guy and that's what's on her mind, night and day. She's in love with a dead man.'

The coffee arrived at that moment and James noticed that Morgana was strangely still.

'What is it?' he asked as soon as the waitress had left. 'You want to tell me something...'

Morgana shrugged again, but James could see by the look in her eyes that she attached more importance to what she was about to say than she was letting on.

'It's nothing, just that I'm taking a psychology module as part of my course. There's a name for what you just described...' She stared out of the window for a moment, a frown scoring deep vertical lines between her eyes as she tried to recall it. '*Spectrophilia*, that's it. A morbid attraction to ghosts, especially involving fantasy or illusion of having sex with phantoms... Christ, James, are you all right?'

James shook his head, trying to dispel the sudden nausea which had gripped him.

'Emma thinks she's fucking Jago Pengarron?'

Morgan shrugged helplessly.

'I don't know – it's just psycho-babble, after all.'

James thought of the times when Emma had initiated sex with him and he had felt used by her, as if she neither knew nor cared who he was. Could she have been substituting him for Jago Pengarron?

'Is it?' he replied with a shudder. 'I'm not so sure.'

'Oh come on, James!' Draining her coffee, Morgana stood up. 'I'd better go. If you're right, though, you'd better keep an eye on Emma.'

'Oh? Why's that?'

'His wife jumped, but what happened to Jago Pengarron himself? Nobody knows. He simply disappeared into thin air – *poof!*' Morgana laughed. 'Lighten up, James! Tell you what, I've got to take some groceries up to the Folly tomorrow. If you like, I'll try to find out how Emma's doing, then call in here on my way home. Okay?'

'Would you? That'd be good of you,' James said, painfully aware that he was relieved to be spared an uncomfortable encounter with Emma for one more day. He wanted to reflect on the new angle Morgana had unwittingly given him on the situation.

Standing up, he walked Morgana to the front door, pecking her briefly on the cheek as she reached the door.

'Oh, I almost forgot,' she said as he opened the door. 'I'll have a friend of mine with me tomorrow. Her name is Helene – would you mind if she came for *coffee* too?'

The emphasis she put on the word *coffee* made James feel warm again.

'Sure,' he answered, trying not to let his imagination run away with him. 'The more the merrier.'

Morgana laughed, then, with a brief wave, she ran

down the steps and over the road to where she'd parked the car.

Emma sat in the garden within a garden where she had first seen Jago and enjoyed the feeling of being bathed in sunlight. It was peaceful here. Initially she had come out to escape the sounds of Morgana Helston moving about the house, but she had heard the girl's car draw away long before. She had no excuse to stay, yet she found she wanted to linger on the bench.

A movement caught her eye in the shadowed recesses of the summerhouse and her heart skipped a beat. Could it be . . .?'

Slowly, tentatively, Emma walked towards the summerhouse. She'd never really noticed it before, now she regarded it with interest. It was very old, the wood gnarled and weather-beaten. Where once there had been a door there was now no more than a gaping opening draped with thick cobwebs. They brushed against her face as she stepped inside, making her shudder.

It was very, very dark inside, so much so that she couldn't see the far wall at all. Trying to ignore the cobwebs that clutched at her hair and arms, Emma groped her way towards the back. Suddenly she noticed a circle of light, greenish in colour, reflecting off the rear wall. As she watched, the circle grew and moved closer, until it seemed that it would swallow her up.

As it enclosed her, Emma shut her eyes, hugging herself for reassurance. When she opened them again, she saw that she was in another garden. A circular stone trough filled with crystal-clear water held a fountain which cascaded majestically over the statue of a cherub. Looking closely, Emma saw that, though the statue had the face of a cherub, its body was that of a man, with a full-sized stone penis, carved with loving detail.

Walking slowly towards the fountain, Emma saw through the curtain of water that there was a hammock strung between two trees in the middle of an immaculate lawn. In the hammock, dressed in plain trousers and a frilled white shirt, lay Jago.

Emma's heart leapt and she stepped forward, a smile spreading across her face.

'Are you real again?'

Jago quirked an eyebrow at her.

'Real? My lady – come and feel for yourself!'

Emma ran across the lawn and laid her hand gently in his lap. She felt him harden at her touch and she smiled.

'You're pleased to see me!' she said, delighted.

'I thought you would never come,' he replied, his voice husky.

Emma climbed carefully into the canvas hammock which rocked alarmingly as she eased herself into a supine position beside him. They laughed like children as Emma clung to him, closing her eyes against the spinning sky.

'Oh, Jago – I thought I'd never find you again!' she murmured against the warm, brown column of his neck.

Jago was silent, though he stroked her hair, lifting her face by the chin so that he could kiss her lips. His mouth tasted of rum and tobacco and Emma sought his tongue with hers, wanting to reassure herself that he lived again. Slipping her hand inside the opening of his shirt, she felt the warmth of his skin and did not doubt it.

Everything that had been troubling her before – James's departure, Morgana's duplicity – fell away like an unwanted layer of clothing. Nothing mattered to her except this moment, this time which she could spend held in Jago's strong arms.

He seemed to be in a lazy mood as he ran his hands slowly over her upper body.

'Are you tired?' she asked him, smiling as she realised that she sounded like an over-solicitous wife.

'Aye, 'twas a long crossing.'

Realising at once that he must have just returned home from a voyage, Emma raised herself up awkwardly so that she could see his face.

'Where did you go?'

'Italy.'

Emma thought his reply rather short, so she pressed him, intrigued by the life he led away from the Folly.

'Did you bring back a good cargo?'

Stiffening beside her, he frowned.

'Good enough.'

'Well?' Emma laughed lightly. 'What was in your fine ship, sir?'

'Nothing that need concern you.'

'Jago!' she pulled back, as far as the hammock would allow, appalled by his tone.

'I meant only that it is not a fit subject to discuss with a lady,' he said, his tone conciliatory, but firm.

'And if I want to discuss it?' she persisted stubbornly.

Jago raised an eyebrow at her.

'Then I should have to persuade my lady that there

are far more interesting things for us to discuss.'

Emma sighed as he covered her breast with his hand and squeezed gently.

'Do you think I am that easily distracted?' she murmured, her breath catching in her chest as Jago began to kiss the breast he held through the thin fabric of her blouse.

'For certain,' he whispered, his tongue swirling round the burgeoning, cotton-covered nipple. 'Why, would you have me stop?' He raised his head and looked at her, his expression teasing. 'I could stop, if it would please you?'

'Oh no,' Emma groaned, urging his head back down again, 'oh no, don't stop!'

Jago chuckled. It was a very masculine, self-satisfied sound which sent shivers up and down Emma's spine. She wriggled slightly as his head moved lower, finding a small patch of bare skin where her blouse had parted from the waistband of her skirt.

'Oh yes!' she whispered, lifting her hips slightly, her skin rising in goosebumps as his lips moved across it. 'Oh, Jago – please . . .!'

'Patience, my love,' he told her, raising his head so that he could see her face.

His fingers took the place of his lips, stroking and smoothing her skin, gradually working the elasticated waistband of her skirt over her hips and down her legs. Emma sighed as she felt the warmth of the sun on her naked skin. Jago looked askance at her minuscule panties, pulling them off and holding them up to the light. Emma could see the evidence of her arousal darkening the gusset and she flushed.

'Jago . . .'

'What garment is this?'

He brought the panties up to her face and wafted them beneath her nose. She caught the sweet, piquant aroma of her own arousal and sucked in her breath. Jago smiled. Burying the lower part of his face in the skimpy, silky fabric, he closed his eyes for a moment and inhaled deeply. Watching him, Emma felt a hard knot of desire form in her belly.

Opening his eyes, Jago caught her expression and his own eyes darkened. Flinging the panties aside, he bent his head to capture her mouth with his. The kiss was deep, yearning, invested with so much emotion that Emma felt tears prick her eyes. The hammock swayed beneath them as he stroked a path down her body to the shiny, slippery folds of her sex.

'Oh!' Emma whispered as he found the hardening bud at the apex of her labia.

Jago moved the pad of his middle finger round and round on the tip of her clitoris, watching her face as if to gauge the extent of her pleasure. Before too long she was panting, the lips of her sex opening and closing round his fingers, sucking him deeper into her body, until a kaleidoscope of light seemed to explode before her eyes and she came, gasping.,

At once Jago brought his hand up to her mouth and smeared her lips with the honeyed secretions of her body. Holding his eye, Emma parted her lips and slowly drew his wet fingers into her mouth. Jago gave a low, shuddering sigh as she licked his fingers clean and she saw that he was losing the steely control he was exerting over himself.

Slowly, so as not to rock the hammock too violently, he lay down on his back, easing her across him. Running his thumbpad firmly over the soft inner flesh of her bottom lip, he unfastened the front of his breeches and released his cock. Emma slid down his body until his penis was on a level with her face. It trembled slightly as she touched it, seeming to swell still more as she enclosed it in her palm.

The skin covering the rigid core was so soft, so silky smooth it was a pleasure to run her hand up and down the shaft. With her other hand Emma cupped the hair-roughened sacs which hung below it, feeling their heat, their weight as they too swelled against her palm.

Slowly, prolonging the anticipation as long as she could, she lowered her head and licked lightly along the underside of his shaft. Jago gasped and a single teardrop of fluid leaked from the slit at the end. Dabbing at it with her tongue, Emma was soon unable to stop the flow.

Opening her mouth wide, she slowly fed the bulbous head of his penis into her mouth. The warm, salty fluid coated her tongue, trickling stickily down the back of her throat. Jago cursed aloud as Emma gently manipulated the hard little balls within the wrinkled pouch of his scrotum before easing his cock further into her mouth, inch by inch.

She sensed he was already close to coming, so she began to suck him in earnest, moving her head up and down and flicking her tongue firmly around the head on each upward stroke. Jago was breathing heavily now and his skin felt hot and damp beneath her fingers.

Increasing her rhythm, Emma fancied she could feel

the vibration in his balls as the seed gathered there, before it was forced along the length of his shaft. She swallowed quickly as the first viscous jets of ejaculate hit the back of her throat. His sperm was hot and milky, flooding her mouth as his fingers tangled in her hair and caressed her scalp.

When the last tremors of orgasm had stilled, Jago pulled Emma up into his arms. Looking deep into her eyes, he kissed her hard on the lips, his tongue raking the tender inside of her cheeks and sweeping over her gums.

'My own,' he whispered, 'Emma.'

She could see that fatigue was fast overtaking him and she stroked back the hair which had fallen across his cheek. With a tired smile, Jago turned his head and pressed his lips against her palm.

Emma held him in her arms, watching his face as he drifted into sleep. His eyelashes were long, resting against his cheekbones. Asleep he looked very young, and Emma felt a protective surge of love for him. She didn't want to go back to the loneliness and pain of the twentieth century, she wanted to stay right here, with Jago.

The thought shocked her, sending a wave of sadness sweeping over her for she knew it was impossible. He had known her this time, had called her by her name. His feelings for her seemed to have developed, deepened as had hers for him. In this curious twilight world where they met it seemed as though time telescoped into haphazard pockets. It seemed to Emma to be a miracle that they had ever managed to meet at all.

With that sense of wonder though there was the strong, inescapable realisation that time was running out for them. That, once used up, these brief blips in the chronology of time could not be revisited.

Resting her cheek against his, Emma closed her eyes and, after a few moments, she too slept.

Thirteen

James was waiting for Morgana when she arrived at ten the following morning.

'Hi, James – this is Helene. Helene – James Lawrence.'

'Pleased to meet you, James,' Helene said, holding out her hand.

James took it, noticing at once how her soft palm moved suggestively against his. He looked at her in surprise and she smiled at him. It was a wide, friendly smile which showed her perfect white teeth. Scanning her face, James saw a fringe of gold-blonde hair above pansy-blue eyes framed by a double row of blonde lashes. Her hair was drawn back into a hairband and fell softly to her shoulders.

There was a look in those ostensibly guileless blue eyes that made James glance at Morgana with suspicion. What had she told this girl about him? Morgana merely smiled at him. He did not trust that smile, he recognised it as the one that showed she was up to something.

'Come through here and I'll see if I can rustle us up some coffee,' he said, showing the way through to the lounge.

There was no one in there apart from the cleaner. Clad in a pink nylon overall and grubby white plimsolls, she was pushing a vacuum cleaner in front of her with one hand while holding up a paperback romance in the other. So engrossed in it was she that she didn't even notice them come in.

James looked round as Morgana touched his arm.

'C'mon, James, we can't hear ourselves think in here with that racket going on! Let's go to your room. Don't worry,' she added, laughing as she saw his expression, 'you'll be perfectly safe with us!'

James felt strangely reluctant to take the girls up to his bedroom, but Morgana was right, it would be ridiculous to try to talk over the noise of the vacuum cleaner. He wondered if Morgana had remembered the reason she had called in to see him this morning – that she was supposed to be telling him how Emma had been when she saw her earlier. He opened his mouth to ask her, but she was already running up the stairs, her boots making an unholy row on the thinly carpeted stairs.

It was obvious to James that Helene had come along anticipating more than a quick coffee. Her hips swayed provocatively as she walked up the stairs in front of him, reminding him of a cat on heat.

What was the matter with him? He was being offered something here, something exciting, yet his body had barely reacted to the stimulus at all. Could it be that now he had been away from the Folly for a while its insidious effect on his libido had begun to wear off?

James found himself hoping fervently that this was the case. Sex had taken over his thoughts lately, affecting his judgement, altering his behaviour, jeopardising every area of his life. He hadn't let Jeff Brawn, his editor, know how he had lost the Andrew Joiner story yet. And as for Emma, well, the fact that he was here at all was eloquent enough an explanation of how he had affected his marriage.

Once inside the room, Helene went to sit on the bed and Morgana perched on its end. She watched as James filled the kettle in the small bathroom and plugged it in. Steam billowed into the little bedroom as the kettle boiled.

'Did you go up to the Folly this morning?' he asked Morgana, wanting to steer the conversation towards the subject she was supposed to have come to discuss.

'Yeah. I didn't stay long, I just put the groceries away and came straight here.'

'How did Emma look?' he asked, aware of the eagerness colouring his tone.

Morgana gave one of her infuriating shrugs.

'I didn't see her.'

James stopped what he was doing and stared at her.

'You didn't see her?' he repeated incredulously. 'But you said you'd check she was all right, you said—'

'Hey, if she wasn't there then it stands to reason that she's all right, doesn't it? Come on, James – she's probably gone for a walk, strolled down to the village or gone down to the beach.'

James saw that what she said was reasonable. Emma could have done any one of those things. Morgana was right, if she'd still been feeling ill she'd have stayed in the house or garden. Forcing himself to stay calm, he made coffee and passed it round to the two women who were both watching him intently.

He noticed a tension in the room and, in spite of himself, his body reacted to it. Morgana took only one sip of her coffee before putting her cup and saucer down on the bedside table and walking over to where James stood, leaning against the wardrobe. Watching her through half-closed eyes, he did not react when she reached up and pressed her lips against the corner of his mouth.

'You worry too much,' she whispered.

Her breath was warm and sweet as it brushed across his skin. James felt an inner trembling as she stroked a finger down the side of his face.

'Emma is my wife,' he reminded her shortly.

Morgana's smile told him what she thought of his sudden concern for Emma.

'What do you think of Helene?' she asked, her voice soft, for his ears only.

James looked across to where Helene was reclining on the bed. Her short white skirt had ridden up over her shapely thighs and he could see a glimpse of white lace panties at her crotch. He swallowed.

'She's very pretty,' he admitted.

Morgana kissed the centre of his throat, licking down to the dip between his collarbones. Her tongue was warm and wet, its surface slightly abrasive against his skin.

'I told her about you,' she said, moving her attention to his earlobe.

'Told her what?' he asked, his voice hoarse.

'That you'd like doing it with two women.'

James felt his stomach plummet with excitement.

Glancing across at Helene, she winked at him and he felt his legs turn to water.

'Jesus, Morgana—'

'Ssh!' she said, placing her finger against his lips. 'Let's just relax and enjoy this, shall we? There's no one going to walk in on us here.'

James immediately thought of Emma and he began to wonder again where she could have gone. He ought to go straight to the Folly to check she was all right. But Morgana was removing his clothes, her hands deft and uncompromising, her fingertips caressing each area of skin as it was exposed.

Climbing off the bed, Helene was busy pulling off her minuscule skirt and T-shirt to reveal high, small breasts above a narrow ribcage, a taut, flat belly and long, lithe legs that met in a fluff of blonde curls.

Once James was naked, Morgana quickly threw off her own clothes and went over to her friend. As he watched, the two women embraced. Morgana's larger breasts jostled with Helene's, flattening against them as they pressed close to each other. Helene's hands slipped down to cup Morgana's buttocks, the fingers making dents in the firm flesh, kneading and separating the two halves. James's eyes lingered on the dark cleft, remembering how she had looked on all fours in front of him, her sex open and ready for the thrust of his cock.

He knew the emotion clouding his reason now was lust, pure and simple. The obsession was gone, but the physical allure Morgana held for him was still there. And, of course, today there was the added delight of Helene.

James watched her as she caressed Morgana, her long, artistic fingers stroking and kneading, and he imagined those same fingers moving over his own body. He noticed that her bottom was taut and firm like the rest of her, with very little flesh to soften it. No matter – he would take her face to face and save the rear entry for Morgana...

When at last they broke the kiss, the two women turned their heads as one and smiled at James in blatant invitation. Visions flashed through his head of himself sandwiched, naked, between the two soft, pliable female bodies and he swallowed. All he had to do was cross the room...

Meanwhile Emma could be lying sick somewhere – the cliffs were treacherous, supposing she'd fallen, or, having climbed down, found that she was still too weak to climb up again? What if she had had more hallucinations, weakening her already fragile grip on reality? He should be there, looking after her, not indulging himself by taking advantage of every sexual opportunity which presented itself! What kind of husband was he, for Christ's sake? What kind of friend?

Seized by a sudden urgent desire to go to her, he picked up his clothes and began pulling them on.

'James?' Morgana was watching him with surprise.

'I'm sorry... I have to go back to the Folly. I should never have left... I'm sorry,' he finished with an inadequate shrug.

'It's all right,' Morgana said, picking his belt up off the floor and handing it to him.

James took it from her and caught her eye. He read

regret there, and affection, and something he had never seen before when Morgana had looked at him. The beginnings of respect.

'Thanks,' he said softly, bending impulsively to kiss her on the cheek.

She smiled.

'Since you don't need the room at the moment, would you mind . . .?'

She gestured at Helene who was reclining on the double bed, unselfconsciously naked. James smiled as he thought of what they would be doing together in a few minutes. He felt a pang of regret that he could not join them.

'Be my guest,' he said lightly.

As he closed the door behind him, he saw them sink together onto the bed, limbs entwined, mouths meeting and melding, and shook his head. Despite the calamitous outcome of their meeting, he knew he would never forget Morgana Helston. Just as he knew that it was now over.

The Folly was quiet as James opened the big double doors, the kind of quiet that could only mean there was no one at home. Nevertheless, he walked from room to room, looking for her.

'Emma! Emma where are you?'

His voice seemed to echo around the high-ceilinged rooms, bouncing off the walls and mocking him. When he was satisfied that she wasn't inside, he went out into the garden and began to search methodically through it.

It wasn't until he reached the garden where they had made love the first time, the time when he had first heard Emma mention Jago, that he saw her. She was lying on the grass in the middle of the lawn, curled up on her side apparently unconscious.

'Emma!'

His stomach plummeted as he ran to her side and fell to his knees. Hesitating slightly, he stroked the hair away from her eyes and picked up her wrist to find her pulse. To his relief, he realised that she was only sleeping, but in such a strange place, in such a strange position...?

Cursing under his breath, James lifted her into his arms and struggled to his feet. She had lost weight, he hadn't realised how much, and he scanned her face now with concern as he carried her into the house. She looked drawn, her skin, always pale, looked almost translucent in the sunlight.

Emma did not stir as James took her into the house. She lay like a dead weight in his arms, oblivious to everything. In her bedroom, he lowered her gently onto the covers and stood for a moment gazing down on her while he struggled to catch his breath.

A surge of love for her overwhelmed him, so strong it took him by surprise. Perhaps it was the realisation of how close he had come to losing her that had made him understand how deeply he cared for her. It puzzled him that he had been so quick to respond to the advances made to him by both Morgana and Monica. The quick, sexual thrills he had shared with them were insignificant when compared to the deep and abiding love he felt for Emma.

'Forgive me,' he murmured, stroking her cool cheek.

Leaning over her, he kissed her lips, drawing back

when he detected the unmistakable hint of tobacco on her breath. He frowned. Emma had never smoked. She stirred in her sleep, distracting him, but she did not wake, merely murmured something he couldn't quite catch.

James laid his hand on her forehead and was relieved to find it felt cool and dry. Though her sleep was very deep, it clearly wasn't the result of illness. Deciding that she would be better off inside the bed, James began to undress her. He frowned as he realised that she was naked beneath her long floral skirt.

Emma simply wasn't the sort of woman who would leave the house pantyless and it bothered James as he eased her nightdress over her head and smoothed it down over her body. He hadn't noticed the missing undergarments lying on the grass near her – what on earth had happened to them?

Even now she did not waken and he began to worry that perhaps it wasn't sleep that claimed her, but something far more sinister. A trance, perhaps? Or maybe she'd been attacked – God, that would explain why she was half naked!

Frantically, James began to examine her for injuries. A lump on her head, a bruise, signs of a struggle. To his relief he found nothing to suggest that anyone had hurt her. Telling himself he was allowing his imagination to run away with him, he ran a hand through his hair and forced himself to calm down.

Folding the covers up to Emma's chin, James sat beside her bed and watched her for a long time. He could see her eyes moving beneath the closed lids. Every now and again her fingers would flex, then curl into fists so tight that the knuckles showed white. Once or twice she muttered something incoherent, as if she was battling her way through a particularly vivid dream.

Remembering what she had said about her dreams, James felt worried. It wasn't natural for her to have slept for so long, not to have been disturbed when he had carried her to the bedroom, when he had undressed her. Something was wrong, he was sure of it.

Sitting and watching her was driving him crazy. He had to *do* something. Deciding that he would telephone Doctor Abbott for advice, he left her alone.

In her dreams Emma concealed herself behind some rocks and watched as the rowing boats cut silently through the night-black water. The masts of the ship which lay at anchor just beyond the cove looked skeletal, dark against the navy blue blotches of the sky.

There were two boats gliding silently towards the shore. As they came nearer, Emma could hear the rush of the waves as they were cut through by the oars. The men, a half dozen in each, were silent, motionless silhouettes.

It was cold, a bitter wind blowing in across the Atlantic carrying a smattering of sleet. Emma knew that it was cold, and yet she was not affected by it. It was as if she watched, but was not really there – like watching a scene in a snowstorm dome, a world within a world, protected by perspex.

A movement to her left caught Emma's attention, and she peered into the gloom at the gaping mouth of the cave. There was a man there, sinister in his dark cloak and tricorn hat, holding a single lantern at shoulder height. The beam of the light caught his face, once, just long enough for her to recognise him.

'Jago!' she whispered.

Something that felt very like alarm travelled through her as she recognised him. Something about the scene felt wrong and all her instincts told her that there was danger on the beach. Did Jago feel it too? Was that why he was standing so still and silent at the mouth of the cave?

The rowing boats reached the shallow water and a man jumped from each to tow it to the shoreline. As the men climbed out of the boats, Emma saw that all were armed. The atmosphere on the beach was threatening, evil, and Emma felt the cold fingers of terror play up and down her spine.

Jago stood, motionless, in the mouth of the cave while the men unloaded their cargo. Not until they had finished did he step forward to examine what they had brought with them. Motioning silently for the lids to be lifted on the chests, he bent down to examine the merchandise.

By the faint light of the lamp, Emma saw his face clearly. It was gaunt, far thinner than when she had seen it before, and his beard and hair both needed attention. He picked something out of a trunk and examined it in the light of the lamp. Emma saw that it was some kind of bottle – brandy perhaps? She frowned. Why would a shipment of brandy be unloaded in the dead of night by armed sailors?

A second trunk was opened and she saw that it contained lace and silks. Jago barely glanced at the fine materials, moving on to check the next trunk which contained tea and tobacco. Emma knew then that these goods must be contraband and that these men were not sailors at all, but the smugglers she had heard so much about. And Jago was one of them.

Emma was aware of disappointment that her suspicions had been confirmed. Her ghost lover had, in life, been no more than a common criminal. It didn't alter her feelings for him, but she was aware that it would colour her view of him from now on. She hadn't realised how much she had hoped the old rumours would not be true, that Jago Pengarron would have been an honest, upright citizen after all.

Jago rose and gave a curt nod. One man stepped forward and accepted a fat pouch which Emma assumed contained his payment for the cargo. He signalled to his men to carry the trunks through to the cave and Jago turned away.

As he turned, Emma saw the man he had paid take something out of his breeches. Too late, she saw it was a knife. She screamed a warning, though whether Jago heard it she could not tell. He turned, so he saw the blade slicing through the air towards him, but he made no move to save himself. As the knife hit home, he seemed to crumple, falling to his knees and doubling over. Then he collapsed on the wet sand and Emma knew at once that he was dead.

The men, unconcerned at the killing, merely reloaded their boats with the contraband. One of them even whistled softly as he worked, until he was silenced by a curse and a rough blow from the man in charge. Once they were ready to head back to the ship, two of them walked calmly over to Jago's body and picked him up beneath the arms, one either side of him. His feet dragged along the ground, churning up the wet sand in two deep grooves.

Emma watched, shaking uncontrollably as they threw him unceremoniously to the floor of one of the boats. She watched, frozen to the spot, as they rowed away as silently as they had come. When they reached the ship, she heard a splash and realised that they must have tipped Jago's body over the side. It was then that she lost control, tearing at her hair and sobbing.

'Oh no! No, no, no!'

Someone was shaking her, trying to make her stop screaming. Emma heard her name being called urgently by a voice she recognised, but could not quite place.

'Emma, wake up! For the love of God, honey, you must wake up! It's a dream, only a dream!'

She opened her eyes and found herself staring at James. She did not have time to analyse how glad she was to see him, she merely threw herself into his arms and allowed him to soothe her. When, at last, she had managed to stop shaking, she looked at him and said, 'I know what happened to Jago Pengarron.'

James's face registered anguish, but he did not try to stop her from talking.

'Another dream?' he said.

She nodded and he sat beside her on the bed, drawing her into the safe crook of his arm.

'Tell me,' he insisted.

Emma related the events she had seen, sparing herself no detail. When she had finished, James sighed.

'Poor guy.'

'Rich as he was, Jago still continued to smuggle goods in from abroad. I can't come to terms with the fact that his death was so pointless. He paid the man and he was murdered – all for the sake of a few contraband goods.' Her voice broke on a sob and she swallowed it down fiercely. 'What a waste. What a bloody waste!'

James put her head on his shoulder and stroked her hair. He didn't tell her to pull herself together, or deny what she had seen, he merely held her until her tears had dried.

'He didn't even defend himself,' Emma said as she blew her nose and wiped her tear-streaked face. 'He saw the knife – there must have been a split second when he could have fought back. But he didn't, he just stood there, as if waiting for the inevitable to happen. Almost as if he had been waiting for it, expecting it to happen.'

'Perhaps he didn't care,' James suggested gently.

'What do you mean?'

'He'd lost his wife, his child – maybe he didn't much care what happened to him.'

Emma was appalled.

'How could you say such a thing?'

James shrugged.

'I lost my child. I almost lost the woman I love, through my own foolishness. I have some idea how he might have felt.'

Emma stared at him.

'Oh, James!' she whispered.

He reached for her and their lips touched in the briefest of kisses before the shrill ring of the telephone cut into the moment.

'That'll be Doctor Abbott,' he told her. 'I left a message with his receptionist asking him to call.'

'Go and tell him I'm fine, James,' Emma told him. 'Go on,' she said, interpreting the look in his eye. 'I'll be all right.'

James nodded and ran to pick up the telephone. The moment the door closed behind him, the air thickened and moved and Jago appeared out of the shadows. Emma forgot James at once and turned to her dream lover.

'Jago – I know what happened to you!' she whispered.

His image was strong today, his sexual magnetism cloaking him like a glowing nebula. Emma recalled the last time they had made love and immediately her thoughts were full of how they might arrange it again.

'What do you mean?' he asked her, a frown marring his smooth skin.

'I was on the beach – I saw the man who killed you ... I guess the tide must have washed your body out to sea, that's why you were never found.'

'Aye, that would be how it was.'

He looked sad, rather wistful as he ran his eyes over Emma's face, lingering on her slightly parted lips.

'Have you come to tell me when we will meet again?' she asked him eagerly.

Jago shook his head.

'No, Emma, it cannot happen again,' he said, regret colouring every word.

Emma stared at him, not quite taking in what he had said.

'What do you mean, Jago? Surely you can't want to abandon me now?'

'I would never abandon you, my lady. I will always be with you, in a small corner of your heart. But you must understand that it is too dangerous for us to cross over now.'

'Why?' she cried, 'why is it too dangerous now?'

Jago shook his head and his eyes resting on her were filled with sadness.

'We have too little control, dear heart. Supposing you had walked out onto the beach on that night, the night of my death? We have no way of knowing the time or the location of our meetings. If you had appeared there instead of merely witnessing the event, you might have been killed too.'

Emma took a few moments to digest this.

'But I want to be with you,' she said at last. 'There is nothing for me here – I would rather die with you than live in my time without you.'

'Ah, Emma, Emma,' he whispered.

Reaching out, he touched her face. Emma felt the caress as lightly as the kiss of a butterfly's wings and she knew that she had not swayed him.

'You are wrong,' he said gently. 'Your place is here, in this time, with your husband.'

'James?'

'Aye. I have been watching him and I see that he cares for you.'

'How can you tell?' Emma asked cynically, seeing again

the vision of Morgana Helston sprawled across the table while she sucked at James's cock.

Jago smiled at her.

'He has been foolish, 'tis true. But think you that he does not know that? Listen—'

Emma heard James knock on the door.

'Em – why have you locked me out? Are you all right?'

Emma glanced quizzically at Jago who quirked an eyebrow at her.

'I have barred the door. I needed to speak with you,' he offered by way of an explanation.

Emma smiled.

'It's all right, James. Give me ten minutes will you?' she asked him, amazed at how calm and sane she sounded when inside she was a mass of seething emotion.

James complied, reluctantly, and she turned back to Jago.

'Every man is entitled to one mistake in his life, Emma. Can you forgive James for his?'

'Can you forgive yourself for the mistake you made in your life?' Emma countered, noticing the way Jago's eyes clouded with sadness.

'Demelza killed herself because of my unreasonable jealousy. That is not a mistake I have been able to put right, in my time or this. Your James has a second chance. Let him take it.'

Emma stared at him. She wanted nothing more than to go to him, to feel again the throb of his heart against her cheek.

'Can we not meet just once more?' she pleaded.

Jago shook his head.

'We cannot risk it. Can you not find any love in your heart for your husband?'

Emma dropped her eyes as she thought of James. She had been so wrapped up in her quest for Jago that she had not allowed herself time to consider James at all.

'I do love him,' she answered truthfully, 'but I am afraid.'

Jago smiled.

'Fear is part of life, my lady,' he replied.

She smiled.

'I guess it is. Can there be no rest for you, Jago?'

He shook his head.

'It is my destiny to search for Demelza, to make amends for the wrong I did her. For, like you, I still love.'

Emma nodded, feeling that she understood. Her heart ached for him as he gave her a small, courtly bow. Then he stepped back, and faded into nothingness.

'Goodbye, Jago,' she whispered. 'Good luck.'

Fourteen

James was relieved when he tried the door again to find that it was open.

'It was *him*, wasn't it?' he said.

Emma nodded.

'He's gone now though, James.'

'For good?'

His heart squeezed painfully in his chest as he saw the sadness which passed across Emma's features before she nodded.

'Yes,' she admitted. 'He's gone for good.'

'I'm glad.' He went to sit on the edge of the bed and stroked the hair back off her forehead. 'That will be the end of the dreams then?'

Emma looked at him. She saw that he still didn't entirely believe her story, but knew now that it did not matter. To her or to him. All that James really wanted was reassurance that whatever had ailed her had passed.

'I expect so.'

His smile was tender and, for the first time, Emma saw what Jago had so clearly seen. James loved her, and his concern for her was very real.

'James?' she said, lying back on the pillows, 'do you think you could make love to me?'

He looked at her with such surprise that she realised that it was the last thing he had expected her to say.

'Please?'

A smile spread across his face and, without a word, he undressed. Emma watched through half-closed eyes as he removed his shirt. He had a good physique, muscular without being over-pumped, the skin naturally tanned and lightly spattered with freckles.

The flat brown discs of his nipples hardened as they were exposed to the air, the dark hairs on his chest rising slightly in response. Emma could smell the light cologne he always wore and she inhaled deeply, wanting to recall the things she had always loved about him. Wanting to reactivate her desire.

Her eyes followed his fingers as he unbuttoned his flies and eased his jeans down, over his narrow hips. The soft bulge beneath the plain white jersey boxers grew harder beneath her gaze, springing semi-erect from his belly as he dispensed with his underwear.

Climbing into bed beside her, James turned to her almost reverently, as if he was afraid that she could change her mind at any moment. Emma snuggled into his familiar embrace, feeling his penis press more urgently against the soft flesh of her belly.

James's hands were gentle as he explored her body through the voluminous folds of her nightdress, but she was encouraged by the fact that his touch made her feel warm and loving, if not exactly passionate. The rest would come, with time, she was sure.

After a few minutes, James helped her out of the nightdress. Feeling the warmth of his naked skin against hers, Emma felt something begin to stir in the pit of her stomach. James's heart beat a steady tattoo against her breast and she dipped her head so that she could press her lips against it.

His fingers exploring the semi-aroused folds of her sex were gentle, as if he sensed that she was still holding back. Emma sighed against his chest as he opened her, closing her eyes as she felt the juices begin to flow. As he edged towards her clitoris though, she pulled back. She wasn't ready for that, not yet.

'Come inside me,' she whispered.

James kissed her, brushing his lips lightly across hers. 'Are you sure?'

'Yes. I want to feel you inside me,' she whispered, not wanting him to talk, just to take her, make his mark on her as Jago had done.

James slipped inside her body as if he was coming home. Once inside, he lay still for a few moments, stroking her face, her eyelids, trying to tell her with his eyes how glad he was that she had begun to forgive him.

Emma moved her hips, encouraging him to move, and he began to slide in and out of her in a steady, increasing rhythm. She watched his face become less sharp, almost blurred around the edges as his concentration focused on the melding of their bodies. The earth did not move, but it was a start, and she held him to her as he came, soothing him as he murmured her name.

'Are you all right?' he asked her when they separated.

Emma smiled.

'Of course.'

James looked unconvinced and so she settled down in the crook of his arm. Stroking her arm slowly, he relaxed against her.

'Will you move back in here tonight?' she asked him softly.

James pulled back slightly so that he could see her face.

'Do you want me to?'

Emma felt her heart contract at the uncharacteristic vulnerability on his face.

'Yes.'

James's face broke into a grin and he looked more like his usual self.

'I'd like that, Em.'

Emma returned his smile, hoping that this would be the beginning of a new understanding between them.

'What did the doctor say when he phoned?' she asked after a while.

'He was kind of brusque, actually. Said you should rest, take plenty of fluids, the usual stuff. He was quite adamant that he wasn't going to come out to see you here again.'

Emma smiled to herself. She couldn't blame the doctor for staying away after the fright that Jago had given him.

'I *am* pretty tired,' she admitted.

'You sleep then. I need to go into St Ives to sort out my bill at the guest house – will you be all right? I shouldn't be more than an hour.'

'I'll be fine.'

James didn't look convinced.

'Maybe Morgana would come in while I've gone—'

'I don't need a babysitter, James,' Emma interrupted him wearily, 'particularly not Morgana Helston.'

'You don't have to worry about her – it *is* over now, I promise you.'

Emma sighed.

'I don't disbelieve you, James. But I really am okay. You go and do what you need to do and leave me to sleep.'

James leaned over and kissed her tenderly on the forehead.

'We'll see,' he said noncommittally.

Emma didn't have enough energy left to debate the issue, she was already slipping into a deep, deep sleep. Vaguely, she heard James walk out of the room and go downstairs. As she lingered at the blurred edges of sleep, she realised that she was falling, slipping towards the kind of dream she thought would leave her now that Jago had gone. Briefly, her subconscious fought against it, but its pull was too strong, sucking her in relentlessly.

She could see the empty fields which must have surrounded Pengarron two centuries before. The grass was very green, very tall, scattered with wild flowers which nodded their heads in the summer breeze.

In the middle of the field was an old oak tree, its spreading branches supplying a small oasis of shade. Above, the sky was a peerless blue, without a cloud in sight, and the air was sweet and clean with a salty tang which told her the ocean was not far away, though in this field she could not tell in which direction it lay.

Suddenly she heard the sound of horse's hooves pounding across the dry earth. Closer and closer it came, the rhythm setting up an answering thumping in Emma's heart as it appeared, a sleek black mare with a white flash down the centre of its face, being given its head by its rider.

There were two people astride the horse, a man, and a woman riding side saddle. Emma knew before they came close enough for her to recognise them that it was Jago and Demelza. Jago reined the horse in by the tree and Demelza slipped, laughing, to the ground.

Emma saw that her cheeks were pink with exertion, her eyes bright with the excitement of her exhilarating ride. Her glorious red hair, set afire by the midday sun, was wind-whipped, flying out from her head in disarray. Her breasts were heaving as she watched Jago dismount and secure the horse. Emma could see the milky white globes quivering above the low-cut bodice of her dress and realised that its fastenings had been loosened some time before.

Jago was a dashing sight, his close-cut riding breeches outlining the manly contours of his body, the white frilled shirt giving him a rakish air. His long, thick brown hair was drawn back in a ponytail, secured at the nape with a neat black bow. Seeing him again, albeit in a dream, gave Emma a jolt of regret.

Jago's eyes, as he turned them on Demelza, were black with passion. Emma could see the tension in him as he walked towards her and she felt a pang of loneliness. Why was she being shown this scene, when she had already agreed to say goodbye?

Demelza squealed as he approached, evading his grasp

as he took a playful lunge at her. Picking up her skirts, she began to run, leading him round the tree in an unequal race that, Emma knew, she did not even hope to win. Jago laughed as he pursued her.

'Come here, you flighty minx!' he said, making another grab for her.

Demelza evaded him again, laughing breathlessly.

'Take me home, husband!' she gasped. 'This is not seemly behaviour for the mistress of Pengarron's Folly!'

Jago growled deep in his throat, and this time when he reached for her, he caught her and pulled her to him. Demelza gasped as her body slammed against his and the air was knocked out of her. She reached her arms around him to steady herself and Jago buried his face in the hollow of her neck, nuzzling the damp skin at her throat.

'Not seemly?' he repeated. 'Since when have you cared for seemliness, my wanton maid? Besides – who is here to see us? Look around you.'

Keeping her clamped tightly to his side, he swept his free arm round to indicate the vast, empty spaces surrounding them. 'No one trespasses on Pengarron land!'

Emma caught the note of almost boastful pride in his voice, as did his wife.

'They are all afraid of you,' she responded, a little reproachfully, Emma thought.

Jago laughed again.

'Ignorant peasants! Are you afraid of me, Demelza Pengarron?'

Demelza smiled, a coquettish, flirtatious smile.

'Always!' she replied with patent untruth.

'So you should be!' Jago growled before capturing her lips with his.

There was hunger in the kiss, an urgent passion which made Demelza clutch at his shirt with her fingers, bunching the fabric at his back so that it pulled out of his breeches. Emma saw the muscular expanse of smooth brown skin and tossed restlessly in her bed.

'It is not fear I see in your eyes, my lady,' Jago said huskily when he broke off the kiss.

'No? What is it you can see, sir?'

He smiled and caressed her cheek tenderly with one hand.

'Could it be that I see love?' he said softly.

'Aye – could be.'

'And lust?'

'Most certainly, sir!'

Demelza laughed as he buried his face in the deep valley between her breasts, entwining her fingers in his hair and pressing him closer to her heart. Emma could see the mounting passion on her lovely face as she turned it up to the sun and felt an answering pull deep in her own womb.

'We cannot – not here!' Demelza protested half-heartedly as he lifted her breasts free of her bodice.

Jago ignored her, lathing her taut nipples with his tongue and walking her gradually back towards the tree.

'Jago . . .!'

Demelza's head fell back on her shoulders and she leaned heavily against the gnarled old trunk as he suckled at her breasts, moulding them into shiny wet cones which hardened still more as the air dried them.

'Lift your skirts for me,' he whispered urgently.

Murmuring an incoherent protest, Demelza complied, bunching her skirts around her waist so that he had access to what lay beneath them.

'You are ready for me,' Jago whispered, his satisfaction evident as his fingers played with the fiery red curls at her groin.

'Yes!' Demelza moaned as he lifted her against the tree trunk and entered her with one sure, swift thrust.

Her legs, still in their cream-coloured stockings, wrapped around his waist as they moved in unison. Even their breathing seemed to be in time, so in tune with each other were they. It was all over very quickly, with a shuddering sigh and a lingering kiss.

As they peeled apart, Emma saw the lips of Demelza's sex close over the combined secretions of their bodies and she imagined how it felt to clench her muscles and try to hold onto the sperm which must be seeping out of her. As she watched, a thin trail trickled down Demelza's thigh. Jago dropped to his knees and caught it with his tongue.

Demelza gasped as he pushed the viscous fluid back up into the tight purse of her sex, probing her closed labia with his tongue until Demelza began to writhe with renewed pleasure. Bending her legs at the knees, she leaned heavily against the solid trunk of the oak tree, tilting her pelvis so that Jago could slide his tongue into the hot, sticky channel of her vagina.

Closing her eyes, she moaned softly, her breath coming in deep, sighing gasps. Her cheeks grew flushed, a stain spreading blotchily over her neck and chest as Jago moved his head from side to side, moving the tip of his nose against her clitoris while he shafted her with his stiffened tongue. Suddenly her eyes opened wide, staring, unfocused at the perfect blue sky.

'Ah!' she cried, the breath exploding from her lungs as she doubled over, trapping Jago's head between her legs and circling her hips wildly, grinding her sex against his face.

As the last waves of orgasm ebbed away, Demelza sank to her knees and cupped Jago's face with her hands. Slowly, she began to lick it clean, just as he had licked her sex, removing all trace of their combined juices from his skin. Jago knelt, passive for a few moments, then with a low, primeval growl, he turned her so that her soft white buttocks were tilted up towards his face.

Demelza gasped as he smacked the flat of his hand across one fleshy globe, making it shiver and shake. He waited until it had stilled before repeating the action on the other buttock. The sound of flesh smacking against flesh was loud in the open air, and before too long Demelza's bottom was flushed a deep, warm rose pink. The deep colour provided a curiously erotic contrast with the pure white skin of her thighs and back.

She had clearly enjoyed the spanking, enthusiastically given, for she thrust her buttocks up higher, waggling her bottom lewdly in Jago's face. He chuckled softly.

'No, no more,' he told her, his voice low and silky. 'You're warm enough now. Time for me to quench your fire.'

Emma saw then that the game they had played had brought Jago erect again. The tip of his penis pushed against the soft folds of Demelza's sex and he sank into her with a low groan. With one arm beneath her belly, he steadied them against the tree trunk with the other as he began to thrust in and out of her.

Demelza reached down and pressed her fingers against her clitoris. Pushing between them, she caressed Jago's moisture-slick cock as it moved in and out of her, cupping his balls and kneading and squeezing them in time with his increasingly urgent thrusting.

They came together this time, collapsing in a tangle of sweaty arms and legs, hugging each other close as they rolled onto the soft, loamy soil. Emma saw the sated expressions on their faces and felt a sharp stab of envy. They had been so much in love, so utterly right for each other. After a few minutes, Jago rolled over onto his stomach so that he could gaze into Demelza's eyes.

'My own love,' Jago murmured, tracing the contours of her face with his fingertips. 'No one could give me more than you have given me.'

Demelza smiled and rearranged her clothing with shaky fingers. When she was decent again, she looked at Jago calmly and said, 'I will give you more, my husband. I will give you a son.'

Incomprehension was soon chased away by incredulity, then joy as Jago realised what she was saying.

'A son ... but I could have hurt you ... Demelza?' He placed a protective palm over the still-flat planes of her belly, his face full of wonder.

Demelza laughed, hugging him to her to hide the relief on her face. It was obvious she had not been sure how he would take the news.

'You could never hurt me,' she whispered.

Emma woke up with a jolt, Demelza's whispered words

ringing in her ears like a shout. *You could never hurt me.* Why then did she jump from the cliffs no more than a year later, with the baby she apparently wanted so much clutched to her breast?

Emma knew she couldn't let it go, she had to know the truth behind the tragedy which had haunted this house for so many years. For she felt such an empathy with Demelza, sensed that in her story she would find the key to getting over her own tragedy. What was it Jago had said? That he had thought that helping her might redeem him. The thought swirled in her mind as she lay staring up at the ceiling. Could the converse also be true? If she could ease Jago's pain, would she find redemption herself?

She looked up as James came through the door.

'You're awake!' he said unnecessarily.

'Just. Is that coffee?'

'Yes. I thought I'd bring you a cup before I go back into town. You will be okay?'

'Sure – don't fuss!' Emma smiled to take the sting out of the words. She didn't want him to suspect that she was eager for him to go. He wouldn't understand that she needed to be alone to see this thing through to the end. Whatever that might be.

She drank her coffee with James and listened as he went back downstairs. As soon as she heard the front door slam, she got out of bed and went over to the trunk. Closing her eyes, she held Demelza's wedding dress against her face, as if she could get some sense of the dead woman through the stiff fabric.

'What happened, Demelza?' she whispered. 'Why did you do it?'

There was a rushing sound in her ears and a sudden draught whipped around her bare ankles. A subtle shift in the atmosphere of the room made Emma open her eyes cautiously. What she saw made her suck in her breath.

She was still in the bedroom. It was the same, yet not the same – the worn furnishings appeared brighter, as if brand new and the electric light fittings had disappeared. In front of her, in the bed, Demelza Pengarron lay nursing her infant son.

Emma watched, hardly daring to breathe as the baby sucked at the swollen, blue-veined breast. Pain cramped in her belly as she passed her eyes over the downy head, the tiny fingers clutching at his mother's breast as he sucked contentedly at her nipple.

Then suddenly, shockingly, he pulled back his head and let out an unearthly yell which froze Emma's blood. The milk spurted from Demelza's breast for a second after the contact was broken and fell across the sheets in a watery stain.

Emma could see the anguish on Demelza's face and saw from her response that this was a frequent occurrence. She could sense her despair as she tried to comfort the screaming infant. All her efforts were in vain; the child thrashed its arms and legs, flinging its head back repeatedly so that it set up a monotonous rhythm on the counterpane.

Some instinct, some sixth sense, told Emma that the child's behaviour was far from normal. He seemed to have the strength of a child three times his age, fighting against his mother as she tried to hold him against her chest. Caring for such a child must be exhausting, Emma knew, and her heart went out to Demelza who was now crying softly, her lips pressing kisses against the soft fuzz on top of the screaming baby's head.

The scene faded, swimming in and out of focus before Emma's eyes. She was relieved to be rid of the sound of the baby's eerie screams and she wondered how Demelza had felt, listening to them night and day.

As the scene refocused, Emma realised that the bedroom had faded and that the location she now saw was the drawing room downstairs. Demelza was standing by the fireplace, the baby, sleeping now, held on her shoulder.

Emma saw that Demelza seemed to have shrunk, somehow. Her eyes were like two green pools, sunk in the sockets of her pale face, shadowed with pain. Her body beneath the cotton gown was thin and undernourished. The contrast between this poor creature and the plump, happy young woman she had seen with Jago in the fields only a short twelve months before was stark. Emma wondered if Jago had ever seen her like this since he was obviously away. She found herself hoping that he had not.

There was a man with her, dressed formally. It wasn't Jago – this man was portly, middle-aged with an officious air.

'There's no good to be had nurturing the child,' he was saying. Though his words brooked no nonsense, his tone held some sympathy.

'No!' Demelza cried, clutching the baby to her so hard that he woke and began to scream again.

A look of horror passed across the physician's face.

'Your husband will agree with me when he

returns. 'Twould be the kindest thing to allow the child to die.'

'I cannot – I will not stop feeding him!' Demelza said, trying desperately to soothe the baby.

'He cannot hear, he cannot see – rest assured he can feel nothing either. I will see you again when your husband's ship comes in. Good day to you, mistress.'

The physician made a hasty exit and Emma found herself alone in her room again. Though two hundred years had passed, she could still sense Demelza's despair. She knew at once that her death had been no fault of Jago's. He hadn't known about the child, had probably been in no fit state to be told after the event. So he had dreamed up reasons of his own, reasons which had kept him earthbound for two centuries, searching for redemption.

Would it make a difference if he knew that it was for the love of their child that Demelza had taken the desperate action of jumping from the cliffs?

'Jago . . . Jago, come to me,' she whispered.

It was useless – he had quite resolutely moved away from her. They had said their goodbyes and he could not come to her again.

Emma felt impotent fury rise up in her. Why had she been shown these scenes too late to help him? Now she had to live with the knowledge of what really happened on the cliffs by Pengarron's Folly.

Restless now, she decided to go for a walk in the fresh air. James would not be back for an hour or so – she had plenty of time.

As James walked into the foyer of the Meridian Guest

House, Morgana was just walking down the stairs. She looked as if she had only just woken; her spiky hair stood up in tufts and her lips were swollen, as if she had just been thoroughly kissed. Which she probably had, he acknowledged wryly.

'I thought you'd be long gone,' he said as she saw him.

She smiled and stretched like a satisfied cat.

'Sorry. Helene's still sleeping. Did you find my purse?'

'Your purse?'

'Yeah – it must have dropped out of my bag when I was at your place this morning.'

'Sorry – I haven't seen it. I was just about to check out, do you think Helene would mind if I woke her?'

Morgana grinned.

'I'm sure she wouldn't mind at all,' she purred, 'but I'd let the poor girl sleep a bit longer first.'

Conscious of the sour-faced receptionist listening, slack-jawed, to their conversation, James sighed.

'Behave, Morgana.'

She made a face.

'Ugh – never!'

James laughed.

'Has anyone ever told you you're incorrigible? Don't answer that! Why don't you go back to the Folly and look for your purse? Emma was in bed when I left her, but you've got a key haven't you?'

'Yeah. Thanks, James. Tell Helene where I've gone will you? Tell her that if she waits for me by the sea wall I'll give her a lift home.'

James watched her walk out of the guest house, her hips swinging jauntily beneath her summer skirt and he shook his head, filled with a sudden affection for her. Once she had gone, he went to turn Helene out of his nice, warm bed so that he could settle his bill and get back to his wife.

Emma walked along the cliff path, watching the gulls as they wheeled noisily below her. The pock-marked granite cliffs housed an entire colony and the grey rock was spattered with bird droppings, like white paint.

She thought of Demelza and empathised with her loss. To have given birth to a child with such problems, especially two hundred years ago when ignorance and prejudice would have made her life impossible, must have been even worse than losing a child before it was born, as Emma had done.

Jago had known right from the start that Emma and Demelza were similarly afflicted. Hadn't he said that, coupled with the physical resemblance, that had been what had drawn him to her? *Jago*. She had loved him, during those all-too-brief encounters when he had lived for her. Loving him had reawakened her, paved the way for a reconciliation with James.

Emma smiled sadly as she thought of James. Could they really breach the months of misunderstanding that had driven them apart? He seemed willing to try and she was hopeful that they could. They had Jago and Demelza Pengarron to thank for that.

She would probably never find an explanation for what had happened here at the Folly. There probably *was* no explanation, and Emma resolved that she would not even try to find one. She would simply accept that all had worked out as it should, and be grateful.

James would be back soon from St Ives and she didn't want to worry him by not being there when he arrived. She was just about to turn back when something caught her attention on the headland. A lone figure, wearing an unseasonal black cloak and holding a bundle in her arms, was standing dangerously close to the edge.

Emma was about to call out a warning when a sudden gust of wind whipped the hood of the cloak back to reveal a shock of red-gold hair. The blood rushed in Emma's ears and she froze to the spot.

'Oh my God!' she whispered.

For a moment she stood, frozen to the spot. She didn't want to watch this last chapter of the story that had been replayed for her since she arrived at the Folly. Suddenly she knew that she was being given a chance to set Jago free.

Wrenching her eyes away from the woman on the cliff, Emma began to run back towards the Folly. Praying that she wouldn't be too late, she instinctively went straight to the garden within a garden where she had found Jago so many times before.

'Jago! Jago – you have to hear me!'

Her voice carried on the breeze, whipping round the bushes and whispering through the branches of the trees.

'I've found Demelza! Jago – she's on the cliffs. She didn't jump because of you, Jago. Your baby was sick and Demelza was desperate . . . She's on the cliffs! You have to save her, Jago, you have to stop her from jumping this time.'

Emma's voice broke on a sob as her entreaties were met by a relentless silence.

POSSESSION

There was nothing for her to do but turn back, try to reach Demelza herself. She knew she wouldn't be able to do anything to stop her, that what she had seen was merely a mirror image of what had happened in the past, unchangeable. Yet everything in her argued that she couldn't let Demelza jump to her death alone. Not this time.

She was still there, teetering on the brink of the cliffs. Emma ran faster than she had ever run before, oblivious to the stitch in her side, wanting only to reach Demelza, before it was too late.

Pulling into the driveway, James was startled to see Morgana hurtling towards him. The expression on her face told him that something was very wrong and he caught hold of her by the shoulders, shaking her as she stumbled over her words.

'What is it? Is it Emma?'

Morgana nodded, pointing towards the headland.

'The cliffs!' she gasped. 'She's going to jump from the cliffs!'

James began to run, blind panic urging him on. Morgana was right – he could see Emma standing right on the very edge of a sheer drop.

'Emma!' he breathed, fear preventing him from shouting out.

He had to reach her – he had to!

Emma reached Demelza's side just before she jumped into the void. It was several seconds before she realised that the sound of screaming was coming from her, not Demelza. Demelza was falling, as if in slow motion. Then she saw him. Jago, large as life, waiting to break Demelza's fall.

Emma bit on her fist as she saw him catch Demelza and the baby in his arms, holding them safe. Her heart leapt as he looked up and saluted her and she saw the joy on his handsome features.

She jumped as strong arms pulled her back from the edge and she found herself looking up into James's white face. She touched his cheek and realised it was wet.

'Jesus, Emma – why? Why?'

She shook her head as she realised what he had thought. That she was going to jump.

'I wouldn't do that to you, James,' she said wonderingly. 'It's Demelza and Jago and their child – they're together now – look.'

Together they moved closer to the edge again and looked over. The beach was deserted, the virgin sand pure and unmarked.

'But I saw them . . .' Emma protested.

'Come away now, love – it's over,' James said gently.

Emma stepped back a safe distance away from the cliff and stared at him. The adrenalin was still pumping through her veins and slowly, inexorably, she felt the fear turn into desire. James saw her expression change and his heart missed a beat.

'Emma—'

'Now, James. I want you *now*.'

Fifteen

The grass at the top of the cliff was sparse and sharp, but Emma seemed not to notice as she knelt down and began to unfasten James's trousers. He was hard already, relief and the aftermath of fear sharpening his senses, quickening his pulse.

Glancing back towards the Folly, he saw Morgana Helston turn and walk away, relief apparent in every line of her body. Silently, he wished her farewell.

Then Emma reached into the gap she had made and eased his cock out of his pants, and James forgot about the young Cornishwoman. His cock felt hot and swollen and the coolness of Emma's hand was blissful as it closed around it. James's breath caught in his chest as Emma planted a dozen tiny kisses along its length before licking round the smooth, exposed glans, flicking her tongue into the slit and swirling it around the underside.

Looking down he could see the deep, shadowed cleft between her breasts down the front of her blouse. It seemed to him that it was the most erotic sight he had ever seen, far more so than total nakedness would have been.

Emma raised her head and looked up at him. Just the expression on her face made his cock weep. Pure lust darkened her eyes, and the fact that it was for him made him feel like a king.

Crouching down, he kissed her, breaching the barrier of her teeth with his tongue and raking the tender skin inside her mouth. He wanted to devour her, draw all the sweetness from her until all her thoughts were filled with him to the exclusion of everything and everyone else.

Her hands worked on his cock as he fondled her breasts, slipping one hand into the valley between them and drawing one out of the lacy cup of her bra. The nipple crested on contact with the air and he circled it with the tip of his finger, pressing lightly on the very end in the way he knew she liked.

Emma gasped and pressed towards him, lifting her face for another kiss. James nibbled gently at her lower lip, opening her mouth with his tongue. Moving back slightly, he gazed at her.

'God, you're beautiful,' he breathed.

He thought she had never looked so lovely, with her soft lips parted, one breast hanging out of her blouse, the nipple pointing yearningly at him. He reached out and pinched it, not hard, but firmly enough to make her gasp aloud. Taking advantage of her moistly parted lips, James nudged at the corner of her mouth with the tip of his cock, drawing it slowly across her lips.

Holding his eye, Emma opened her mouth wide and sucked him in. He groaned, conscious of the rhythm of the waves below them keeping time with the pounding of his heart. Emma's lips moved back and forth along his shaft, sending little shocks of sensation rippling along its length. He felt the sweat break out all over his body as he raced towards his climax.

Normally he would try to hold back, to spend time giving as well as receiving pleasure, but this time he did not want to stop. He watched Emma's face as he increased his speed, clenching his stomach muscles to suppress the urge to thrust too deeply into her mouth. She must have known he was close to coming, yet she made no move to let him go. Encouraged by her acceptance, James held her head still as the sperm surged along his penis and spurted into her mouth.

As it began to jet out of him, he was overwhelmed by a sudden urge to come over her skin. Pulling out of her mouth, he watched as the milky fluid landed on her exposed breast, rolling towards the tip and dripping slowly off the end.

Emma looked up at him and smiled. Slowly, she rubbed the sticky fluid into her skin, massaging it into her puckered aureola. Then she lifted her hand to her lips and licked her fingers clean. With a muffled groan, James cupped her face in his hands and kissed her deeply. He could taste his sperm on her tongue as she thrust it into his mouth.

Running his hands over her body, he could feel the vibration of her own arousal and excitement stabbed at him.

'Jesus, Emma . . . Jesus Christ!'

Emma looked at him, her gaze unfocused, blurred by

desire. Pulling at the front of her blouse, she felt a button fly off as she yanked it off her shoulders. James helped her out of her bra and skirt, his fingers curling into the waistband of her damp panties.

'You're so wet,' he breathed in her ear, his fingers sinking into her hot, pulpy flesh, stroking along her labia.

Emma moved her buttocks restlessly on the stony ground, wanting more than the gentle caress. Reaching down, she rubbed at her clitoris, thrusting her hips up towards James's face in a blatant gesture of need.

His tongue was rougher than his fingers, pressing on the tiny mass of nerve endings and flicking deliciously back and forth across it. Emma bore down, pushing out the hard little bead as the sensations gathered at its base.

'Harder,' she grated as she teetered on the brink, frustrated by her inability to take the leap into climax.

James replaced his tongue with a finger and licked down to her vagina. He penetrated her with his tongue, thrusting in and out of the lubricated channel, faster and faster as he sensed her imminent orgasm.

'Yes!' she hissed as, at last, it crested and broke, an explosion of sensation that spread outwards from the central point, bathing her in warmth.

They lay panting on top of the cliff for several minutes.

'Let's get back to the house,' James said urgently.

Emma turned her head and looked at him.

'Why?'

'Because I want to fuck you every way I can and I don't want to chance the local Ramblers' Association choosing this path as their "walk for the day".'

Emma chuckled.

'Every way you can? All right, we'll go back.'

They pulled on their clothes haphazardly and, hand in hand, ran back to the house. As soon as they got through the door, James tore at Emma's clothes and they sank together onto the fourth step of the stairs. He was hard again, his cock pressing uncomfortably against the front of his jeans.

As soon as he had undressed, he grasped Emma by the knees and pushed them back, opening her like a split peach. Despite her recent orgasm, Emma felt the juices begin to flow again as he stared at her, his eyes hot as they raked the intricate folds of flesh. He probed her entrance with the tip of his cock, easing himself into her so that just the bulb of his penis was inside her.

Emma breathed shallowly as she waited for the inevitable thrust. The anticipation was excruciating, stringing her body tight as a bow. James held her gaze, compelling her not to break eye contact as, with a sudden, savage thrust of his hips, he sank into her, right up to the hilt. She felt a response deep in her womb and clutched him to her, wriggling her bottom on the stairs to give him deeper access.

They were both burning hot, their skin sticking and peeling apart, adding to the wet, lascivious noises of their bodies as they joined and separated over and over again. Reaching down between them, James smeared the juices now running freely from her along the stretched membranes of her perineum and up to where her anus pulsed eagerly beneath his fingers.

She was stretched wide open, every orifice available to

him as he eased his fingertip into the hot, tight channel of her back passage. He could feel his own cock moving in and out of her, separated only by the thinnest wall inside her. The sensation excited him beyond control and he twisted his finger, easing it in further, up to the second knuckle.

Emma cried out, her fingernails raking sharply across his shoulders as she came. Her sheath convulsed around his cock, rippling along its length and forcing the gathering sperm to overspill.

'U-uh! Emma . . .!'

They collapsed against the stairs, momentarily exhausted. After a few minutes, Emma realised the hard stairs were bruising her back and she shifted uncomfortably. James helped her to her feet and they both looked up, as one, to where the portrait of Jago and Demelza stared down at them.

'Do you think they're at peace now?' Emma mused.

James pulled her into his arms and kissed her.

'I hope so,' he said. 'Come on – let's go up to the bedroom.'

They slept for a while, then Emma was woken by the feel of soft hands stroking her naked skin. She lay very still, not daring to open her eyes, listening to James's deep, even breathing beside her. She could smell lavender and the evocative, familiar scent of cinnamon and tobacco lingering on the air.

The soft, feminine fingers tweaked at her nipples before moving down to part the tender folds of her labia. Emma sighed, desire reverberating through her body. She felt masculine hands stroking her cheek as a small, wet tongue lapped delicately at the combined secretions between her legs. Opening her mouth, Emma welcomed the masterful thrust of a firmer tongue between her lips.

She felt filled by them, they were all around her, touching, tasting, tantalising her senses. Realising they had probably come to say goodbye, Emma opened her legs wider, inviting a deeper caress.

The benign succubus did not disappoint her, entering her with her fingers while she lathed her clitoris with her tongue. Emma raised herself up on her shoulders, offering her breasts to the ghostly fingers which were stroking her neck. Long fingers pinched and pulled at her nipples, creating a chain of sensation which seemed to run from the tips of her breasts right through her to her clitoris.

She came, gasping and writhing. Opening her eyes, she saw Jago and Demelza, standing together at the end of the bed. They were both smiling at her, a nebula of light shining like a crown around their heads.

'Goodbye,' Emma mouthed, understanding at once that this truly was the last time she would see them.

The air of sadness, of tragedy, which had always accompanied Jago's forays into this world was tangibly absent. Emma smiled, happy that they had at last found peace. She watched as gradually, hand in hand, they faded into the shadows for the last time – together.

Emma rolled over towards James and, easing down under the covers, woke him as quickly as she knew how. As soon as he was fully erect, she climbed on top of him and slipped him inside her. James gazed up at her, still groggy with sleep, as she rode him. He arched his back, his eyes glazing over as she squeezed him, bringing him swiftly to a long, shuddering climax.

Afterwards, Emma raised herself up on one elbow so that she could look at him.

'I'd like to go home tomorrow,' she said.

She watched as a smile spread across James's face.

'Whatever you want, honey,' he replied happily.

Emma snuggled down in his arms.

'I have what I want right here,' she whispered, then, silently, she thanked Jago and Demelza for reuniting her with James just as they had been reunited in another time, another place.